CRUSHED

The Witch Game Novels Book One

KASI BLAKE

Crushed

ISBN: 978-1-63422-083-5

Cover Design by: Marya Heiman

Interior Design by: Cassy Roop of Pink Ink Designs

& Courtney Nuckels

Editing by: Cynthia Shepp

For more information about our content disclosure, please utilize the QR code above with your smart phone or visit us at

www.CleanTeenPublishing.com.

From Kristen Noah's notebook:
HOW TO PLAY CRUSHED

TO BEGIN THE GAME: Each witch needs to choose a (boy) mark. Choose wisely. A weak-minded boy without a rebellious or stubborn streak will be a lot easier to control than a boy with a strong personality. Each witch needs to prepare her own potion with care using the usual components.

At the agreed-upon time, each witch will blow the dust-like substance into the face of her mark. Everyone must use a different color. Colors will be assigned at the beginning of the game.

RULES:

1. No cheating or sabotaging other players.
2. No other spells may be used to manipulate the boys.
3. You may not crush a boy you have dated, are dating, or want to date in the future.
4. You cannot make the boy do anything that will endanger him.
5. You must not mention the game to anyone not playing.
6. The game begins and ends at a time agreed upon by all players.
8. You cannot use the Crushed game to get revenge.
9. Winner gets the agreed-upon prize.

HOW TO WIN: The power of the crushed spell increases with every successful use. Boys must be given tasks to complete in order to grow the spell, but choose tasks wisely—the boy may refuse to comply. If he does, the spell will be broken, and that witch forfeits the game. Once the power of the spell has increased, the witch can order the boy to do harder things, things he would not normally do.

Once the end date has arrived, each witch will call her spell back to the original bottle. The dust should return as smoke. At home, in the privacy of an agreed-upon bedroom, the witches will release their smoke into the air, and the colors will mingle. Two of the colors will die out. The remaining color reveals the winner.

1

Broken

"Witch!" The word echoed down Titan High's main hallway. Kristen stumbled in her red stilettos, almost tripping the sibling to her left. She recovered her footing quickly and tried to maintain an air of dignity, but it was too late. Giggles assaulted her ears. Anger burned below the surface, and her blood heated. The laughing students didn't need to worry about retaliation because she had bigger problems at the moment—someone was calling her out on *her* turf.

Unbelievable!

Her secret had finally been discovered. The anonymous person with the loud voice was going to reveal her identity to her unsuspecting peers. If she turned around, if she dared to look, she would find a finger pointed straight at her. Then it would be over. She'd lose her powers forever.

Could this day get any worse?

She slowly revolved, a spell waiting on her eager tongue. The anonymous shouter would be sorry they'd messed with her today. There wasn't a thing she could do to stop them from publicly accusing her of being a witch, but she could certainly make them pay a hefty price for the big reveal.

Brittany grabbed her arm just above the elbow and dragged her around the corner. Shoving her against a row of lockers, Brittany whispered, even though it was apparent she wanted to scream. "OMG! Could you be any more obvious? Why don't you just carry a big sign?"

They were the Noah sisters, Titan High royalty. There were three of them, triplets. Brittany and Cyndi shared the same facial features, while Kristen had an original face. She was a respectable five foot six, but her skyscraper-tall sisters made her look like a hobbit in comparison. Maybe that was why she'd developed such a high level of confidence, for survival.

She looked at Brittany and cringed. How could anyone willingly leave the house dressed in purple pajama bottoms, a Black Metal T-shirt, and a hundred silver bangles on their arms? Brittany's waist-length, blonde hair didn't look like it had seen a comb in weeks, and if that weren't bad enough, she'd applied thick eyeliner and black shadow with a heavy hand to both eyes. The girl looked like a raccoon.

Poor Cyndi did, too, because Brittany forced her twin to dress like her.

Kristen wouldn't have been caught dead in that outfit. For her first day of senior year, she'd chosen a stylish pair of skinny jeans with a man's button-down shirt, a borrowed tie from her dad, a black vest, and a hat that she wore tilted to the side. Each of her fingernails was painted a different color. Rainbow nails were her invention, a new trend that she vowed to make popular by the end of the first semester.

If she died today, at least she'd die looking good.

Kristen had tried numerous times to get Cyndi to stand up to Brittany and tell her replica she wasn't going to be dressed like a store-front mannequin, but Cyndi refused to go against Brittany in even the smallest way. When she disagreed with her twin, she did it in a feeble voice. Like now.

"Leave her alone, Britt." Cyndi sighed. "It's not her fault she thought we'd been found out. I almost wet my pants until I realized it was only Tina Jenkins, and she wasn't even looking at us."

Brittany's hands continued to pin Kristen to the lockers. Kristen allowed it because punching another student—even her own sister—could get her suspended. She swallowed the anger before it could consume her and said, "I'm okay now. Back off."

"All summer long, you have been yammering nonstop about how awesome this year is going to be. Then you try to ruin it five seconds through the door. *Get* a *grip*! What is wrong with you, anyway?"

Kristen shuddered. "I had that dream again last night."

Cyndi patted her arm, immediately sympathetic.

Brittany released her but continued to scowl.

"It's the second dream," Kristen said. Her dreams came true once she had them three times. It was her (curse) gift. "I couldn't see anyone's face, but there were dozens of fingers pointed at me, and one person yelled the word loud and clear. You know I don't usually freak, but this has got me really scared." She made sure no one was close enough to hear before she continued in a voice tinged with desperation. "They publicly accused me. You know what that means."

"Paranoid much? We're super careful. No one knows about us."

"Britt's right," Cyndi said. She gestured to the passing students who stared at them with open fascination. "Calm down and enjoy the adoration."

"Sticking up for your twin? Big surprise." Glares from both sides hit Kristen. The girls hated it when she referred to them as "the twins," but she was going to keep doing it until they stopped dressing alike. Even though the three of them had been born the same day, she was her own person, while they were reflections of each other.

Cyndi changed the subject. "Do either of you know who you're going to crush this year? I already have mine picked out." Smug grin in place, she added, "Rufus McDillion. He's a freshman this year, and I've been waiting for him to hit high school. I'm giving you notice. He's mine."

Brittany snorted.

Kristen's mind shifted gears. She pushed her worry over being accused to the side and concentrated on living in the moment. She didn't find Cyndi's choice amusing. Rufus was as dorky as his name implied, and he would be ultra-easy for Cyndi to control. If Kristen didn't make an equally wise choice, she'd lose the game. She'd won three years in a row, but this year was the most important one. She needed the money to buy her prom dress, a designer original from New York. Her mom could get her a sweet deal with a top designer, but it was still going to be expensive.

Brittany stared at something over Kristen's shoulder, a hungry look on her face. "I know who I'd love to crush. Don't look now, but there's tall, dark, and scary."

Kristen didn't have to look to know whom Brittany meant. Disturbing rumors followed Zach Bevian like a bad odor, and his terrible attitude didn't exactly contradict them. Her mouth went dry at the mere thought of him. She tried to resist the temptation to glance his way, but the magnetic pull was too strong. Although she hated Zach to the core of her being, she couldn't keep her eyes off him.

Hot didn't come close to describing him. Every time she saw him, it was like seeing him for the first time. It should have been a sin to be so incredibly gorgeous and such a jerk. Everything about him seemed dangerous, from his dark hair, spiked on top, razor sharp—it didn't exactly invite feminine fingers to delve into it—to the tattoo peeking from beneath the short sleeve of his black T-shirt. Although she hadn't seen it with her own eyes, a few students claimed he carried a switchblade.

His clear blue eyes looked deceptively sleepy, disinterested in his surroundings. Kristen knew that was a lie. He was always watching, always waiting for something that never seemed to happen. And every time those eyes rested on her or one of her sisters, they took on a heavily disapproving darkness that was close to suffocating.

Zach stopped at his locker. He swung the metal door open but didn't peer inside. Instead, he slowly turned in her direction. She tried to look away, but it was too late. The jerk had caught her staring. His eyes narrowed on her face, and his lips twisted into a sneer.

She lifted her chin a fraction and met his gaze head-on, silently daring him to do something about it. Zach Bevian had better watch his attitude. Titan High was her playground, and she could annihilate him if she got the urge.

Brittany intruded on her thoughts by saying, "I think I might hook up with Bevian this year."

"Forget it," Kristen said. "He has a worse reputation than you do."

Brittany stuck her tongue out, showing off her tongue piercing. She stared at the object of her desire with a secretive smile. "Why do you think I like him? He's so extreme."

"Dad would hit the roof, and you know it. He would ground you for an entire year. You'd miss senior prom and everything."

In a singsong voice, Brittany said, "I bet it would be worth it."

Kristen preferred to fly solo, while Brittany made out with every guy she got near, and Cyndi had a steady boyfriend named Jake Petrie going on two years now. They were talking marriage. It would be a cold day in hell before Kristen fell into *that* trap. Someday, the twins would learn the lesson she had learned long ago. Love didn't exist. People often mistook physical attraction for love and wound up in deep trouble, but that wasn't going to happen to her. She certainly wasn't going to let some guy ruin her future plans.

The first class of the day went well for Kristen. She had one of her favorite teachers for World History and was looking forward to the challenging assignments. Familiar faces surrounded her as she reached her locker. Since she'd arrived fashionably late to school, she hadn't had the chance to catch up with friends. There were hugs, laughter, and plenty of comments about what she was wearing. Everyone talked at once, rushing because they only had ten minutes between classes. She'd been in New York with her mom all summer and hadn't seen the gang in months. Questions flew at her, and she did her best to answer them.

Cyndi shooed away the crowd after a short time. Once everyone was out of earshot, she searched Kristen's face as if looking for something important. Hugging her books to her chest, she said, "Britt's not here, so you can talk to me. What's up with you?"

"Nothing."

"Right," Cyndi scoffed. She leaned close and lowered her voice. "I can see your aura, you know. It's usually a soft blue or green pastel, but right now it's a yucky, greenish brown."

"Dad called me *reliable* this morning." Kristen slammed her locker, annoyed with the memory.

"I'm sorry." Cyndi frowned in confusion. "What?"

Kristen fumed. "You call a middle-aged woman reliable, or an old, faithful car, not a girl in her teens. I'm not even going to be an official adult for another eight months."

"Yeah, it's kind of my birthday, too." Cyndi apologized after being hit by a heavy glare from Kristen. "Sorry. Jokes aside, you have been acting pissed off since we left Mom's. Did she say something to you?"

"She did say something, yes, and I think she was right."

"That's crazy talk. Mom's never right… about anything."

Kristen scowled, remembering her mother's words. "She pointed out that Dad has been *grooming* me to follow in his footsteps since I was in diapers. He *told* me that I wanted to be a businesswoman. He *insisted* that I was born to run the Hong Kong offices. He brainwashed me!"

"That's ridiculous."

"Is it?" Kristen made a face. "Do you remember our tea parties? Do you? I remember them. I remember Dad making my teddy bear into a Japanese businessman."

"Maybe he did that because that's what he's comfortable with. If he were a dentist, we would have been having tea with a patient. You know, you should just be happy that we have a dad who cared enough to play with us."

"I still think Mom was right, and I'm tired of being his little puppet."

"You seriously need to stop listening to Mom."

"It's not just Mom. Dad called me reliable, and teachers always look to me to run for office, oversee committees, and tutor failing students. They don't even ask if I'll do it anymore. They just assume I will because they think I'm *reliable*."

"Wow. You really don't like that word, do you?"

Kristen wasn't listening. Ever since her enlightening conversation with her mother, she'd been rethinking her priorities. She was going to make some changes. Thinking aloud, she said, "I'm not going to completely blow my grade point average this year, but I want to try something new just in case I decide later that I don't want to be a businesswoman. Maybe I'll even decide I don't want to go to college. I don't want to be known as Miss Perfect anymore. I'm thinking maybe I should have a little fun this year."

Brittany caught the end of the conversation. Stepping between her two sisters, she swung her gaze back and forth between them. Her mouth curved, and a wicked glint entered her eyes. "Did I just hear someone say they want to have fun?"

"I wasn't talking to you." Kristen glared at Brittany. The other girl would give her endless crap over wasting her life if she found out about Kristen's doubts. No way was she going to let Brittany know what their mom had said to her over the summer.

"If you really want to have fun, I can help you."

"No thanks. Your kind of fun gets people arrested."

Brittany rolled her eyes. "Relax. I'm not talking about *that* kind of fun. I'm talking about the game. We can make it more interesting. Let's have a side bet this year, just you and me."

Kristen's eyes narrowed. "Side bet?"

"You get to pick my mark, and I'll pick yours. I want you to crush tall, dark, and scary. If you win, I'll give you my allowance for the whole year, every cent, and you can take the car to college with you."

Cyndi's soft gasp slipped between Brittany's outrageous statement and Kristen's reply.

"You're out of your mind."

Brittany laughed. "I knew you didn't have the balls to do it. You're always bragging about being the queen of Crushed, always bragging that you can put a spell on anyone and make it work. Well, it's time to prove it, sis. I dare you to crush him." She winked at Cyndi before adding, "I double-dare you."

"What, are we in kindergarten now?"

Cyndi took a step away from them. "This is getting a little too intense for me. I'm going to find Jake. I haven't seen him all summer, and I can't get him on his cell."

"Do you want to—" Brittany started to ask.

Before the question was out of her mouth, Cyndi nodded. "Then after school, we can—"

"Right. Make sure you—"

"Don't I always?"

It was that weird, twin thing again. As if dressing alike weren't enough, the girls had to talk in code. Kristen wouldn't admit it to anyone, but their telepathic conversations made her feel like an outsider.

She retrieved a yellow notebook and matching mechanical pencil from her locker. Then she hesitated. She needed to talk to Ms. Wilson after math class. Should she take the red notebook and pencil for English, or would she have time to stop at her locker again?

Reading her mind, Brittany sighed. "Yeah, you're going to have fun this year. You won't be able to pull your nose out of the schoolbooks long enough to notice if your pants are on fire. You're too afraid of getting into trouble. Face it, Kris. You're a good girl, and good girls can't be bad."

Kristen threw the yellow notebook and pencil back into the locker, slamming it shut for the second time. She'd show Brittany she didn't have to be perfect. "I'm going to class unprepared today because I don't care what anyone thinks."

"Yes, you do. Don't be stupid. Take the notebook and pencil, or risk having a heart attack."

"I can be fun, Britt. Just watch me."

"Whatever. I hope you aren't going to freak out anymore today.

I want to relax and have a good time this year, not babysit a crazy person. I'm a senior, too, you know. So chill." She put her sunglasses on and wiggled her fingers. "TTFN."

The hair at the base of Kristen's neck prickled, signaling Zach was nearby, probably at his locker. She didn't understand why she felt his presence like a tangible force. It was ridiculous.

Brittany strutted down the hallway like a model in Paris working the runway. She went in Zach's direction, and for one horrible second, Kristen thought her sister was actually going to engage him in some stupid form of conversation, one idiot to another.

Kristen let her pent-up breath out in relief as Brittany passed him by.

Satisfied, she reopened her locker and retrieved her supplies. Still, the hairs on the back of her neck continued to bristle. She hated Zach Bevian. So why couldn't she stop thinking about him? Her nerves sizzled whenever he was close by. It wasn't normal.

She headed for class before her eyes could wander back to him again. A familiar face caught her attention and held it. It was Cyndi's boyfriend, Jake. Kristen started in his direction but stopped cold when a feminine hand touched his cheek, caressing him, and it wasn't Cyndi's. He laughed and bent down to whisper something in the brunette's ear. Kristen's biggest rival, Gina Bentley, laughed up at him. The sound was more painful than fingernails on a chalkboard.

Kristen's heart dropped to her feet, and the blood drained from her face. That lowdown loser had betrayed her sister!

The two cheaters turned at the same time and looked directly at her. Jake at least had the good sense to flush guiltily, but Gina's smile widened. The nasty girl knew exactly what she was doing. For the past five years, she'd tried to take Kristen's place in everything from the cheerleading squad to head of the junior prom committee. She'd worked hard to get under Kristen's skin and failed, so now she was coming at her through her sister. *Big mistake*.

Kristen had seen enough.

She made a mad dash for the restroom, half-afraid she might kill

Jake and Gina on the spot. Her hands slammed against the door when she reached it. There were a few students inside the small room, some smoking, others talking. They saw her furious face and decided to make a quick exit. *Smart girls.* Kristen marched back and forth in front of the row of sinks. She couldn't control the anger anymore. She wanted to kill somebody.

Not just somebody.

She wanted to kill Jake and Gina.

But first, she had to break the news to Cyndi. How was she supposed to do that? Poor Cyndi had a big heart that broke over the slightest bad news. She couldn't possibly withstand this kind of pain. Kristen hissed between her teeth, releasing some of the rage, just enough to keep from exploding.

The mirrors above the sinks began to rattle. Kristen watched as her image rippled. The mirrors shook harder and harder until they shattered. Pieces fell to the floor like jagged raindrops. Her hands trembled. Now what was she going to do with the *rest* of her building fury?

2

Stunned

Kristen paced in front of the broken mirrors while absently biting her lower lip. Her mind conjured the image of Jake and Gina together again and again. That jerk was going to break Cyndi's heart, and there wasn't a thing she could do about it. She had to warn her sister. If she didn't tell Cyndi, Gina would. That stupid girl would probably take an ad out in the school paper.

Kristen… wanted… to… *scream!*

The door opened, and both of her sisters rushed in just in time to keep her from blowing up the toilets. Cyndi stopped cold and gasped at the sight of the mirrors, but Brittany didn't look surprised. She rolled her eyes before ordering Cyndi to take care of the mess.

"Fix the mirrors," Brittany instructed her twin, "and do it fast. I heard one of the kids telling Mr. Gleason about the noise, so we only have a short time before he gets a female teacher in here."

Cyndi moved to the center of the room and waved her hands in the air. The glass slowly floated up. Pieces, big and small, returned to the wall and fit together like a puzzle. In seconds, the mirrors were restored to their original state. Each of the girls had a special talent, and Cyndi was the fixer. She could salvage almost anything.

Good thing for them, since they unintentionally broke stuff when they got angry.

"What is it with you today?" Brittany asked Kristen. "Since when did you become such a freak?"

Kristen turned to Cyndi in desperation, the truth on her lips. She tried to find the words, but she couldn't do it. She couldn't hurt her sister. It would be so much better if Cyndi could be the one to dump Jake. A sly idea curved the ends of Kristen's mouth. Smiling, she asked, "Can I borrow your brush?" Cyndi started to open her purse, but Kristen snatched it out of her hands. "It's okay. I'll get it."

She reached inside and grabbed the bottle of Crushed powder instead. Turning away from the girls, she poured a small amount of green dust into her hand and slipped it into the side pocket of her own purse. She was going to save her sister from heartache even if she had to be sneaky about it.

The door opened, and a teacher stepped inside.

"What is going on in here?" Miss Young asked. "Students reported hearing glass break."

"I don't know why they would say that." Kristen flashed a confident smile at the teacher as she went to the sink. She turned a faucet on and squirted a quarter-sized amount of liquid soap into one hand. Her sisters followed her lead. She added, "You know how some kids are on the first day of school. It's probably just a prank."

"Yes, well, you'd better get to class. All of you."

"We're on our way now."

The teacher left, satisfied.

"Are you going to tell us why you smashed the mirrors?" Brittany asked with arms folded over her chest and a pinched look to her face.

"Simple," Kristen said while drying her hands on a brown paper towel. "I'm just trying to shake my good girl image and have fun like you wanted."

Brittany raised her voice. "Why did you break the stinking mirrors?"

"I already told you."

"I don't believe you. Try again."

Kristen left the restroom, still blinded by fury and in no mood for a game of Twenty Questions. Brittany's annoying voice trailed after her. "What are you planning to do now?"

The hallway was empty, with one huge exception. Zach Bevian.

It didn't surprise her to see him talking on his cell. She'd had a class with him once. Tardy was his middle name. If he were going to show up at all, it would be five to ten minutes late. The loser probably wanted to make a grand entrance so everyone would look at him. He finished his conversation and tucked the cell phone into his snug jeans. She was surprised there was enough room in those pockets for something wider than a quarter.

Too bad for him that he was in the wrong place at the wrong time.

She could be wild and fun and impulsive. She would show Brittany that Kristen Noah was not your typical good girl. There wasn't any reason why she couldn't get decent grades and have fun at the same time. When she was done experimenting with her wild side, Brittany would beg her to play nice again. Reaching into her purse, Kristen pulled a long, skinny, glass vial out. Emptying the pink dust into one hand, she walked straight up to Zach. Before she had the chance to come to her senses or count the number of ways this could go wrong, she blew the dust into his face. A pink cloud floated around him for a second. It dissipated quickly. He stared at her in stunned silence.

The Crushed spell had that effect on people. Boys gazed into space once they were hit with it. The spell momentarily distorted their thinking. Soon, he would be following her around, doing her bidding, making puppy-love eyes at her. She could hardly wait.

The vision of him following her around brought a smile to her face. She continued to walk, barely missing a step.

Cyndi's shocked voice reached her ears. "She didn't."

"She did," Brittany said.

"But we aren't supposed to start the game until next week."

"Tell that to the cheater."

Kristen felt better already. She felt so good that she stopped to fix her face. She pulled a mirror from her purse and reapplied her signature lipstick before going to class. Candy Apple Crush. It was deep red, her favorite color, with diamond-like sparkles and a hint of gloss. Her mother had it specially made for her in New York.

She compressed her lips to evenly distribute the color. The mirror caught Zach Bevian's reflection. He was still standing there with wide eyes and an open mouth. The poor guy didn't look like he even remembered his own name.

Regrets began to pile on top of her head. Someone with a will as strong as Zach's was going to be hard to control. She might actually lose the game this year. She really shouldn't have crushed him, but she needed the money that a side bet with Brittany would give her.

His expression changed from puzzlement to pure hatred. He glared at her with a murderous glint in his eyes. Startled, she whipped around to look at him, but he was rummaging around in his locker again.

She must have imagined the hatred in his eyes. Victims of the Crushed spell were instantly in love with the witch who brewed the potion. A painful lump lodged in her throat, and remorse hung over her like a dark cloud. Blowing the dust into his face had been a huge mistake. This could ruin everything.

Zach slammed the door so hard that it rattled the diamond-cut windows. He stormed through the foyer and thundered past the hand-carved staircase on his way to the study where he could contemplate his revenge in private. That little witch was going to be sorry.

Little witch was his nickname for her, what he called her in his head, where no one else could hear. Last year, while watching her abuse her powers and lead a boy around like a dog on a leash, the nickname had been his only solace. He couldn't accuse her without giving away his secret, so he mocked her instead. But the insult wasn't in the word 'witch'. The put-down was in the 'little', spoken with contempt beneath his breath. She and her sisters thought they were powerful, but they had no idea what true power was.

Fists clenched, he walked past the stone fireplace without looking at it. Changing direction with a sharp turn, he went into the family room instead.

Furious, he stood in the center of the massive room and released a slow, audible breath.

The mansion quaked. A picture fell from the mantle, and a vase toppled off the corner table. Hearing the glass break fueled his anger. The mansion shook harder, but he didn't care if the roof caved in on his head. He was so angry that not even a ton of wood and stone could hurt him.

He turned around slowly and found his sister below the great arch between rooms, hands covering her head in an effort to protect it from the falling debris she probably imagined was on its way. In his need to blow off steam, he had forgotten she was in the house. Her dark brown eyes were wide, terrified.

"Are you okay?" he asked, immediately concerned.

"In an earthquake you are supposed to stand in a doorway. There are earthquakes in California. We live in California now. You should stand over here in the doorway. You're supposed to stand in the doorway during an earthquake, and this is an earthquake. I've never been in one, but I've read about them."

Physically, his sister was twenty; mentally, she was a great deal younger. His parents had figured out there was something wrong with her when she turned five, but they couldn't take her to a doctor because she was already using her powers by then. Their mother had turned to the Internet, researching Morgan's behavior, and she'd come up with a few possibilities. Autism had been at the top of the list.

Morgan thought as a child, but she could do some amazing things, like remember everything she read word for word. Other people called it a photographic memory. He just called it awesome.

Shame filled him, and the house stopped shaking. "It wasn't an earthquake, Morgan. It was just me. I'm sorry. I lost control of my powers for a second. It won't happen again."

"Why are you home?" She lowered her hands. "This morning you told me you would be here at three o'clock. I wrote it down." Morgan marched over to the coffee table where she'd left her notebook. She opened it and showed him a page. "See? It says right here that Zach is going to be home at three. We're going to have a snack together, and then you're going to make dinner for me at six."

"I had a small problem at school."

"But you told me you had to go to school and blend in. You said you needed to fly below the radar. You told me we had to be careful so no one would figure out our secret."

Leave it to Morgan to remember every single word he ever spoke. She probably wrote it down in her notebook, every syllable. He sighed and rubbed the throbbing place between his eyes. No one could make his head ache like Morgan. He said, "I tried to stick to the plan, but something happened."

"You aren't supposed to be home until three o'clock. It isn't three o'clock yet. I haven't had lunch. I was about to have my morning snack, peanut butter and graham crackers, but the house started shaking. I forgot to eat."

Zach dropped on the sofa, arms crossed, feeling guiltier by the second. It was his job to take care of Morgan, not to scare her to death. He stared at the paneled wall without seeing it and mumbled, "You can have your snack now."

Morgan dipped her head to look at her watch. Dark brown hair fell forward, covering her quizzical face. "I can't eat my snack now. The time is six minutes after ten. I have to eat my snack at ten o'clock."

"It will be okay, Morgan. This one time you can eat a few minutes late."

She shook her head stubbornly. "I can't eat my peanut butter and graham crackers. The time is six minutes after ten. I eat my snack at ten o'clock."

The anger began to build in his chest again, but he swallowed it quickly.

She was the reason he hadn't done anything about the Noah sisters. He didn't want anyone to find out about Morgan and tell the witches' council, so he had watched those girls from a distance as they'd played their stupid game. No one knew it, not even Morgan, but he had a small vial of blue dust hidden in a secret drawer in his cherry-wood headboard upstairs.

He had made his own love spell potion after realizing what the Noah sisters were doing. Daydreaming about enchanting the triplets and making them do humiliating things had gotten him through some tough times his junior year, but he'd been afraid to actually do it. Love spells had a tendency to not work properly when used on other witches; although, he suspected he had enough power to make it work.

To get her mind off her missed snack, he decided to tell Morgan about his day. "That stupid little witch blew pink crap into my face. I should have melted her on the spot."

Morgan looked faintly alarmed. "Are we allowed to do that? You told me we aren't supposed to hurt people." She flipped her notebook to another page and shoved it under his nose. "See? Right there." She pointed at the neatly printed sentences. "We aren't supposed to hurt anyone. It's an important rule. You said so. I underlined it three times."

Indeed, she had.

Zach swallowed his anger at Kristen Noah and chose his words carefully. Empathy was a foreign concept to Morgan. If he didn't spell it out for her, she might use her powers to hurt somebody.

"The girl I'm talking about is a witch, not your average person. She has powers of her own and obviously isn't afraid to use them."

"It's okay to hurt witches, then. Just not regular people."

"No. That isn't what I'm saying." He got up and paced the length of the room while trying to come up with a reasonable argument that Morgan would understand. He needed to keep it simple. "If we are attacked, we have to defend ourselves. Make sense? We shouldn't hurt anyone unless our lives are at stake." He forced a smile and lowered his face a bit so he could stare straight into her eyes in order to keep her attention focused on him long enough to get his point across. "I was joking about melting her. We don't do that, not ever. Okay?"

"Will you get in trouble for leaving school early? You told me you wanted to look normal. I wrote it down in my notebook, but I remember it, too. I remember you telling me you had to act like a normal teen."

"Cutting school is what normal teens do. The wild ones, anyway." He shrugged and dropped his hands back to his sides. "Remember me telling you about the witches at school last year?" Once Morgan nodded he said, "Well, one of them tried to enchant me today."

Morgan's brows knitted together. "But you can't be enchanted."

"I know that."

"She doesn't know."

Her usual, matter-of-fact tone fell on his ears like a cat's claws on metal. He sighed. "No, the witch doesn't know about me."

"Do you want some wood? You're mad right now, and making an angel helps relax you. You should get some wood."

He didn't think his hobby could relax him at the moment. "I need to figure out what to do about that little witch."

"What are you going to do to the girl with the pink crap?"

A fair question. The deed was done. There wasn't any point in getting mad about it, but he needed to deal with the fallout. His mouth stretched into a slow smile. "I'm going to make that little witch wish she was never born."

"How?"

"I think I have to accuse her of being a witch in public and take away her powers. People like her shouldn't have access to magic in the first place. I'll deal with her, and then I'll get her sisters, too, to keep them from retaliating." He rubbed his jaw and tried to picture Kristen Noah's expression as the power left her body. "Maybe there'll even be a hunter nearby to lop off her head."

"Hunter?"

Zach's smile deserted his lips. In his glee at the thought of destroying the Noah sisters, he'd forgotten about Morgan's fear of hunters. In order to keep her from wandering off or getting into trouble using her powers, their mother had told her awful stories about hunters. Instead of Snow White, Morgan had listened to bedtime stories about evil witches hunting down other witches. It had been an awful thing to do to a little girl, but it had worked. It was still working. Morgan stayed inside the house unless he was with her.

He wanted to recall the word, but it was too late. Morgan was already racing from the room as if the devil were chasing her. She knocked over a vase on her way to the stairs and didn't even stop to look at what she'd done.

"Morgan?" He dashed after her. "Morgan, it's okay. I'm sorry. Come back."

She ran up the stairs, went straight to her bedroom, and tried to slam the door shut, but he caught it. Curling up at the top of her bed, she drew her knees close to her chest and held her pillow in front of her like a shield. Her eyes darted around the room as if she expected a hunter to be hiding behind the gold drapes or under the heavy, antique desk. Zach wanted to comfort her, but Morgan didn't like to be touched.

Instead, he stayed close enough to talk to her, yet far enough away not to upset her further. Holding his hands out, he said, "I'm sorry for scaring you. It's okay. There are no hunters in this area. I checked before we moved here, remember? I double-checked. Then I triple checked. There are no hunters anywhere nearby. I swear to you. No hunters."

"No hunters." Her lips barely moved as she repeated the phrase.

"You don't have to worry about hunters, Morgan. Hunters kill vampires, and we don't like vampires. Hunters are good." Perhaps if he changed the subject he could get her to calm down. "What happened to Bear? I thought he was going to keep you company while I was at school."

Bear was the ratty teddy bear she'd had since she was a baby. She carried it with her more often than not, using the thing as a security blanket. It was kind of cute and kind of sad at the same time.

Her lifeless eyes drifted to his. "Bear is in the kitchen. I was going to have a snack of peanut butter and graham crackers. Then the house started to shake. I thought it was an earthquake. You were mad, and you made me forget what I was doing."

Zach took the same care in approaching her as he would in approaching a frightened rabbit. He slowly lowered himself onto the bed next to her, careful not to touch her. "I'm sorry for all the drama. It's over now. Promise. You can go get Bear, and I'll go back to school."

"Okay." She nodded. "I can't have my snack now. It was peanut butter and graham crackers, but I can't eat it now."

"I have an idea." He smiled as he took the pillow from her. "You can eat it with your lunch."

Morgan crawled off the bed, went to the desk in the corner of her room, and picked up a physics textbook. It was his. She handed it to him and said, "I read it."

"The whole thing? Already?"

"Yes. I finished it last night."

"Okay. I have about thirty questions to fill out this weekend. Do you think you'll feel like helping me with it?"

Morgan nodded. She got up and walked away as if he had already left. She didn't look back, didn't say goodbye.

As soon as she vanished from his sight, his thoughts returned to the witches at school. What was he going to do about them? Those ignorant girls had no idea the damage they could cause. For over a year he had let them get away with it because interfering could cause problems for him and Morgan. He wished he could permanently stop them.

More than anything, he wanted to publicly accuse Kristen and take away her powers, but it wasn't worth the risk to Morgan. He couldn't afford to draw attention to himself. Not yet. Maybe he could accuse the sisters at the end of the school year. Until then, he would have to be careful to extract vengeance slowly.

If he wanted to keep Morgan safe, he had to pretend to be under Kristen's spell. Hopefully she wouldn't ask him to do anything too humiliating. It was going to be a long, hard year for both of them. If he was going to suffer, so was she, one way or another.

3

Vengeful

At lunchtime, Kristen reclined on the hood of Jake's crappy, lime green car, waiting for the jerk to show his cheating face. Titan High had an open campus, allowing students to eat lunch in town provided they returned to school on time, and Jake always took advantage of it. No reason today should be any different.

To the untrained eye, Kristen looked calm and relaxed, with one leg draped over the other and her back resting against the windshield. However, on the inside she was an erupting volcano. She tore the wrapper off a bar of chocolate with a vicious yank and bit off a huge chunk. Chewing it slowly, she thought about all the terrible things she wanted to do to Jake Petrie.

She spotted the cheating couple before they saw her. Jake and Gina headed her way, hand in hand. Faces close, as if they were going to kiss, they giggled without a thought or a shred of remorse over what this was going to do to poor Cyndi. They looked up at the same time. His smile froze, but Gina's mouth twisted into a knowing smirk.

"What do you want?" Jake asked as he neared the driver's side door while Gina went to the other side.

Kristen slid off the hood to confront him. She reached into her purse, scooped up as much green dust as she possibly could, and blew it into his face without saying a word. Fortunately, no one without powers could see the dust. To them it would look like she'd blown him a simple kiss.

Jake's expression went blank. His jaw went slack, and his eyes stared into space for a couple seconds. Slowly, a blissful smile formed. With both hands, he grabbed Kristen by the shoulders and asked, "Where is Cyndi? I have to see her."

"She's in the cafeteria."

"I have to see her. I have to tell her how much I love her."

He began to run back to school, but Gina's voice stopped him cold. "Where are you going?" She stood next to the car, hands on hips. "I thought you were taking me out to lunch."

Jake turned, and a light of recognition dawned in his eyes. "I'm sorry. I forgot about you." He scratched the back of his head. "I love Cyndi. You were a mistake. I don't even like you. Your hair is stringy, you need to lose a few pounds, and you smell bad. Cyndi is an angel. I need her. I have to tell her before it's too late."

Kristen bit back the laughter threatening to explode from her chest. She turned away as Jake sprinted off to find his true love. Of course, this was only to save Cyndi from public humiliation. Kristen knew she was going to have to tell Cyndi the truth sooner or later. No getting around that. The girl couldn't marry a brainwashed boy under the Crushed spell. She needed to find someone who would treat her like a queen.

"What did you say to him?" Gina rounded the car, chest heaving and fists clenched.

"I didn't say anything. You were here. I guess he just came to his senses." She leaned forward and took an exaggerated sniff. "He was right, by the way. You do smell. Cheap perfume and desperation."

"That's it!" Gina shoved her backwards, and a crowd of spectators began to form. "I am going to kick your stupid butt all over this parking lot!"

Kristen shook her head, remaining calm. Smile in place, she said, "I'll fight you anytime, anywhere. Name it. But I won't fight you here. I'm not getting kicked out of school on the first day."

"I think you're chicken."

Gina began to cluck while Kristen stood her ground. In the third grade, this maneuver might have worked on her. Kristen would have thrown the first punch and gotten into big trouble, but she'd grown up since then, unlike some people. Her main concern was what the other students were going to think. Would they understand she was doing the smart thing? Or would they think she was afraid of the brown-haired loser?

A low chant rumbled through the crowd. *Fight! Fight! Fight!* It brought her nightmare back like a screaming jet roaring through her mind. The students in her dream had been chanting a different word. Kristen shook off the unhealthy residue of negative emotion. She had to be extra careful to keep her temper in check and not cause something unexplainable to happen, not in front of this many witnesses.

Gina reached out a finger and purposely flicked the hat off Kristen's head with a nasty twist on her big lips.

A round of "Oooohs" passed through the crowd.

"Uh-uh. She cannot get away with that," said Lori, one of Kristen's oldest friends.

"Get her, Kristen," another girl said.

"Kick her butt," yet another student said.

"Not here," Kristen repeated in a louder, firmer voice. "You want to fight? I'll meet you after school in the park."

When Gina shook her head, Kristen realized what the girl's game plan was, and it was worse than fighting on school grounds. This wasn't about hitting her. Gina wanted to make Kristen look bad. The girl wasn't as stupid as Kristen had originally believed. Now how was Kristen supposed to get out of this one without being expelled or losing her hard-earned reputation?

Before Kristen could think of something, Gina renewed her verbal attack. She spoke as loud as she could to the other students. "Isn't it funny how Kristen never has a boyfriend? Guys talk, you know. Lots of boys ask her out, but she turns them down every time. She wants you to think it's because she's picky, but we all know the truth deep down, don't we?"

Kristen stood frozen to the ground, unable to breathe. Her mind raced in violent circles, trying desperately to find a way out of this mess. Gina was about to start a nasty rumor. Rumors could kill an otherwise-perfect image and plunge a person into a sea of unpopularity. She had to think fast, had to act fast, before Gina said something they'd both regret.

"Kristen doesn't like boys." Gina folded arms over her chest, looking more pleased than a cat with a bowl of fresh cream. "She prefers girls."

A murmur of surprise floated through the growing crowd. Some students shook their heads in disbelief, but others frowned as they considered the possibility. Several took their cell phones out and started calling contacts to spread the news. Kristen knew she had to squash this rumor like a bug before it got out of control.

It was then she noticed Zach Bevian. Like an answer to her unspoken prayer, he stood in front of the crowd, a grim twist to his mouth. It was his usual expression, and that worried her. Shouldn't he be wearing a dopey grin by now?

Of course, the other victims of her spell had been weak and easily manipulated. Maybe Zach was acting normal for someone with a strong personality under the Crushed spell. Unfortunately, there wasn't a manual to consult, and she definitely wasn't asking her grandmother about it. Grandma Noah would totally freak if she found out her granddaughters were using their powers to play games.

Kristen mentally crossed her fingers, hoping her powers were strong enough to make Zach comply. If this didn't work, she was going to have to change schools.

"For your information," she said just as loud, "I do have a boyfriend. I've been seeing him in secret for a long time."

Gina snorted. "Right. Who is this secret boyfriend, then?"

"That's really none of your business, but I'll tell you just to shut your big, fat mouth." Kristen stood taller and announced, "I'm dating Zach Bevian."

An explosion of excited gasps and shouts came out of the crowd this time. Fingers worked faster on cell phones. Happy voices filled in friends who weren't there to witness the event. She heard a couple people say they were putting it on Facebook.

Gina held a hand up. "She's lying. The girl is desperate for you to think she's a boy magnet. Everyone here knows Bevian only dates women in their twenties."

"Zach." Kristen went to him, praying with every step that the spell had worked and her power was strong enough to make him do what she asked. Usually, she would build up slowly to something this big by asking him to carry her books or pay for her lunch or do her homework. What she was about to ask him for would take a lot of power. Hopefully, her spell was stronger than usual, and Zach was weaker than he seemed.

His eyes held a flood of contempt, and every ounce was directed at her. The two of them faced off like opposing soldiers from different camps. They sized each other up in silence. The hatred in his gaze seemed to grow brighter by the second.

Kristen's confidence took a nosedive. The spell hadn't worked. He was going to rip her life apart and make her the joke of the entire school. Her world was about to collapse, and she couldn't stop it.

There was no turning back now. Like it or not, she had to push this to the bitter end. In the next few seconds, her future would be decided. Either she would continue on the path to success, or she'd lose everything she'd worked her butt off for. She would keep her place at the top of the social food chain or fall into a pit of unpopularity.

She took a deep breath and lowered her voice just a tad, even though she wanted to demand that Zach obey her. If she was going to convince these people Zach was her boyfriend, then she needed to speak to him like he was one.

"We don't have to hide our love anymore." She could barely

breathe and dug her fingernails into the fleshy palms of her hands. The pain helped her focus. "You can give me your jacket now."

She wanted his jacket?

Zach blinked at her, completely thrown by her softly spoken command. She had obviously lost her mind. He didn't like anyone touching his jacket, let alone wearing it. It had been the last gift his mother had given him before she'd died. Kristen Noah could pry it out of his cold, lifeless fingers if she wanted it. He certainly wasn't handing it over to her like a lovesick idiot.

He'd planned to play along with her silly game, but now he didn't think he could. He wasn't going to pretend to *date* her. She was taking things too far. If she continued to push, he was going to push back.

Gina spoke in a loud, cutting voice. "You are not dating Bevian, you total loser. What a joke! He wouldn't touch something like you with gloves on."

"He *is* my boyfriend!" She looked directly at Zach, locked eyes with him, and repeated the command. She seemed to be trying her best to keep it from sounding like an order, but that's exactly what it was, and they both knew it. "We can let everyone know we're together now and be a real couple, just like we talked about. Give me your jacket."

There was a quiet desperation in her wide eyes along with a heavy fear that made him think of Morgan. That was the only thing about this girl that reminded him of his sister. For the first time, he noticed Kristen Noah—really noticed her. She wasn't his type, but there was something extraordinary about her.

Her golden hair fell over her shoulders in soft waves, and it shimmered in the sun, producing a halo effect around her head. She had wide, generous lips that seemed to curve at the ends in a secretive smile even when she wasn't happy, and her eyes seemed to change color with her mood. At the moment, they were a stormy gray, dark like a thundercloud.

Then there was her body.

Her sisters were too skinny for his taste, but Kristen had nice curves exactly where they should be. He wondered what it would feel like to hold her close and kiss her. She had a reputation for being tough as leather when it came to the opposite sex. The girl could take care of herself. Would she want to dominate the kiss, or would she melt like ice cream on a hot day?

What was he *thinking*? Kristen Noah was the most selfish, heartless witch he'd ever stumbled over. There was no way he was attracted to her. She played games with people's emotions. He was a firm believer in "what goes around comes around." The universe should be ready to take her down a notch, and if not, then he would be glad to help the universe out.

Everyone stared at him, obviously waiting for him to confirm or deny Kristen's claim. All eyes were on him, forcing him to make a quick decision.

Zach shrugged out of the jacket, resigned to play along for now. He walked around Kristen Noah and placed the jacket on her shoulders. Then he continued around until he was standing in front of her. Taking both sides of the jacket in his hands, he pulled them together.

She stared at him with wide, unblinking eyes. The distrust in them was like a neon sign. She had expected him to blow her dreams apart. In fact, she still seemed to be waiting for him to pull the proverbial rug out from under her and tell them all the truth.

She's waiting for me to smack her down, he thought with a tinge of satisfaction. He wished he could do it, flatten her on the spot, but Morgan's face floated through his mind. No matter what it cost, he had to protect his sister.

"It looks good on you." He almost choked on the words. "Beautiful as always."

Relief stole over her features. "Thank you."

"No way," Gina said, shaking her head. "I don't believe it. This is a setup or a prank or something. No way have you been dating him without everyone in the school knowing about it."

Kristen shrugged as she snuggled close to him, arm around his waist. She relaxed against his side and played her part to the hilt. A smug smile parted her lips. "I guess we're better at hiding our feelings than most."

Left without a choice, Zach draped an arm around her shoulders as if he'd done it a million times. He hated giving in to her. The arm around her showed they were together, but his hand dangled on the other side rather than touching her. It was a small display of rebellion, one he was sure no one would notice.

The crowd had grown to about a quarter of the school. Several students began to text the juicy news to their friends. Others blatantly started calling people. A few used their camera phones to take pictures of Kristen in Zach's arms. She smiled for the photos.

Zach didn't smile. His jaw tightened instead. There were grenades exploding inside his stomach. If he didn't squelch his temper fast, a massive quake would turn the parking lot into a giant sinkhole that no one could explain. He took a few deep, slow breaths. His hands itched to rip the little witch's head off. She was going to be very sorry she'd picked him to mess with.

Gina's eyes reluctantly shifted to Zach. He recognized the fear and awe in her gaze. He'd worked hard to receive that look from his fellow Titan Warriors. She swallowed, obviously uncomfortable confronting him, but her notorious hatred for Kristen pushed her to the extreme. Last year, he'd watched this girl make problems for the little witch, and he had secretly cheered her on. They were on the same side, but he couldn't let that show.

"When did this happen?" Gina asked. She stared straight into his eyes, demanding answers. "Why do you glare at her all the time if you're dating? It doesn't make any sense. Why would you date her when you only date older women? What is so special about her?"

Kristen Noah is a witch! The words waited at the back of his throat, begging for release. He wanted to shout them at the top of his lungs. Hands clenched, he took another deep breath. It would be so easy to let go and yell the accusation, but then someone would alert the council. Witches weren't accused that often these days. They'd become geniuses at hiding in plain sight. So, when it happened, the council demanded every detail. If he accused her of being a witch, the council would discover his secret, and Morgan would die.

Even if it cost him his sanity, he had to keep his mouth shut.

He hit Gina with a hard glare, turning his fury on her since he couldn't blast Kristen with it. The dark-haired girl folded in an instant. He imagined she was remembering the stories about him blowing up houses and killing people. Her survival instinct won out over her hatred for Kristen.

She stormed off without another word.

Zach's murderous stare went to the spectators. Laughter died. Smiles faded. The kids scattered like cockroaches at night when a light is turned on. Unfortunately, that left him alone with Kristen, his arm stiff around her shoulders. What now? What was he supposed to do in order to keep up the charade? How would an 'enchanted' boy act under these circumstances?

Kristen sighed, a wistful sound. She rested her head against his shoulder for a moment. The small token of intimacy pushed him over the edge. He couldn't do it. There was no way in hell he was going to be nice to her.

He stepped aside, and she lost her balance, almost falling. Almost. When she looked up at him with a question in her eyes, he grabbed the jacket sleeve closest to him and gave it a vicious yank, stripping the jacket off her in one quick motion.

She gasped.

He walked away, leaving her to stare after him while mentally giving himself a point on the invisible scoreboard in his mind. Bevian: 1. Noah: 0.

4

Falling

Somehow, Kristen made it to her last class, gym, without losing her temper again. Titan High kept the boys and girls separated for physical education, and the activities changed every month. Today, the boys were playing basketball while the girls ran laps in the gymnasium. They were supposed to be running on the track across the street, but it had rained last night, and the track was flooded—which was fine with Kristen. If she had to run, she'd rather do it inside.

Dressed in the school's colors, red shorts and white shirts, Kristen and Brittany chose to walk so they could talk to each other. Brittany complained, "You weren't supposed to crush anyone until Monday."

"Sorry." Kristen shrugged, and her ponytail bobbed. "Guess I got carried away."

"Give me the 4-1-1. How's it going with tall, dark, and scary? Have you asked him to do anything yet?"

Kristen's eyes drifted to the boy in question, and she realized with disgust that she'd been waiting for a reason to cast her gaze in his direction. What was the matter with her? She couldn't possibly be attracted to that hopeless, brain-dead jerk.

Zach stood off to the side of the basketball court, too cool to fight for the ball. They had split into two teams, skins against shirts. Naturally, he was on the topless team. His lean muscles glistened with perspiration.

There was a tattoo on his left arm. Kristen squinted, trying to figure out what it was without openly staring at him for more than five seconds. The tattoo had been put on with black ink, no color, and it seemed to have fluid curves like a long sentence written in cursive. It totally wrapped around his upper arm. She frowned, a bit disappointed; she'd expected him to have a dagger or dragon or some other wicked picture.

He called out to one of his teammates, demanding the ball. The boy turned and threw it to Zach without hesitation. No one from the other team tried to block him. Two of the players were supposed to be covering Zach, but they gave him a wide berth, obvious fear in their eyes.

A born athlete, Zach caught the ball with ease, bounced it once, and threw it hard. His teammates watched it sail over their heads and sink into the basket. A few of them smiled and gave each other high fives as if they'd had something to do with the two points.

"Good job," the boys' coach yelled encouragement from the sidelines.

Brittany repeated, "Have you asked him to do anything?"

Feeling smug, Kristen smiled as she gave her answer. "I got him to give me his precious leather jacket."

"No way." Brittany gaped at her for a moment. Then her eyes narrowed in suspicion. "So where is it?"

"Shut up."

"You are such a liar." Brittany said with a snicker.

"Am not. He gave it to me at lunchtime," Kristen explained, "and half the school saw him do it. You can ask around if you don't believe me. But after everyone walked away, he sort of took it back."

"You can always order him to take me out this Saturday night.

There's a party I want to go to, and it would be super cool if he went with me."

"In your dreams."

Brittany formed an *L* for "loser" on her forehead. "Whatever. You probably couldn't make him do it, anyway. You are weak, and you're pushing him too hard. If you keep it up, you'll break the spell before the semester ends. You are so going to lose this year."

"If I were you, I'd be more worried about who you have to crush. I haven't told you who your mark is yet."

Cyndi ran past them. Making a sharp U-turn, she jogged in a circle around them and said, "You're supposed to be running, not walking."

"Teacher's pet." Brittany rolled her eyes in mock disgust. "Teacher's pet."

"What are you two talking about?" Cyndi asked, running backwards so she could face them while they talked to her.

"Kristen was just about to tell me who she wants me to crush this year. It's for our side bet, you know."

Cyndi nodded.

"Bobby Heckler," Kristen said with a neutral expression, even though she knew she'd just dropped a massive bomb.

Cyndi gasped.

Brittany's mouth tightened.

Bobby Heckler had publicly humiliated Brittany their sophomore year by dumping her at a crowded beach party. Since then, she'd gotten revenge by hitting him with several bad-luck spells. He was the last person Brittany would want following her around. Hopefully, their past relationship would make it difficult, if not impossible, for Brittany to give him orders, and Kristen would win.

Spinning around on one foot, Cyndi raced away from them.

Smart girl. Kristen stiffened, preparing for her sister's wrath. There was no way Brittany was going to be a good sport and let it go. She was going to want vengeance, immediate vengeance.

"Bitch!" Brittany shoved Kristen hard.

Kristen flew backwards, and her feet slipped on the shiny, wood floor. Any second that floor would rise up to smack her. It happened too fast for her to use a spell to cushion her fall. One second she was standing, and the next, she was flying through the air. She squeezed her eyes shut and braced for impact.

It didn't happen.

Instead, two strong arms caught her. She opened her eyes to find Zach Bevian glaring down at her. He had saved her from a nasty fall and possible injury. He had caught her on her way to the floor, so she was leaning backwards like a dancer being dipped by her partner. She stared up into his eyes, afraid to blink or move or speak and risk destroying the moment.

Slowly, the contempt drained from his gaze, and his features softened. His teeth raked over his bottom lip. Everything around them seemed to dissolve into nothing until they were the only two people left in the gym.

She stared at his mouth and wondered what it would be like to kiss him. Trying hard to figure out what she should do next, she searched for something intelligent to say.

A piercing whistle blew apart the romantic illusion.

A flash of hatred crossed Zach's face half a second before he pulled her up and shoved her away from himself as if he were afraid he'd get a disease from touching her. He started to walk away, but she grabbed him by the wrist. No one looked at her like she was scum and got away with it.

Maybe a little public humiliation would knock him off his invisible throne. Plus, she was starting to get a bad feeling about him, like maybe the spell hadn't worked after all. Maybe the spell had been broken by his strong will and her outrageous demand for his leather jacket. "Pat your head and rub your stomach."

"What?" He blinked at her.

"Pat your head and rub your stomach while hopping on one foot. Do it now."

For a second she thought he might actually take a swing at her. His eyes glazed over with violent hostility. One of his feet left the ground by slow inches, and he began to hop while rubbing his stomach with one hand and patting the top of his head with the other. There was no way Zach Bevian would do something like that in public unless he were hopelessly enchanted. Her fears faded.

Students stared at Zach, eyebrows raised, but no one dared to laugh.

Changing the order to a nicer one, she said, "I want to see you play basketball."

He put his foot and arms down. "What?"

"You heard me." Had the spell made him deaf? She leaned close and whispered the demands while twirling the end of her ponytail. Having Zach under her spell was kind of fun. Besides, she wanted Brittany to see how much power she had over Zach. She wanted Brittany to know she was going to lose this year—again. "I want you to go out there and play. Play hard. Get the ball and make basket after basket. Do it for me."

Resentment filled Zach's eyes again. His spine straightened, and he scowled at her until she thought she'd taken it too far. Maybe she should have quit while she was ahead. She had a whole year to build up her power through successfully completed tasks. There was no sense in breaking the spell on the first day just to show off in front of her sister.

Zach turned away. He went straight into the middle of the playing boys, stole the ball from the rival team, and made a basket with ease. The other students gaped at him but didn't say a word. The coach encouraged him to do it again, beaming as if silently taking credit for Zach's natural ability.

"Noah!" the girls' coach shouted. "The boys aren't here to entertain you. Move your butt!"

With a smile firmly in place, Kristen joined the other girls on their tenth lap. She weaved around a few until she reached Cyndi. The two of them ran together. Brittany had ducked out without anyone noticing, including Kristen. It was only the first day, and she was already up to her old tricks.

Deep in thought, Kristen didn't hear the shouts to look out. The basketball blasted by her face, an inch from her nose. It almost took off her head. Stopping cold, she looked around to see who'd thrown the ball. It was impossible to tell because several boys were standing around, staring in her direction, including Zach. Hands on hips, he glared at her.

Could he have thrown the ball at her?

No way. Boys under the Crushed spell would rather die than hurt the witch who'd brewed the potion. On the other hand, he had that look of pure hatred in his eyes again. She had a sinking feeling that Zach Bevian was going to be harder to control than she'd thought, and Brittany was right about one thing. If she pushed him too far, she'd break the spell.

Zach was relieved beyond measure when class ended. Kristen Noah had been asking for it, taunting him with stupid demands. He'd wanted to burn her on the spot. Fortunately, he had learned to control his temper long ago. But how much more could he possibly take? It was only the first day, and she'd already ordered him to pull a humiliating stunt.

As fast as he could, he changed into his street clothes before ducking out of the boys' locker room. He was eager to get home to Morgan. Although she seemed to be improving on a daily basis, he didn't like leaving her alone. He stepped into the hallway and got another nasty surprise.

Kristen Noah was waiting for him. Leaning against the wall outside the girls' locker room, her eyes were glued to the boys' door as he walked out. Hoping she would leave him alone, he began to move fast in the opposite direction, but she raced to catch up with him. Her hand latched on to his arm, and she jerked him to an abrupt halt.

"I need a ride home," she said.

He shoved his hands deep into the pockets of his jeans and stared at her. The girl had no shame. If he didn't hate her so much, he might actually like her. "Don't you have a car that you share with your sisters?"

"Britt took it. She's pissed off at me right now, and..." Clamping her lips shut, Kristen glared up at him for a moment. Then she said, "Why am I explaining myself to *you*? Just give me a ride home."

Another order. Zach glanced around the empty hallway. If they'd had an audience, he would have accused her on the spot. Morgan's face popped into his mind, reminding him of his duty to her. He couldn't expose Kristen no matter how bitchy she got. He wasn't going to risk his sister's life. Until he could come up with a sensible way out of this mess, he would have to play along.

"Follow me," he mumbled.

Zach led the way through the double-glass doors and across the parking lot. When they neared his motorcycle, he gestured to it for Kristen's benefit. She eyed his baby with distaste. The fearful expression on her face brought a grin to his. Maybe he wouldn't have to give her a ride home after all. He handed her the helmet before swinging a leg over the seat to the other side.

"Wait a second." She stared daggers at Zach. "I thought you had a car. I'm sure I've seen you driving a black sports car."

"It's a nice day, so I decided to ride the bike instead. Hop on."

"No way am I getting on that thing." She put a hand on her hip and gave his baby another dirty look. "I'd rather not die today."

He grabbed the handlebars and prepared to start the engine. "I guess you're walking, then."

She glanced around the parking lot as if searching for someone else she could bum a ride from. Zach didn't know why, but he suddenly wanted her to get on the bike. He wanted to drive her home. Maybe it was because he wanted to scare the crap out of her so she'd remove the spell and never speak to him again.

"Chicken?" He grinned up at her.

She shook her head and lifted her chin high. "No. I'm not *chicken*. The motorcycle doesn't worry me, but the driver does."

“Excuse me? I happen to be an excellent driver.”

“Yeah. That’s what they all say.”

“I’m not going to beg you to let me drive you home. If you don’t want a ride, that’s fine with me. You be a good little girl and go find a nice, safe car to ride home in.”

Her face paled, and for a moment, he thought she might actually ball up a fist and slam it into his mouth. Instead, she shoved her head into the helmet. Feeling triumphant, he stood long enough to kick-start the engine. The vibration of the bike felt incredible beneath him. He waited for Kristen to climb onto the back and wrap her arms around his waist, but he’d forgotten that Kristen Noah could be unpredictable.

Putting a hand on his chest, she pushed him backwards. “Get out of my way.”

“What are you doing?” He had to yell to be heard over the engine.

She climbed on in front of him, taking over the role of driver while he sat there, stunned. She wrapped her hands around the handlebars and gunned the engine.

He shouted, “Hey, have you ever driven one of these before?”

She smiled over her shoulder. “Now who’s being a chicken?”

They took off faster than he was comfortable with, and he grabbed on to part of the seat behind him to keep from tumbling off. The last thing he wanted was to touch Kristen Noah, so he chose not to hold on to her. They drove past a multitude of staring students. If the kids hadn’t believed they were a couple before, they believed it now.

A few shouts of encouragement and one wolf-whistle followed them out to the busy street. Terrified she was going to crash into another vehicle, Zach stopped worrying what would happen if he touched her. He wrapped his arms tightly around her waist and leaned to the right so he could see over her shoulder, keeping one hand ready to emit a powerful spell if the need arose. It was the last thing he wanted to do. He could save their lives if he saw an accident coming, but he would expose himself in the process. Then Kristen would have a ton of questions.

The tension in his body slowly eased as he realized she knew what she was doing. Kristen Noah was full of surprises. She pulled into the left-turn lane at a four-lane intersection. Both pairs of feet rested on the ground as they waited for the light to change. Neither of them tried to talk over the noisy engine.

The light finally changed, but Kristen didn't budge. Keeping her feet on the ground, she glanced up the street one way and down the other. There wasn't any traffic, so Zach didn't know what she was waiting for. He glanced behind them. There was a white car approaching in the lane to the right. He moved his mouth close to where her ear would be inside the helmet, and he shouted, "The light is green! That means '*Go*'."

Instead of turning left like she was supposed to, she made an illegal move and cut in front of the white car to turn right at the last second. The car's horn blasted at them. Zach's arms tightened around her, and the tension returned to his body full-force.

They drove for ten minutes, traveling around winding hills until they eventually made it to the coastal highway. Kristen opened the throttle then. The motorcycle jerked beneath them as it picked up speed at an incredible rate. Zach glued his body to the back of hers and continued to watch over her shoulder for trouble. It was hard to concentrate. For some unknown reason, he was becoming more and more attracted to her.

Relief flooded his system when Kristen slowed the bike down and pulled off to the side of the highway. There was a scenic outlook that had been created for tourists. As they drove in, there was a family driving out. Tension returned yet again as Zach realized they were going to be totally alone for the first time.

Kristen switched off the engine, and Zach hopped off the back. He couldn't put enough distance between them. Going over to the railing, he pretended to be fascinated by the ocean view. The silence became a palpable thing, building until he couldn't stand it. He had to know what Kristen was doing, what she was thinking, so he turned to face her. What he saw completely knocked him off balance. Tough-as-nails Kristen Noah was crying.

Still sitting on the bike, shoulders slumped forward, Kristen stared at the ground. Her vision blurred, and she couldn't see through the tears. The last conversation she'd had with her mother replayed in her head. The woman had laid into her big time, telling her she was ruining her life and was going to wind up alone, like her father. Although her mother had been in a multitude of relationships since the divorce, her dad didn't date at all.

Was he lonely? Was her mother right about that? She'd told Kristen that her dad was afraid to open his heart to anyone. According to her mother, that had been the main problem in their marriage. Her dad had been closed off, too wrapped up in his career to see past his own nose.

For the first time in her life, Kristen felt like a boat that had come loose from the pier—adrift, tossing and turning without anyone to guide it. For the first time, she didn't have a comforting list of future goals to strive for. If her mother was right and those goals actually belonged to her father, then she had nothing that belonged solely to her.

Feeling Zach's eyes on her, she looked up and caught him staring. Embarrassed about crying in front of him, she wiped away the tears with the backs of both hands. Tears were a weakness. She hadn't cried in front of another person in years. Why, when she finally broke down, did it have to be in front of Zach Bevian? She blurted out, "Do you ever get tired of people thinking you're a useless waste of space?"

He blinked at her. "What?"

"Do you ever get tired of wearing the bad-boy label?"

"I have no idea what you're talking about." He kicked at a small rock with the toe of his boot, looking uncomfortable with the turn the conversation had taken.

More than anything, she wanted to be able to talk to someone about her feelings.

An epiphany eased her confusion and pain. Zach Bevian was under her control. She could order him to keep his mouth shut. It would be almost like talking to a shrink. In fact, she could probably even order him to forget the conversation had ever happened. She went straight up to him, eyes still locked on his, and said, "You can't tell anyone what I'm about to tell you."

"I understand."

"Seriously, just don't talk about me at all."

"Got it. My lips are sealed."

The mere thought of being able to talk to someone without being judged or having to listen to endless advice made her feel better. Nervous energy pushed her to walk circles around Zach as she laid her troubles at his feet.

"When I was little, I used to get up early just to make my bed. I had to help Cyndi with hers because she couldn't do it, and I made Brittany's bed because she refused. In school, I worked hard to get the best grades.

"I remember coming home in tears because I got a ninety-six percent on a test instead of a hundred. All these years, I thought I was born to be special, but now I wonder how much of it comes from my dad pushing me to be the best. He's a perfectionist, and I think it rubbed off on me. My mom shined a light on some things this summer and got me thinking about my future.

"People expect so much out of me, and I don't want to let them down, but I have to live for me, don't I? They expect me to take charge of everything and do a good job. I guess I'm just sick of it. When do I get to be irresponsible? When do I get to lean on someone else?"

Zach stared at her through narrowed eyes, saying nothing.

She added, "So I was wondering about you."

"Me?"

"Yes, you. I'm kind of stuck with being the good girl, but you have the bad-boy label hanging around your neck. Do you like it? Are you happy with it? I guess the most important thing I want to know is—if you weren't happy with it anymore, how would you get rid of it?"

He shook his head. "I don't think you can. Once people think they have you figured out, it takes a lot to change their minds. You'd have to do something really, really bad to lose the good-girl label, and I don't recommend you blow up the school or anything."

It wasn't what Kristen wanted to hear. Another thought occurred to her, and she smiled. "Well, maybe your bad reputation will rub off on me. Everyone thinks we're dating. It's a start in the right direction." She went to the railing and took in the magnificent view. "What do I do about my future? How do I figure out if it's my dream to be a businesswoman or my dad's dream?"

Zach seemed to take her question seriously. Thinking about it, he rubbed his chin. His eyes slid over her and went to the ocean again. But when he answered her, he looked straight at her. "Okay. You're planning to go to college, obviously. A degree will take at least four years. That gives you a lot of time to think about what you want to do with your life. My advice to you is to follow your heart."

Sighing in frustration, she spoke aloud, but she was talking more to herself than to Zach. "What about love? I've never even been on a date because my mom goes through one bad relationship after another, and my dad says love is an illusion. They brainwashed me. Now I'm a social retard."

"You've never been on a date?" Zach openly gaped at her. "Seriously?"

"That's what I just said."

"Have you ever kissed a guy?"

"If I haven't been on a date, Einstein, I haven't kissed anyone, either."

He got a weird look on his face but didn't say a word. Instead, Zach cupped her face between his hands and stared down at her mouth with longing. He was going to kiss her. It was totally against the rules, and she should order him to take a step back.

Her tongue snaked out to lick her upper lip.

She wanted him to kiss her. More than anything, she wanted to feel his mouth on hers. She wanted to experience the things her sisters went on and on about and get some first-hand knowledge of the passion she'd only read about in books.

A loud screech made them jump apart. Kristen's eyes went to the pale blue sky. A huge, brown owl with yellow eyes circled above them once before plunging straight down. The owl headed straight for her. Hands in the air, she tried to defend herself, but it happened so fast she didn't have time to even think of a spell.

She had to get out of its way. Turning, she ran in the wrong direction, smacked into the protective railing, and her feet left the ground. She tumbled over the side, and before she knew what was happening, she was airborne. Her stomach flipped over. Spying the jagged rocks waiting below, a sickening dizziness forced her eyes closed. She couldn't believe she was going to die like this.

It wasn't Zach's fault, but they would blame him. His reputation would grow, while hers would remain untarnished in death. She was going to die, and she'd never even been kissed.

5

Tired

"Then what happened?"

Cyndi slid to the edge of Kristen's white, wrought-iron daybed, eager to hear the rest of the terrifying tale. Her hands clutched at the thick comforter. A couple of the decorative pillows fell over when she moved. Kristen didn't immediately speak, so Cyndi asked, "How did you survive it? Did you do a spell?"

"There wasn't time for that," Kristen admitted. "If it wasn't for Zach and his quick reflexes, I literally wouldn't be here. I wouldn't be anywhere."

"He saved you? That is *so* romantic."

"It didn't feel romantic. One minute we were talking, and the next, a stupid owl knocked me right off the cliff. It came out of nowhere. I've never seen an owl during the day before."

"Do you like him now?"

"Who? Zach? No." Kristen shook her head and added conviction to her voice. "*Hell* no. I just don't hate him quite as much anymore. Okay?"

Cyndi laughed. "You like him."

"I do not."

"I can see your aura, Kris. It's all soft and blush-pink right now. You are so into him you can't even think straight."

Ignoring her, Kristen fixed the pillows, placing her favorite ones—red squares covered with white lace and tiny, red bows—to the side so Cyndi wouldn't recline on them. Her sisters had a bad habit of messing with them even though they knew it drove her crazy. Once the pillows were exactly where they should be again, she returned to her desk.

It was early evening. The sun shone through her two floor-to-ceiling windows as it put in a last appearance before sinking into the ocean. The sound of waves rolling onto their private beach soothed Kristen's otherwise frayed nerves as she picked up her gold pen and continued writing a letter to her dad. She probably wouldn't give it to him, but it felt good to put her true feelings in writing.

Kristen formed each word slowly in cursive, writing as neatly as possible on the floral stationary. She still needed to do her homework, cook dinner—Brittany obviously wasn't going to—and pick out tomorrow's outfit and accessories. Old habits were hard to break. If she were going to have fun this year, she would have to let some of her responsibilities slide.

But it was so hard to stop being good.

"Did your life flash before your eyes?" Cyndi asked.

"You watch way too many movies. It happened too fast for me to think about anything. I was flying through the air, and then I felt his hand on my wrist. He pulled me up before I could even wonder if he was strong enough."

She owed Zach Bevian her life. Another brick of guilt was added to the ten-foot-high wall. He had saved her from certain death after she'd crushed him. She didn't even want to think about ordering him to hop up and down while rubbing his stomach and patting his head. He should have let her fall and die. It was what she deserved.

"I want to un-crush him," she blurted out.

Cyndi gasped. "You know Britt won't stand for you backing out after you already did the deed. She's still mad at you, you know, and I mean super mad. If I were you, I'd avoid her for as long as possible. You should have seen how red her face got after you crushed Zach before it was time. She called you a cheater." Cyndi's cheeks flushed pink. "She called you a lot of things. If you try to un-crush Zach now, she'll make you forfeit the game."

Kristen tried to conjure up a good reason for un-crushing Zach other than the obvious, but she couldn't think of anything that would convince Brittany to let her do it. Her sister would love an excuse to kick her out of the game. Brittany wanted to win this year more than she wanted to breathe.

Kristen reminded herself what was at stake. If she lost, she would lose use of the car. Then there was prom, the single most important event of the whole school year. She wouldn't be able to buy a designer original, and those pictures would be floating around forever, especially if she were voted prom queen. Someday, at the worst possible time, they would resurface. They could ruin her career.

She wanted to have some fun this year, but she didn't want to destroy her future while doing it.

She reasoned aloud, "I guess I'm not really hurting him. I mean, Zach doesn't seem to mind that he's under my spell. In fact, he's been surprisingly charming."

"Really?" Cyndi frowned. She grabbed one of the pillows and put it on her knees so she could lean her elbows on it. "All of my marks have followed me around like puppies begging for constant attention. I wouldn't call that charming."

That was how they usually behaved, but Zach was different. There was something off about him. Kristen wished she could figure it out. She opened her mouth to ask Cyndi what she thought it meant.

The first syllable emerged and was cut short as the door flew open and their father stuck his head in. Eyebrows furrowed, he looked this way and that. "What are you two doing?"

Their father had been a marine before attending business school. He thought they were up to something twenty-four-seven. Without warning, he would peek into their rooms. They knew not to change clothes unless they were in the bathroom, the only door he would actually knock on. He also searched their rooms on a regular basis, but he didn't think they knew about that.

Brittany kept her cigarettes and occasional bottle of beer in a box beneath the front porch. So far, he hadn't found it.

"Nothing, Dad," Cyndi said with a sigh. "We were just talking about school and stuff."

"Yes, today was your first day as seniors." He entered the room and walked around, hands clasped behind his back. His eyes took everything in like a cop searching for contraband, but he wasn't dressed like an officer of the law. His expensive suit made him look more like a politician. He spoke to them without looking directly at them. "And how was it?"

"Good," Kristen said.

She worked hard to keep from looking guilty. Part of her wanted to confess on the spot and get it over with. Somehow, he was going to find out she'd driven a motorcycle. Or worse, he could learn she'd been with Titan High's bad boy. He'd never trust her again. She watched her dad move around the room, and she held her breath when he neared her dresser. If he pulled the bottom drawer open, he would find Zach's jacket. That would be hard to explain.

After her near-death experience, Zach had wrapped the jacket around her, insisting she wear it home.

"School was okay," Cyndi replied with a shrug. "Same old same old."

Daniel Noah walked past the windows to the tall, white dresser in-between. His eyes swept over the surface: a close-up photograph of the girls wrapped in a gold frame, a black-lacquer jewelry box with a neon-pink butterfly on the lid, her landline phone in the shape of two red lips, and the small tray where she tossed her keys every day as soon as she got home.

Grabbing the gold handles, he opened her dual closet doors and stepped into the huge walk-in. Her clothes hung neatly on both sides, evenly spaced and color coordinated, starting with her favorite color—red—and ending at the back with her least favorite—yellow. Shoes were lined in neat rows beneath the clothes, with her purses on the shelf above. When he came out of the closet, he was smiling. For some reason, her room always seemed to cheer him up.

Their father stopped in front of Cyndi. "Where is the other one at?"

Cyndi shrugged. "I think Britt is downstairs."

"If she snuck out of the house again, she's toast."

"She didn't sneak out. She's around here somewhere."

"She had better be." He nodded at Kristen before leaving.

Once the door was completely shut and they heard his footsteps fading down the hallway, Kristen asked, "*Did* Britt take off again?"

"Naturally."

"He's going to kill her this time. Then he's going to ground her for three months. I can't believe she is such an idiot. School just started. What is wrong with her?"

"Don't worry. I have it covered."

Cyndi headed for the door with a knowing smile.

"Where are you going?" Kristen asked as she stuffed the letter into the waiting envelope.

"I'm going to take the back stairs down to the kitchen and pretend to be Britt. He won't know the difference."

"Why do you always look out for her when she's begging to get caught?"

"If Britt gets busted, he'll put us all on lockdown. You know that. Now give me a sec to become her."

Cyndi's eyes drifted shut before snapping open again. She wore a haughty, almost hostile expression. "OMG! Don't have a cow. I'll be right back."

Kristen shivered with distaste, hating it when Cyndi played the part of her twin. The girl was way too good at it, making Kristen wonder if Cyndi had ever played the trick on her.

Cyndi left, and Kristen stood up. She stretched with her arms overhead, back arched. A yawn closed her eyes and opened her mouth wide. It had been a long and exhausting day. She went to the bed and fell down on it, promising herself it would just be for a few minutes as her eyes drifted shut.

Although she didn't have much homework, it being the first day, she wanted to get a jump on reading some chapters from her new schoolbooks. It was her style to work ahead, and the teachers had come to expect it from her. But she was so tired. Her limbs grew heavy, and she began to float.

Zach slammed the front door for the second time that day.

He had dropped Kristen off five blocks from her house because she'd been afraid her father would catch them together. Sometimes his bad rep was a distinct disadvantage. Zach had wanted to make sure she was safe, so he'd looped around the block a few times. For some reason, the urge to protect Kristen was riding him hard. He couldn't shake it.

But there were bigger things to worry about now. When he'd seen Kristen fall off the cliff, it had scared ten years off his life. He had wanted to see her suffer, not die. Someone had intentionally tried to kill her today. He was sure of it. That hadn't been an ordinary owl at the cliff. Someone wanted her dead, and he was afraid he already knew the identity of that 'someone'.

Moving quickly from room to room, he searched for his sister. He finally found her in the family room. Still dressed in pajamas, she was lying on the sofa with a hand on her stomach.

When she saw him appear in the doorway, she looked pointedly to the grandfather clock across the room. "You're late. You told me you would be here at three o'clock. I wrote it down in my notebook. We were going to have a snack together."

Hiding his suspicions about her, he said, "I can fix you something now if you want."

"My stomach hurts. I don't want anything."

"Are you okay?" The incident with Kristen momentarily forgotten, he crossed the room to sit next to his sister. Once again, she became his top priority. "Are you sick?"

"My stomach hurts," she repeated. "I ate my snack with my lunch the way you told me to, but it made my stomach hurt. I threw up."

"What exactly did you eat?"

"I had a tuna sandwich, apple, peanut butter, and graham crackers."

He made a face. "Next time I make a suggestion like that, I'll make sure it isn't such a disgusting combination."

Morgan groaned and closed her eyes. "I had a glass of milk, too."

Zach moved to the end of the sofa where her head was resting and placed a pillow on his lap, careful not to touch Morgan because sometimes a simple touch set her off on a rampage. She placed her head on the pillow. He sang the song their mother used to sing to them when they were sick. It had always helped him.

"Did you go out today?" he asked after the song ended.

"Hmm?"

"Did you stay inside the house, or did you go somewhere?"

"I was home all day. I was sick."

He stiffened, wondering if she was lying to him. "Are you sure?"

Morgan sprung off the couch like an activated jack-in-the-box. She crossed the room to grab her treasured notebook. Holding it to her chest, she returned to Zach's side. "I write everything I do down in my notebook. Look."

She flipped the book open to the last page and shoved it at him. "After I ate lunch, I didn't feel good. My stomach hurt. I had tuna, peanut butter, graham crackers—"

"I know," he said, cutting her off.

It was true. According to the notebook, she had decided to rest after eating the unfortunate lunch and hadn't gotten up to write in her journal since. So, who had conjured an owl to attack Kristen? Was there another witch in the vicinity, one with a nasty disposition, or had one of Kristen's own sisters sent the owl as a warning to her?

And why an owl?

It was possible there was an outsider with information on his sister, information they should not have. If that were true, both girls were in danger.

"Did you have a good day?" Morgan asked. "This morning was bad. You had pink crap blown into your face." She turned back one page in her notebook and showed him a new entry. "See? It says Zach had pink crap blown in his face."

Indeed it did. "I had a much better afternoon, thank you," he said, trying hard not to smile.

"Why were you late?"

Should he tell her that Kristen Noah wasn't an evil witch after all? He decided against it. Morgan could be weird when it came to new people, especially if it was someone he was spending time with.

"I had to talk to somebody after school. I'm sorry. I promise not to be late again."

"That's okay. I didn't want an afternoon snack anyway. My stomach hurts because of lunch."

Zach interrupted her before she could list off the foods again. "I know. But you feel better now, right?"

A surprised smile took over her face. "Yes. I do feel better."

Morgan plopped down next to him and wound her arms around his middle. It was okay for her to touch him, but she didn't like him touching her. Hugging him tightly, she added, "I always feel better when you're here. I wish you didn't have to go to school. You could stay home with me. We could watch television."

It was too bad he couldn't spend more time with her. School wasn't just an option for him. He had to go. Otherwise, someone might get suspicious. If the council found out Morgan was with him, they'd both be in trouble.

"I can't drop out of school, Morgan, but I'm here now. We can watch a movie if you want."

Her face brightened. "I'll find one."

"Okay. I'll be back in a minute."

Zach went out the back door. The moon shed enough light to make the search for a piece of wood easy. A variety of wood—every shape and size imaginable—formed a short pyramid on the other side of the gray, stone terrace. He chose a small piece and went back inside.

While Morgan curled up on the other side of the couch to watch the movie she'd selected, he took out his knife and started whittling the wood. It took a ton of concentration to make an angel out of nothing. His father had taught him how to do it. In a few minutes, he was totally relaxed.

Kristen walked quickly down the long hallway with endless lockers on both sides. Since starting school at Titan, she'd always had a locker on the top row. She felt kind of bad for the kids with lockers on the bottom because they either had to bend down or squat to turn the dial. She hadn't asked for special treatment, but somehow she always seemed to get it. The principal and teachers loved her. Sometimes being a good girl worked in her favor.

She was on her way to the gymnasium for cheerleading practice, and she was already late. Students stopped to stare. Fingers pointed at her. Because of the mist-covered floor, the students seemed to be floating instead of walking.

A cold, wet fear seeped into Kristen's bones.

"Stop looking at me!" she shouted.

Her heartbeat quickened.

She didn't fully understand what was going on, but she knew she had to get away from them. She began to run. Instead of getting closer, the end of the hallway stretched until it was miles away. Her heart thumped painfully against her ribs. Escape. She had to find a way out before it was too late.

There was Brittany, surrounded by a bunch of boys, talking and laughing. Kristen ran to her.

Brittany turned. Her eyes were big, black holes, nothing but empty voids. With her usual attitude, she said, "What's wrong with you?"

"Show me the way out!"

"There is no way out. You're trapped."

"No!" Kristen grabbed her sister's arm. The appendage fell off in her hands. No blood. No mess. Just a lifeless limb. She screamed.

"Look what you did!" Brittany tore her dead arm out of Kristen's trembling grasp. "What am I supposed to do with this now?"

Kristen couldn't breathe properly. Hands on her throat, she backed away from her sister before spinning around and running for the elusive exit. There was something she had to do, something important, but she couldn't remember what. Why wouldn't the other students tell her?

Why did they keep staring and pointing?

Cyndi waited for her at the end of the hallway, a smug smile on her lips. She lifted a finger and wagged it. "Naughty, naughty. You can't leave school until you finish all of your homework."

"What are you talking about?" Kristen tried to rush past her to get to the doors.

Cyndi stepped to the side, blocking Kristen's way. The other girl started out looking normal, but then she changed. Her hair turned into green slime. It dripped onto her shoulders. "You brought this on yourself, you know."

Kristen backed away as Cyndi reached for her with a slime-covered hand. "Don't touch me."

"*Don't touch me*." The mocking voice belonged to a boy she'd refused to date last year. He appeared at Cyndi's side. The skin on his face began to flake away, revealing the bloody tissue beneath, but he didn't seem to notice. "Don't touch me. That should be your middle name. Kristen Don't-Touch-Me Noah. You are such a frigid witch."

Witch.

The last word reverberated through her brain and echoed down the Titan High hallways. A chorus line of heads snapped up at the same time like a well-executed, musical slash-dance number. The word spread in low whispers.

She cried, "No! Don't say that."

"Don't say what? Witch?"

Witch. Some of the students turned in their direction.

"Please stop! They might hear you."

A whispered mantra began in the background, softly at first. "Witch. Witch. Witch."

The students formed a circle around her. Books fell from their hands. They lifted their arms and pointed their fingers as the chant grew louder. "Witch. Witch. Witch."

"No! Stop it!"

A new figure emerged from the shadows. She couldn't see the face, just a basic outline, but deep down she knew she should recognize this person. They lifted an arm and pointed at her. "Kristen Noah is a witch."

"Witch!" they screamed now, in earnest. "Witch! Witch!"

She cowered in the corner as the powers drained from her quaking body.

Kristen bolted up from her bed, a scream dying on her stiff lips. She pinched her arm to make sure she was awake. Relief at finding she was still in her bedroom didn't last long, because she realized what the dream meant for her. It had been the third dream.

It was going to come true, and there wasn't anything she could do to stop it.

6

Enchanted

Torn. After a restless night of chasing elusive sleep, Zach went to school with a dull headache sawing on a nerve just behind his eyes. He was torn between contempt for Kristen and an unreasonable urge to protect the girl. There was something different about her. He didn't fully understand why, but he wanted to get to know her better. Maybe he wanted the information so he could use it against her later, or maybe he genuinely liked her.

He waited next to her locker and tried hard to ignore the curious stares, quiet giggles, and whispered innuendos. How had he gotten himself into this mess? He had adapted after the explosion, learned to keep a low profile, but Kristen had ruined everything in less than five seconds. Now what? If he were smart, he would run in the opposite direction. Kristen was more dangerous than his sister… dangerous to his peace of mind.

That was his last coherent thought. Then, he saw her. She appeared at the end of the hallway in the center of chaos, definitely in her element. She was with her own kind—cheerleaders. They were dressed in their red-and-white uniforms, but the short skirts and tight sweaters looked ridiculous on everyone except Kristen. He hated to admit it, but she was incredibly hot.

Her eyes met his, and she stumbled.

Bending his head slightly, he bit his lower lip to keep from laughing.

Blood rushed to her face, staining her cheeks nearly the same red as her lips. Her brows drew together in a frown. Lifting her chin high, she continued on as if nothing had happened. Obviously, she hadn't been expecting to see him waiting for her, and Zach wondered if he'd given himself away already. It was possible that enchanted boys didn't normally seek her out. Maybe they waited for her to call for them.

Kristen gave the girls a warning look, and they drifted away. A few watched with knowing smiles in place. They thought he was Kristen's boyfriend—they had no idea what was really going on beneath the surface. They didn't know he was supposed to be under a spell.

Tearing his gaze from her, Zach grabbed the locker dial between his thumb and two fingers. He needed time to mentally regroup before facing her again. He rotated the dial this way and that, hitting each number just right until it clicked. Pulling the metal door open, he smiled at her. She stared at him in stunned amazement, and he shrugged. "You'd be surprised at what I know."

A flicker of fear darkened her eyes.

He could read her like a first-grade textbook. She was wondering if he'd discovered her secret. Good. Let her sweat it out a bit. She had an important lesson to learn. Boys weren't puppets to be used for her amusement.

Kristen slapped her forehead, startling him. "Oh no! I forgot your jacket. I was going to return it to you. Every night, I choose my clothes for the next day and get them ready. I would have put your jacket with them, but I was afraid my dad would see it."

"If you don't mind, it's a bit early in the day to talk about your obsessive-compulsive behavior." His voice sounded raw, as if he hadn't used it in days. He cleared his throat before adding, "I only had one cup of coffee this morning, and I'm not totally awake yet."

"Here." She lifted a large paper cup he'd somehow missed while appraising her. It had an expensive label on it that he immediately recognized, although he'd never purchased anything from that particular establishment.

She added, "I don't mind sharing."

Dying for caffeine, he took a huge mouthful before realizing there was something wrong with it. He swung his body to the right, swung around to the left, desperately searching for a place to spit it out, and found nothing handy. No water fountain. No trash can. He was forced to swallow the nasty concoction. Was it a witch's brew? Was she trying to put another spell on him?

He screwed his face up for a moment, and Kristen laughed.

"That's not coffee," he complained.

"Sorry." She rolled her eyes, soft gray today. "I should have known you were a straight-from-the-pot, strongly brewed, black-with-no-sugar kind of guy."

"Oh yeah?" He leaned back against the locker next to hers. At least things were a bit less awkward between them today. Since he'd saved her life, she was different, less guarded. He liked it. "And what kind of girl are you?"

"I'm a white-chocolate and raspberry soy latté."

He shook his head and handed the nasty thing back to her. That explained the horrible taste in his mouth. "I'd rather drink water from a dog's bowl."

"Stop making fun of my coffee."

"That's not coffee. Someday, I'm going to introduce you to the real thing, and you won't want to drink this girly stuff again."

Her lips twitched as she tried hard not to smile. She probably didn't want to fall for him any more than he wanted to fall for her. He needed to pour on the charm today and make it happen. If she told him to pat his head and rub his stomach one more time, he was going to do something drastic. But if she fell for him, she would want to remove the spell. He was almost one-hundred-percent sure.

Drawn in by her incredible smile, Zach's body moved closer to hers of its own volition. Her eyes crinkled a bit at the sides when she laughed. She was more beautiful than any girl had a right to be. *Damn*. He was supposed to be getting under her skin, not the other way around.

"Hey," he said. His palms began to sweat, so he wiped them on his jeans while talking. "Do you want to see a movie with me this weekend?"

She froze, and her eyes widened by slow fractions. "Are you asking me out on a date?"

"I'm trying to."

"Oh." She turned her face and looked at passing students.

The Noah girls probably had a rule against dating people they had put their little spells on. She had no way of knowing he couldn't be enchanted. He certainly wasn't going to tell her. For his plan to work, he needed to get her alone for a while and romance her. If it was the last thing he did, he was going to get Kristen Noah to fall for him.

She stood straighter and nodded once. "I guess that would be okay."

"Great. I'll pick you up Saturday at four o'clock."

"Sounds like fun." She stared at her fingernails, her gaze on them instead of him. They were painted soft pink now. She said, "Pick me up at the library, not my house. Okay?"

The softly spoken demand didn't surprise him. She didn't want her father to know she was dating and especially not that she was dating someone with a bad reputation. He casually shrugged, even though every fiber of his being was on red alert. She was good at playing games. If he didn't watch himself, she would have him under her spell instead of the other way around.

Spell? He froze, and the bottom dropped out of his world. The little witch might actually have more power than he'd given her credit for. He couldn't breathe. Was he under a spell after all? His feelings had developed awfully fast. Yesterday morning, he'd wanted to kill her. By afternoon, he had saved her life and almost accused his own sister of knocking her off a cliff. Now he wanted to hook up with her?

Either he was enchanted, or he'd lost his mind.

Zach quickly went over every single command she'd given him. He had followed them to the letter, but he'd had his reasons. He'd been pretending to be under the spell. Right? *Just* pretending. But what if that was how the spell worked? What if the enchanted guy always rationalized why he obeyed? It could be part of the magic.

He had given her his jacket so she wouldn't figure out he was onto her. Later, he had patted his head and rubbed his stomach. Then, he'd played basketball for her. The question was—could he have stopped himself? Or was she *that* powerful?

Zach stared at Kristen, jaw tight. Truly scared, his life flashed before his eyes, his life *and* Morgan's. They were both at risk. In a flash, the warm, protective feeling he'd had for Kristen died a quick death. Pure hatred replaced it. If it were the last thing he ever did, he would make her pay for blowing that pink crap into his face.

Cyndi walked by with boyfriend Jake Petrie dogging her footsteps. It was clear to everyone except Jake that he was annoying her. He was babbling like an idiot, asking her all sorts of questions. "Do you like Coke or Pepsi? What about singing in the shower? Do you do that? I like to ice skate. Maybe I can take you with me next time. Do you like to ice skate? If you don't, then I don't like it, either. I would give up anything for you, Cyn."

Cyndi shot him a sideways glare but said nothing. She grabbed the dial on her locker and spun it around. Jake dropped to his knees next to her and cried, "I love you! I love everything about you."

"*Stop it!*" she hissed. "Everyone is looking. What is *wrong* with you today?"

"I want the whole world to know how much I love you."

"Well, I want to be alone for a while. I can't think when you're constantly talking."

"Please, tell me something I can do for you. Anything. I would do absolutely anything to make you happy."

Cyndi turned on him, smoke practically shooting from her nostrils. "You want to do something for me? Go jump off a bridge."

"*No!*"

Kristen screamed the word and dropped her coffee cup on the floor. The lid flew off, and lukewarm liquid splashed Zach's boots. Leaving him standing at her locker alone, she rushed over to her sister and dragged her to an empty corner, where she whispered feverish words in the other girl's ear. Since Zach couldn't hear what was going on, he studied their expressions. Cyndi's went from shock to anger in a split second.

After sharing a vicious glare with Kristen, she went to Jake and asked him to join her outside for a quick chat. Happy to comply, he followed her like a puppy about to get a treat, and that was when the truth hit Zach square between the eyes. Jake Petrie had been enchanted, but not by Cyndi. Kristen had done the dirty deed.

Zach leaned against Kristen's locker, arms folded over his chest. Kristen's unhappy gaze followed her sister. Wrapped up in her own drama, she didn't notice him watching her. He didn't know what to think about this latest development. Once again, Kristen had used her powers to play God, but she'd done it to save her sister from being hurt. As much as he wanted to hate her for it, he understood why she'd done it. He understood crossing the line to protect a sibling.

Brittany strutted up to Kristen with a freshman in tow and a sour expression on her face as if she'd been sucking on lemons. The boy gazed at her with open adoration. Feeling trouble coming, Zach moved closer so he could hear what was going on.

"Tell my sister what you just did for me," Brittany said.

The boy obeyed immediately. "Car-surfing in the parking lot."

Kristen frowned. "You can't ask him to do something dangerous like that, Britt. He could have gotten hurt. What is wrong with you?"

"OMG! Turn the drama-dial down a notch! He's fine. Anyway," she shrugged, "you broke a rule first. What goes around comes around. I'm going to win this year, and there's nothing you can do about it. Marc here just risked his life and pumped up my power. I haven't seen you ask Bevian to do anything lately. What's wrong? Losing your touch?"

"Don't worry about me. Everything is going according to plan."

"Right. If the plan is for you to lose, excellent job."

Kristen's mouth tightened. "I won't lose. I never lose. You know why I don't lose? Because I know how to groom the guy. Slow and steady wins the race."

Brittany chuckled. "Whatever."

"Hey, you were supposed to crush Bobby Heckler. That was our deal."

"I couldn't. FYI, he has the measles and won't be back to school for a while."

Kristen folded arms over her chest. "Measles? I don't believe you. If he has the measles, I know where he got them."

"Prove it." Brittany's eyes widened in feigned innocence. "Anyway, I didn't have a choice. I had to crush someone because you cheated and started the game early."

"What about our side bet?"

"It's still on."

"That isn't fair. You give me an impossible challenge, but you do one of the easiest marks in school?"

Smug smile, Brittany shrugged. "I guess you shouldn't have cheated. Maybe if you had followed the rules, you would have found out I was joking. Now you're screwed. Deal with it."

Kristen went to her locker and retrieved her books. She didn't catch the vicious glare Brittany sent her way, but Zach saw it. Could Brittany have enough power to control an owl? Better question was—did she hate her sister enough to try to kill her?

Brittany walked away and disappeared into the crowd.

Zach considered warning Kristen that her sister was out for blood, but he didn't get the chance.

Kristen returned to his side, mouth tight. Her expression had turned bitter. She pushed her books at him and said, "Carry these and walk me to class."

It was a classic order. In the past, he'd seen boys follow the Noah girls throughout the school year, day after day, carrying their books with blissful smiles on their faces. It had made his blood boil. If he hadn't been working hard to stay below the radar, he would have accused them and stripped them of their powers long ago.

Once again, he had to wonder if he was under her spell, because he took Kristen's books without argument. *Had* he been enchanted? How could he possibly know? He wasn't sure how enchanted boys felt, only how they acted. If he wasn't under the spell, he could throw her books down and refuse to comply. He was sure he could do that if he wanted to, but then she would know something was off about him, and she wouldn't rest until she got to the truth. She could go to the witches' council and destroy everything.

Kristen did a double take.

Purposely changing his expression, covering the resentment in his eyes with warmth—he had to think about his sister to accomplish this—he said, "I'm just waiting for you to lead the way."

Nodding briefly, she walked off, leaving him to follow.

Zach stayed a step behind her, inwardly cursing her and himself for wanting her. It was just physical, of course. His body wanted her, while his mind wanted to get as far away from her as possible. He needed to get himself under control. Then he would take care of her. He would have to step up the plan of seduction because he wasn't sure how much more he could take. At least once he got her to fall for him, she would back off with the orders.

At lunchtime, Kristen entered the cafeteria a few steps ahead of Zach. She'd been afraid he might take her hand, creating a bigger spectacle than the time Brittany had taken on three girls at once over an argument that had started with the simple question, "Who is the best guitar player living and working today?"

Baby elephants did a tap dance in Kristen's stomach. It was more than being with Zach that had her nerves stretched to the point of snapping. Both of her sisters were mad at her. It was a record. Brittany was a dangerous person to fight with, especially without an ally. In the past, Cyndi had always been the voice of reason, albeit a weak one.

This morning, Brittany had left for school unusually early, and she'd taken the car. Fortunately, Brittany was predictable. Knowing her sister would leave her stranded, Kristen had arranged for another ride ahead of time.

Their fights always started like that, mild to begin with, then picking up steam until Brittany either crossed the line and caused an injury or got over being mad, whichever happened first. Step one—Brittany would do something to annoy her. Leaving her without a way to get to school filled that requirement. Step two—Brittany would curse her, something small like embarrassing hiccups. Step three—this was usually the point of injury. Kristen was hoping to avoid Brittany's step three this time around.

A disturbing ripple of excitement traveled from one side of the cafeteria to the other as students noticed that Zach and Kristen were together. Kristen stiffened but managed a cheerful smile. She waved to some friends as Zach led her to an empty table in the corner, his hand on the small of her back. It felt like there were thousands of curious eyes on her. Now she understood why tigers paced in their cages.

Feeling like the most horrible person in the world, she gave Zach another order. If she didn't ask him to do things for her, her spell wouldn't gain power, and she would lose the bet. "Buy me lunch."

She felt dirty, so dirty not even a shower could get her clean again. She played with her fingernails, unable to meet his gaze. He had asked her out on a date, and for a moment she'd thought he liked her, but then she'd remembered he was enchanted. Boys didn't like the witches who crushed them, they *loved* them. He had asked her out because he had a stronger will than most and was showing that love in a different way. That was all there was to it.

The whole thing made her sick. She didn't have the stomach for it anymore. She should just hand the money and car over to Brittany now.

Zach went to get her lunch without hesitation.

She sat at her usual table and watched in fascination as a couple of freshmen gestured for Zach to cut in front of them. It was only the second day, and the newbies already seemed to understand who the major players were.

Her troubles faded with every movement of Zach's lean, flat-muscled abdomen. He loaded up two trays and balanced them with ease. Elbow on the table, she leaned against her hand and smiled in spite of everything else going on in her life. She was going to have her first real date this weekend. She wondered what it would be like.

What were they going to talk about?

Zach returned while she was daydreaming. He dropped the tray onto the table in front of her. The loud bang made her jump. Startled, her gaze flew up to meet his. The look of resentment in his eyes was so incredibly clear that a blind person couldn't miss it. Part of him truly hated her.

She dragged her gaze off him and looked at the tray of food. There was a variety to choose from including a fruit plate, pudding, a slice of pizza, potato chips, and red gelatin. He had also gotten her a bottle of water, orange juice, and a tiny carton of milk. Her appetite totally disappeared.

He sat across from her and gestured to the food. "Well? You asked for it. Aren't you going to eat it?"

Feeling guilty for making him buy her lunch, she picked up the small carton of milk and opened it. Refusing to meet his gaze, she drank it while checking out the other tables. Students continued to stare at them. Kristen wondered how long it would be before the novelty wore off.

When she set the milk down, Zach chuckled. "You have a moustache now."

She reached for a napkin, but before she could use it, Zach wiped the milk from her face with a tanned finger. He stuck the finger into his mouth and sucked on it while she watched in awe. Then, he turned his attention to the food on his own tray. It was such a startling show of intimacy that Kristen forgot to breathe. Sheer panic twisted her stomach muscles into knots.

Was this what falling in love felt like?

Trying to lighten her mood as well as his, Kristen teased him. "Do you have a closet full of T-shirts at home?"

"They're comfortable," he said and shrugged his wide shoulders, "and they're easy to buy. I don't have to try them on or mess with annoying salespeople."

"You do realize they come in colors others than white and black, don't you?"

His lips twitched as if he were trying not to smile. "I have a couple of blue ones, too."

"Do you ever wear them?"

"Only on special occasions." He shook his head at her and added, "It bothers you when other people don't follow your code of perfection, doesn't it?"

"Wear what you want. I was just curious."

"Something's been bugging me about you for the longest time."

Gulp! She almost swallowed her tongue at the thought of Zach wondering anything about her. "What is it?"

"What do you wear when you're at home? Do you ever dress down in sweats or walk around in pajamas all day? Or do you have a favorite piece of clothing that's stained, but you still wear it?"

She made a face. What a disgusting thought. "Of course not. I like to look my best at all times."

"What about when you go to bed?"

"Then, too."

He stared at her as if she had three heads. "Why?"

"My dad has always told us that first impressions are important, and…" The rest of the words stuck in her throat. She'd looked up to her father all her life, idolizing the man, but what if her mom was right? What if being a control-freak businesswoman had been his idea, his dream for her?

Students passed by the table but didn't try to sit with them. Some were probably afraid of Zach. Others would know she always saved two seats for her sisters. She had expected Brittany to show long enough to tell her off at least. It worried her that neither sister had come to the cafeteria for lunch. That meant they were beyond angry with her. She could expect some major vengeance spells to come her way in the next few days.

"You okay?" Zach's eyes narrowed on her face.

She nodded and lied. "I have an essay due at the end of the week, and I was just trying to figure out what I'm going to write about."

"You won't back out on our date, will you?"

"When I say I'm going to do something, I do it. Don't worry. I have cheerleading practice in the afternoon this Saturday, but I'll still have plenty of time to go home and change before meeting you at the library."

Zach grinned. "You don't have to change for me. I wouldn't mind taking a hot cheerleader to a movie."

"In your dreams."

Their laughter mingled before being interrupted by a shriek. The lunchroom went silent. Everyone looked around, curious. It didn't take long to find the reason for the angry sound. One of the basketball players was walking on some girl's food. He kicked the trays out of his way so he could stand in the middle of the table. No one dared say a word to him.

Kristen looked for a teacher but didn't see one.

The basketball player pointed at Kristen. His dark hair dripped with sweat. His large eyes were wider than usual. He laughed like a maniac, showing two rows of uneven teeth. In a loud voice he announced, "Kristen Noah is a…"

The blood drained from her face as dream became reality. It was over. All over. Her entire life was about to end with one little word. Hard work and diligence weren't enough to propel her to the top. She was going to need her powers on occasion to pave the way.

Kristen rose to her feet and prepared to take the bullet.

A small smile touched Zach's lips, smug in nature, but Kristen didn't have time to decipher the reason for it. Dizzy, she grabbed onto the table, half afraid she would faint and hit her head on the way down.

"...a w-w-wonderful cheerleader, and Titan High is proud of her! That's the end of this announcement. Thank you, all."

The basketball player jumped off the table and headed for the doors. Kristen's eyes followed him. She slowly unclenched her fists. Her palms burned where her long fingernails had cut into the flesh, and her entire body trembled. *Why?* It didn't make any sense. Why would a basketball player single her out like that? It was too close to her dream to be a coincidence, and then she spotted the reason why.

Brittany patted the boy on the arm as he walked by her to exit. She turned in Kristen's direction, gave a big smirk, and winked before following him out. Brittany had made her second move. Now it was up to Kristen. She could apologize to Brittany for breaking a rule, or she could let the girl have it with a stunning spell of her own.

Kristen's jaw hurt from clenching her teeth too hard. She released a breath in a slow hiss and considered her options. If she were going to get even, she would have to make it good because Brittany would be out for blood.

7

Deceitful

On Saturday afternoon, Kristen went through half her closet, searching for the perfect outfit to wear on her date with Zach. She stripped several items off their hangers, carried them to the bed, and laid them down before heading back to the walk-in for the next load. She didn't stop until the clothes formed a huge mound in the center of the bed. One at a time, she held them in front of her while gazing into the full-length mirror. She tried to imagine Zach's reaction to each outfit.

She stood behind a red mini dress that fit her like a second skin and stared at her reflection, picturing bare legs and sparkling, red stilettos. What would Zach think if he saw her walking toward him in this hot little number? "Major slut," she said with a wry twist to her mouth.

She tossed it and grabbed the next outfit, a frilly, white prairie skirt with matching top. What did her reflection say now? She made a face. "Don't touch me. I don't like boys."

Next!

Kristen went through at least thirty outfits before deciding to play it safe and go casual. Zach was just going to wear his usual denim and T-shirt, no doubt, so she would look ridiculous if she wore a fancy dress. She chose a simple pair of jeans, gray T-shirt with *AC/DC* scrawled across her chest, and a tan suede jacket.

Why was she nervous? She still didn't trust Zach and had only agreed to go out with him to get information. Something was off about him, and she was determined to find the truth.

She checked with the mirror one last time. Casual was the perfect choice. Zach would feel more relaxed around her, and she didn't look like a clingy girl in need of male attention. In fact, she smiled at herself with confidence; she didn't care if he liked her or not. She was on a fishing expedition. That was it.

"I am Kristen Noah, future CEO." For ten years, she'd repeated the mantra to her reflection while preparing for the day ahead. Now, she added a qualifier. "Maybe." She hated the sound of that, the sound of doubt. "Probably."

"Talk to yourself much?" Brittany stood in the open doorway, hands on narrow hips.

Kristen hadn't seen Brittany since the incident at lunch. She imagined running across the room and strangling the goth-girl wannabe. The visual brought a smile to her freshly tinted red lips, but she couldn't do anything because her father was down the hall in his office. Playing it cool, she turned to face the other girl.

"That was clever," Kristen said. "Having a boy pretend he was going to publicly accuse me? Very clever."

"Glad you liked it."

"I hope you've gotten it out of your system, because I'm not putting up with anything else. I broke a rule, and you put me in my place. We're done now."

Brittany grinned, hands in pockets. "Have you learned your lesson? That cheating is very, very wrong?"

Kristen wanted to knock the smug girl on her skinny butt. She took a deep breath and reminded herself that Brittany was a dangerous person to tangle with. Calling a truce now, swallowing a bit of pride, would be better for all players in the long run. So she nodded. "I'll play nice as long as you do. No more rule breaking."

Except for going out with Zach, of course. What her sisters didn't know couldn't come back to bite her later.

Brittany entered the bedroom without an invite and looked at the clothes on the floor with a pleased curve to her lips. "Riding a motorcycle, breaking rules, and now you're turning into a slob. You and I are growing more and more alike every day."

Kristen rolled her eyes. "There's no need to be insulting."

"Bitch."

"Tramp."

They dissolved into quiet laughter, friends again. It was such a relief to make peace with her sister that Kristen forgot where she was headed for a second. Then Brittany reminded her with an innocent observation.

"If I didn't know better, I would think little Krissy had a date. All the signs are there. Messy room, fidgety hands, and you have a strange new glow. Where are you going?"

Kristen turned away so Brittany wouldn't see the lie in her eyes. "Library. I have an essay to write, remember?"

"Oh yeah. Homework. You're the only girl I know who has to have the perfect outfit for writing essays. Remind me someday to teach you how to have fun."

"Would you like it if I went out on a date?" Kristen held her breath as she waited for the answer.

"Are you kidding? It would be great to have a normal sister instead of a freak in the room next to mine." Brittany knocked the rest of the clothes off Kristen's daybed and sat on the edge. She picked up a square pillow and tossed it into the air while talking. She caught it and threw it again, repeating the game over and over. "I have a confession to make. I was pissed off at you for crushing tall, dark, and scary because I like him. He's my type from the top of his spiky hair to the toes of his biker boots."

A cold fist settled in Kristen's stomach. "But you told me to crush him."

Brittany huffed. "I didn't think you would actually do it. I was just giving you crap, trying to push your buttons. FYI, I was going to tell you I was just kidding, but then you decided to break the rules and crush him early."

Kristen's heart nearly stopped. Her sister liked Zach, and she was dating him on the sly. A situation like that couldn't possibly end well, even if she were only dating him for information. There were a few unwritten rules when it came to being a good sister. The most important one was that you never, ever dated a guy one of your sisters wanted.

What was she going to do now?

Brittany dropped the pillow on the bed and hopped up. She headed for the door with a bright smile. "Have fun studying. Don't do anything I wouldn't do."

Kristen just stood there, feet glued to the floor. She had no idea what to do. Should she call Zach and cancel? Probably. But did she want to? No way. She had to know if he was under her spell. She had to know if he liked her…

…and if she liked him back.

She paced her floor, back and forth between windows and door, while racking her brain for a solution that would make everyone happy. On one hand, Brittany had liked Zach first. That meant Kristen shouldn't have crushed him, shouldn't have even looked at him, but the damage was done. She couldn't undo what had already been done. She hadn't known about Brittany's feelings for him. It was news to her. Although Brittany had mentioned his name occasionally and had threatened to go after him, she'd continued to date every other guy she'd tripped over. How was Kristen supposed to know Brittany had actual feelings for him?

On the other hand, Brittany didn't even know Zach. She hadn't spoken to him, not once. She was infatuated with him. That was all. It would pass as soon as she found someone else she wanted, but for Kristen, this could be real. It could be her only chance to find out if love were something worth pursuing.

Mind made up, she grabbed her purse. She was going out on her first date tonight. It was a shame she couldn't share the news with her family or friends. She was going to get to know Zach, try to figure out if he was crushed or not. In general, she planned on having a great first date. It could be her last date for a long time, especially if her dad found out about it.

If she discovered she didn't like him, or that he didn't like her and was just under the spell, Brittany would never have to know. Case closed.

But if she liked him, if they liked each other, she would just have to deal with the fallout. Hopefully Brittany would understand, but Kristen wasn't going to hold her breath waiting for that day to roll around.

Twenty minutes later, Kristen parked her car in front of the library. It was a necessary, albeit annoying, move. Her father had a LoJack on both the car and her cell phone. With a few quick mouse clicks, he could trace her whereabouts on the computer, and that was why she was leaving both her car and cell phone outside the library. Turning the rearview mirror her way, she reapplied her Candy Apple Crush lipstick. Perfect.

A familiar roar filled her ears and accelerated her heartbeat as Zach's motorcycle rolled to a stop next to her car. Bending over to get a good look at her through his dark sunglasses and her window, he grinned. The sight of him knocked the breath right out of her. He looked incredible in his faded jeans and leather jacket. A strip of blue peeked through the sides of his jacket, and she realized he was wearing a blue T-shirt.

A memory sparked to life in the back of her mind. He had told her over lunch that he had a couple of blue shirts. "*I only wear them on special occasions.*"

Her blood pumped faster. She could barely contain the stupid grin threatening to take over her face at the realization that this was a special occasion and not just to her. Zach was obviously excited, too.

He killed the engine, swung his leg over, and set the kickstand into place. Smiling at her, he opened the car door and leaned in to talk to her. "I thought we'd grab a bite to eat before the movie, if that's okay with you."

"Fine." A huge lump clogged her throat. What was she doing? Lying to her dad and sisters, sneaking off with a boy she barely knew? Had she lost her mind?

He held a hand out, and she took it. She had to work to keep her fingers from trembling against his as he helped her climb out of the car. She took her time in closing the door and locking it, reluctant to face him. When the excuses not to look at him disappeared, she slowly turned, smile in place.

"Do you know what you want to see?" he asked.

She drew a total blank. What was he talking about? She stared at him like an idiot for a second. *Duh,* they were going to a movie. Quickly she shrugged. "I like comedies and action. No teary-eyed chick-flicks please."

He grinned. "A girl who knows what she wants. I like that."

The praise had her beaming at him. Lifting her chin, she boldly said, "I like things about you, too."

"Oh yeah? Like what?"

"I like your confidence and your sense of humor." She grinned. "And the motorcycle doesn't hurt."

The problem of him being crushed resurfaced. She had to know if he was under her spell or not. A test sprang to mind. It was a bit risky. If he wasn't under her spell, he would think she was an idiot, but she had to know. She took a deep breath and said, "Lick the sidewalk."

Zach frowned. "What?"

She repeated the command in a louder voice. "Lick the sidewalk."

He shook his head slowly. His dark brows drew together over ice-blue eyes, and his mouth formed a wide *O* like he understood her but still didn't get it. "You want me to lick a sidewalk? Why?"

He'd passed the test. A boy who'd been crushed would have been on his knees already, tongue out and ready to go. Her smile widened. It was possible he'd been under the spell earlier, but it was over now. Somehow, the spell had been broken. No doubt she'd done it by pushing him too hard and asking for huge things right away instead of working up to them.

She'd never been so happy to lose before. Brittany could have the money and the car. If Kristen had actually found love, it would be worth it.

She circled him, a bounce in her step, and lied. "It's a new musical group I just heard about. I was wondering if you ever listened to their music."

"Can't say that I have." He got on his bike and started the engine. "Do you want to drive again?"

Shaking her head, she climbed on the back and wrapped her arms securely around his waist. Her body fit against his like they were made to be together. Feet up, she held on as the motorcycle turned and headed across the tarmac to the exit.

Cyndi would love this. It was ultra-romantic, her hero riding up on his steel horse so he could sweep her off her feet and carry her away from her boring life.

Too bad there was one thing ruining it for her—Brittany.

8

Kissed

Kristen couldn't remember being this nervous before. Her palms were sweaty, and there were dragons in her stomach breathing fire every other second. She couldn't swallow saliva properly. How was she supposed to eat? Was this what dating always felt like?

It kind of sucked.

Her jangling nerves weren't solely due to having dinner with Zach. Shards of guilt cut into her conscience because she was stabbing Brittany in the back just by being across a table from him. It was true that in the beginning she hadn't realized Brittany liked him enough to feel betrayed, but now that she knew, she shouldn't be dating him.

She glanced up from the Chinese food and choked on the last bite because Zach was watching her. Coughing, she grabbed her soda and drank a third of it. The cold liquid washed the pork down. She gulped in some air, knowing her face had probably turned red. Great, she could see the headlines now—"Head cheerleader dies of embarrassment on first date."

"You okay?" Zach asked with a mixture of concern and amusement.

"Mmm hmm."

"Good. `Cause I don't know the Heimlich."

They both laughed, and Kristen relaxed a bit. She carefully chewed each bite she took after that. They were sitting in the center of the food court at the mall. At least no one seemed to notice her distress. They were focused on their own food and the people eating with them.

He glanced around the food court and said, "I would have taken you somewhere nice, but the movie is starting soon, and the theater is right next door. The food court was too convenient to pass up."

"It's fine," she said, feeling incredibly awkward. "The food is good."

"I guess." With a heavy sigh, he tilted back in his chair, balancing on the rear legs. He rolled his eyes and chuckled. "Being with each other shouldn't be this hard."

She nodded. "I was thinking the same thing."

He played with his half-empty cup, turning it this way and that, sliding the straw in and out. Kristen stared at his hand for a moment, fascinated by it. He had beautiful hands, tanned and smooth with strong fingers. She wondered what they would feel like against her skin.

"What do you think the problem is?" he asked.

Not being one to back down from anything, Kristen took a deep breath before hitting him with the plain, unadulterated truth. "This is my first date. I don't know how to act. I feel like I'm a performer, you're the judge, and I'm waiting for my score. So that's my problem. What's yours?"

She stuck the business end of the straw into her mouth and sucked down some of her carbonated beverage. It had lost its fizz, watered down by melted ice, but her mouth was bone dry, so she didn't care.

His eyes narrowed for a moment, and he stared at her until she thought he wasn't going to answer. He set the front legs of his chair back down. Leaning his elbows on the table, he said, "Truthfully? I feel like I'm totally out of my depth here, like I'm a trash collector taking a princess to the ball. Everything I say comes out wrong. And knowing that this is your first date just adds to the pressure. You don't know how to act? Try the view from this end.

"I want you to remember this as one of the best nights of your life." A cocky grin stretched his lips. "I want this date to be so good that you compare every other date in your life to it, and they all fall short."

Oh my. She was in trouble. In the blink of an eye, he'd turned on the charm, and she couldn't resist. Part of her had been thinking he regretted asking her out because there wasn't any chemistry between them, but he was just as nervous. Happy bubbles filled her throat and quickly turned into a girlish giggle that she immediately hated herself for, but she wasn't going to let a slight imperfection spoil what could be the best night of her life so far.

She put some food on her spoon and carefully floated it across the table to his mouth. It was an intimate gesture, something to build on. "Try some of this. It's delicious."

He did. His gaze locked with hers and stayed that way as his mouth captured the rice and chewed it. His Adam's apple moved as he swallowed. She wanted to crawl across the table and kiss him. What would he do if she took the initiative?

"You need to learn to relax more," he said. "I read an article online yesterday. People with Type-A personalities wind up with ulcers and have heart attacks."

Where did that come from? She was just beginning to feel relaxed, and he ruined it. Feeling like she needed to defend her lifestyle, she said, "I have to get good grades to get into a good school."

"What about all the extra stuff you do? Cheerleading? Drama Club? And I hear you're running for class president."

"My guidance counselor suggested I do those things because they'll look good on the college apps. The best schools don't just wave you in because you get decent grades, you know. You have to be a well-rounded person." She sighed and pushed her food away. "You just don't get it. I've spent my entire life working toward one goal, a college degree. I can't relax and screw it up now, even if I'm not sure what I want to do with it. I don't want to blow it and then figure out it's what I wanted all along."

"Don't worry. You aren't going to fall on your face."

The word 'fall' caused a shiver to vibrate her spine. A vision of plunging off the cliff and almost dying came to mind and refused to be dislodged. She picked up the plastic spoon again and played with the food on her plate. "That was weird what happened the other day, wasn't it? I've never seen an owl in the daytime before. I wonder what caused it to attack me."

"Attack you? Nah. It just lost control and almost ran into you. Maybe it was blind."

"It didn't look blind."

"Did you get a good look at it?" Zach leaned forward, eyes on her face with a new intensity. "I barely caught a glimpse. Can you tell me what color it was?"

She didn't understand his interest in the owl's color. What difference did the color make? And why did she feel like the police were interrogating her? "It was two or three shades of brown, and it had yellow eyes."

His mouth tightened. "Are you sure about the yellow eyes?"

"Yes. What's the big deal? Do you know something about owls that I don't?"

He shrugged and looked away. There was something he wasn't telling her. He continued to stare off in another direction for several minutes, ignoring her. He was making her regret her decision to defy her sisters and go out with him. Maybe the Crushed spell had done something to his brain.

Kristen filled her spoon with more rice. She held it up, grabbed the end, and flicked it at him. Rice sailed across the table. Some hit the side of his face, while the rest landed on his shirt.

That got his attention.

He frowned at her and asked, "Why did you do that?"

"Why do you think? We're supposed to be on a date, but you're not even here. What gives? We were finally starting to get along. At least, I thought we were."

"I just realized I might have a family problem to deal with."

She blinked at him. "An owl reminded you of a family problem?"

Dodging the question, he held his wrist up and pointed to the watch. "It's getting late. When do you want to start walking to the theater?"

Dating was hard.

Zach didn't know how other boys did it. How did they keep a straight face while saying mushy stuff to girls? When he'd told Kristen he wanted this to be the best date of her life, he'd almost gagged on the words. He wasn't a hearts and poetry kind of guy. If he liked a girl, he would show her by fixing her car or painting her house.

Kristen didn't bother to answer his question. She could probably tell he was using his watch to distract her. If he didn't think of something quick, she was going to walk out on him. There was a faraway look in her eyes as she leaned back in her chair and finished her drink. She was either trying to figure out how to successfully pump him for information, or she was about to dump him.

He opened his mouth to compliment her. His dad had always told his mom she looked pretty when they went out, and it had made his mom smile. But a crowd of rowdy teens caught his attention. Lips still parted, his gaze followed them. They surrounded Rufus McDillion in front of the Crispy Chicken. One of the boys knocked his hat off while two others stole food from his tray. Zach hated bullies. He turned to Kristen to tell her he would be back in a second, but she was already halfway across the food court.

Moving like an unstoppable freight train, Kristen rushed over to save the small boy. She stepped between the three overgrown jocks and Rufus. Red faced, she shoved the main guy backwards and shouted, "Leave him alone!"

He asked, "Are you his mommy or his date?"

His friends laughed and high-fived him.

Kristen stood straight, hands on her hips in a battle-ready stance.

Her expression alone should have scared the jerks off, but it was obvious they'd been drinking and weren't currently using their brains. The biggest guy weaved on his feet, while the others giggled like girls at a sleepover.

Kristen jabbed the huge jerk in the chest with her finger and said, "Walk away now before you get hurt."

No longer laughing, the bully took a menacing step forward, crowding her. Another couple of inches, and he'd be standing in the same space she was currently occupying. Zach shot out of his chair, almost knocking it over in the process. A picture of the dangerous teen taking a swing at Kristen took him from one side of the food court to the other in record time.

The guy lifted a beefy arm.

Zach grabbed it and jerked the bully around to face him. "Touch her, and I'll rip your stupid face off!"

Pedestrians gave them a wide berth. Some of them ignored what was happening, not wanting to get involved, while others shot dirty looks at them before continuing on. Most people wouldn't put themselves in physical danger for someone they didn't know. That's why Kristen's actions had stunned Zach. She'd been willing to risk serious injury for a kid she barely noticed at school.

Zach clenched his fists, ready for a fight. The aroma of cooking chicken nauseated him. Or maybe the gigantic rock in his stomach was because of Kristen. The thought of her being hurt ripped at his sanity.

The other boys moved away, quickly abandoning their friend. Zach stared into the bully's eyes. A silent understanding passed between them, and the bully retreated. He tripped over his own feet, staggered, but recovered quickly. Looking clumsy, he turned and ran.

To Kristen, it would look like the boy had heard of Zach's reputation and didn't want to mess with him. In reality, Zach had used a spell, a sort of Jedi mind trick. He'd shown that idiot a vision of what would happen to him if he didn't make a quick exit. The move had zapped Zach's energy. His shoulders sagged a bit, and he forced his lungs to suck in more oxygen. He bent over and retrieved the discarded hat, then handed it to Rufus. Patting the boy on the shoulder, he asked, “You okay?”

Eyes huge, the kid nodded several times. “Y-yes, uh, sir.”

“You can call me Zach.”

“Thanks.”

Rufus spun around and took off at top speed.

“Now you did it,” Kristen said with a smile. “He’s going to tell everyone at school how you’re his best friend. Before you know it, he’ll be saying you’re his big brother.”

“I’m not worried.”

Kristen stared at him for a long moment before saying, “You aren’t at all what I expected.”

Neither was she. The girl had taken on a rowdy group of boys to protect a kid from a possible beating. She seemed to be fearless. He was in awe of her. In that moment, the date became a real one, at least in his mind. He offered his hand to her, and she took it. Both smiling, they walked through the mall and out the main doors. He liked Kristen Noah, and he didn’t care who knew it.

His parents would have liked her. He wished they could have met her. His mom would have loved her compassion and her soft heart. His dad would have admired her strength and spunk. But they were gone because of Morgan.

He pictured the brown, yellow-eyed owl in his head and prayed he was wrong about it. If Morgan had had anything to do with trying to hurt Kristen, he wouldn’t be able to forgive her, not this time.

At least he had one piece of happy news, thanks to Kristen. He wasn’t under her spell. Back at the library, she had ordered him to lick the ground. Although she’d covered with a brilliant lie, he knew exactly what she’d been trying to do. He hadn’t been the only person wondering if he were enchanted, but her command hadn’t affected him in the slightest. There hadn’t been even a teeny, tiny urge to lick concrete.

His feelings for her were genuine.

Of course, he would have to continue pretending to be enchanted, at least until she removed her spell.

They exited the mall and continued down the sidewalk. He saw the crowd waiting in front of the theater three blocks away. Another awkward silence settled over them like a dark cloud. He couldn't think of a single thing to say to her. What was wrong with him? Why did this girl have him tongue-tied and practically shaking in his boots every time he got near her?

"My mom called this morning. She wants me to move to New York after I graduate and take a year off before going to college. My dad would have a cow if I even thought about blowing off school. I think he'd disown me."

Zach stopped walking for a second and stared into her eyes. "And what do you want?"

"Huh?"

"You keep telling me what your parents want you to do. What do you want?"

Instead of answering, Kristen rested her head against his shoulder again. He wrapped an arm around her and held her close as they continued to walk. It felt incredible to know that he was her sole confidant. She hadn't told anyone else about her worries over her future. The revealing talks should be bringing them closer together, but his secrets were keeping them apart. He was beginning to see something amazing in this girl, but he couldn't allow himself to fall in love with her.

Because of Morgan, he couldn't fall for anyone.

The movie wasn't that great, but it wasn't awful, either.

Zach shared a big bucket of popcorn with her, and their hands bumped a couple of times when they both reached for some. She giggled an apology and realized the movie probably wasn't that bad. She just couldn't seem to focus on the screen with Zach sitting beside her. It was kind of cool in the theater, but she felt suffocated by the waves of heat coming off his body.

Out of the corner of her eye, she saw him turn in her direction. He looked at her but didn't say a word. She couldn't see his expression clearly. Was he smiling or frowning? Did he like her or didn't he?

She took a deep breath, swallowed the lump in her throat, and looked his way. His eyes were on the screen again. Maybe she'd imagined the whole thing, and he hadn't even glanced at her. Or maybe he was just trying to find the popcorn.

Disappointed, Kristen returned her gaze to the screen. She couldn't keep up with the characters. There were too many, and she didn't think their gags were funny. She should have suggested a bloody horror film instead. That would have suited her mood better.

Her peripheral vision told her he was staring at her again. Or was he? Maybe she should invest in some glasses. She grabbed a handful of popcorn and stuffed part of it into her mouth. Carefully, she tilted her head in such a way that his face became clearer without looking directly at him. Oh yeah, he was checking her out. Definitely.

That made her smile.

She looked at him.

Once again, his eyes were on the movie.

Kristen sighed, tired of the game. It was like playing phone tag without the phone. Determined to put an end to it, she turned sideways in her seat and blatantly stared at him until he decided to take another look at her. She only had to wait a few seconds. He slowly turned his head, and his eyes widened in surprise. His lips curved.

"Hey," he said.

Her breath caught in her throat. "Hey yourself."

He had to lean closer because the movie was almost loud enough to make their heads explode. With his cheek against hers, he spoke directly into her ear. "You don't look like you're enjoying yourself. Do you want to leave?"

"Not unless you do. I mean, I'm not having a terrible time, but I'm okay with leaving if that's what you want."

What was wrong with her? Since when was she polite and evasive? She should tell him exactly what was on her mind.

"I like being here with you," he said.

One of his hands rested on her bare wrist, sending a shiver up her spine. His thumb absently stroked the skin. Her pulse raced, and she wondered if he could feel it.

He admitted, "It would be nice to just sit somewhere and talk."

She nodded. "Yeah. That'd be good."

For a long, awkward moment, he didn't say another word. His hot breath tickled her ear. Finally, he asked, "Would it be too weird if I kissed you right now?"

He wanted to kiss her? She almost swallowed her tongue.

Kristen's mind raced in frantic circles. What should she say? He wasn't under a spell, so it should be okay. It wasn't like she was making him do it. He wanted to. Zach Bevian wanted to kiss her because he liked her.

She pulled back so he could see her smile and nodded again. More than anything, she wanted to kiss Zach. Her grandma had told her that a kiss could reveal a lot about a person, shed some light on their true feelings, and let you know if there was any chemistry.

They moved at the same time, mutual consent, and their mouths met in a feather-soft kiss. His gentle fingers touched the sides of her face and held her steady as she trembled from head to toe. It was her first real kiss, and it was the most incredible thing ever to happen to her. She felt like she would float right out of her seat if she didn't hold onto something.

His teeth lightly nibbled on her lower lip.

Her hands went around his neck, and she pulled him closer. Not sure of what to do, she tried to remember seeing other people kiss and what they did. She pressed her mouth against his.

It was a good move. With a groan, he kissed her harder. A fierce hunger she hadn't expected grew in the pit of her stomach. It frightened her a little bit. She wondered if he knew she wasn't the type of girl to go all the way on the first date. Or the second, for that matter. Or the third.

His hands cupped her face, holding her steady as the kiss went on and on. His tongue parted her lips. An incredible feeling of bliss lit up her insides like the Fourth of July. Oh yeah, this had definitely been worth the wait.

A bloodcurdling scream filled her ears.

She jumped out of his arms and straight to her feet in the crowded theater. Her heart thundered in her chest at a painful rate. A few people shouted at her to get out of the way. Eyes wide, she visually swept the theater, searching for and finding a familiar face. The scream had been for her ears only. Brittany sat in the back row, alone. Her narrowed eyes pierced Kristen's soul.

Kristen retook her seat as her blood turned to icy slush. She went numb all over. Her life was over. She was so dead. There wouldn't be any reasoning with Brittany, not after she'd seen them kissing. Guilt mounted upon guilt. Kristen didn't know what to do. Reaching for popcorn, she scooped a handful and brought it to her mouth. She chewed automatically without even tasting it.

"Are you okay?" Zach asked. "You look like you saw a ghost."

She kept chewing, no comment. There wasn't anything she could say to explain the change in her demeanor. Her mind was such a chaotic mess she couldn't even think of a good lie.

"Do you want to leave?" he asked.

Did she?

What would be the point? Brittany had already seen them together. The damage was done. No matter how angry her sister was, Kristen was relatively sure the other girl wouldn't attack her in front of this many witnesses. She settled back in her seat and said, "I'm watching the movie. I don't want to leave until it's over."

Zach leaned in again and whispered in her ear. "Did I freak you out?"

Heat suffused her cheeks. "No. I'm not a baby."

"I didn't say you were." He sighed. "I should have waited until our second date to do that. I'm sorry, but your mouth is so very hard to resist."

His husky voice made her nerve endings tingle. She turned to look at him. Their hungry gazes met and held. He wanted to kiss her again, and she wanted it, too, only Brittany would collapse the roof on top of them if their lips met a second time. With a great deal of effort, she tore her gaze off Zach and looked to the screen. How would it end?

Not the movie.

Her life.

9

Smashed

For the next three weeks, Kristen continued to work hard at school in spite of what her mother had said. Every time she tried to slack off, she nearly had a panic attack. Letting go of her good-girl image was proving harder than she'd thought. Then there was Zach. After their date, she'd been sure he wasn't crushed, but he'd behaved like a person under a spell at school. He followed her orders, every one. Something was definitely wrong. He hadn't licked the sidewalk on their date, but he did everything else she asked him to do.

Either he was playing games with her, or the spell hadn't worked.

Confused and scared, she turned to the one person she knew would be able to help. Grandma Noah. Her paternal grandmother lived in San Diego, a three-hour drive from Sol Moreno, so she borrowed her father's car without permission. He was away on a business trip, and she didn't want to face an interrogation from her sisters. She didn't want anyone to know where she'd gone, especially not Brittany. Besides, her car had a LoJack on it. At least this way her father would never have to know she'd broken one of his major rules.

It was beginning to get dark outside. Kristen waited for Grandma Noah to pour the hot tea into two dainty cups. They were beautiful, yet fragile. Kristen remembered staring at the floral pattern as a child, wondering what kind of flowers they were and wishing she were old enough to have afternoon tea with her grandmother.

Grandma Noah lifted a small plate of cookies and held it out to her. "They're oatmeal raisin. Made them myself. Have one, dear."

Kristen took a cookie as her stomach rumbled. She ate part of it before setting the rest on the edge of her plate. Worry stole her appetite. If she didn't find out what was wrong with Zach, she was going to lose her mind.

"Well, I am so happy you're here, dear." Grandma Noah's blue eyes twinkled from the other side of the table. "However, I am not an old fool. I know you didn't drive all the way down here by yourself just for my company. Why are you here?"

Kristen didn't know where to begin. She took a sip of tea and carefully returned the cup to the saucer. "Do you remember when you told us we were witches?"

"Of course I do. I'm not senile, dear, not yet. As I recall, you were twelve at the time. Strange things were happening at your house, and it spooked your father, so he called me. I was both pleased and dismayed to hear you three girls had inherited the family gift."

"You told us if we ever had any questions about our powers, we should ask you."

Grandma Noah's eyes narrowed. "What's on your mind? Spit it out, child, while I'm still young enough to hear it."

"I was just wondering if there was any reason why a person might be immune to spells."

Grandma Noah was the opposite of senile. Sharp as a freshly ground axe, the woman could still do difficult math in her head. "You tried to put a spell on someone, and it didn't take. What sort of spell did you use, and whom did you cast it upon?"

Kristen shifted in the chair, suddenly uncomfortable. She couldn't lie to her grandmother, but she didn't want to spill the whole truth, either. Grandma Noah thought it was okay to practice using their gifts as long as they didn't do anything stupid. Kristen hesitated a second too long.

"If you don't tell me, child, I'll find out some other way. You know all I have to do is pick up the phone and call your sister. Cyndi will tell me everything."

And then some. If Grandma Noah got her hands on Cyndi, the girl would confess to everything short of JFK's assassination. Better to just spill the truth now. "Fine. It's a boy at school. I tried to use a love spell on him, and I don't think it worked."

Grandma Noah gasped. "I told you a million times not to mess with love spells. They are unpredictable and useless. You can't make someone love you. I am in shock right now. Total shock." Her hand went to her chest as if she were expecting a heart attack. "Why in the world would you feel the need to use a love spell? You've told me a hundred times that you like being unattached."

"It's kind of complicated."

"There is no excuse to use a love spell, and I am still waiting to hear a credible explanation as to why you did it. You could have any boy you wanted with a simple smile."

Kristen lowered her eyes, ashamed. "It's part of a game."

Grandma Noah threw her hands up in the air. "Oh, you girls! What in the world were you thinking?"

"Grandma, please, just tell me why it didn't work. Are there people out there who are immune to our powers?"

The elderly woman nodded her gray head. "There are three types you don't want to be messing with."

Kristen leaned forward in her chair. "Who are they?"

"Vampires. You sure don't want to go messing with one of them. They have dark souls, and half of them would love to convert a pretty girl like you."

"I don't think he's a vampire 'cause he goes to my school during the day and doesn't catch fire."

"The second type is like us. The more powerful the witch or wizard, the less likely the spell will work right. Take me, for instance. I am quite powerful in my own right. If someone used a love spell on me, it would have some effect, but wouldn't enchant me entirely."

Kristen slowly shook her head. "I don't think that's it, either. Nothing strange has ever happened around him."

"The only other option is someone who has been enchanted already." Grandma Noah shrugged her bony shoulders. "Perhaps another witch got to him first."

Another witch?

Kristen didn't think that was possible. She and her sisters would know if another witch were at the school, unless the witch in question *was* one of her sisters. Brittany had admitted to having a thing for Zach. She could have used the spell on him outside of the game, hoping to trap him into a romantic relationship.

That didn't seem right, either. Zach wasn't panting after Brittany. He didn't melt when she was around or follow her with those electric blue eyes. He didn't even like her. If he were enchanted, it was by a witch unknown to them.

"Are you quite certain your spell didn't work, dear?"

She wasn't sure about anything. "He just doesn't act like someone who's been cru… put under a spell."

Her grandmother's eyes narrowed at the word her tongue had tripped over, but the elderly woman let it pass. "Tell me exactly how he behaves."

Kristen took a deep breath and began slowly, trying to remember every detail of Zach's suspicious behavior. "Well, I kind of pushed it and asked him to do something right away that he normally wouldn't do in a million years. There was a long hesitation, but then he did it. He gave me his precious leather jacket. He even did an embarrassing little hopping thing in front of our whole gym class.

"Later, when I asked him for a simple favor, to carry my books, he looked at me like he wanted to rip my throat out. Then he asked me out on a date. I didn't make him do it. I swear. He took me to a movie, and he was sweet and seemed to want to get to know me. He even kissed me, which is against all of our rules.

"I don't know what to do. I really like him, but I don't want him to be with me because he has to be, because he's under a spell. Then again, he may not even be under the spell. I tested him when we were on the date, but he didn't do what I asked. I am so confused, Grandma. Sometimes I think he's under the spell, and sometimes I think he's just pretending. Sometimes I get the feeling he's playing his own little game with me."

Grandma Noah looked deeply distressed by the statement. "Remove the spell. Immediately."

"What?"

"It's the only answer, dear. If it's true that he isn't under a spell, removing it won't matter. If he is, then you need to remove it because something has gone terribly wrong."

Kristen wished it were that simple. "I wanted to remove the spell a long time ago, Grandma, but Brittany won't let me."

"Just exactly how is she stopping you?"

"She won't let me enchant anyone else, and I'll lose the game."

Grandma Noah shook her head. "I don't know what is the matter with you three girls, but this nonsense needs to stop now. Tell your sisters I know about the game, and I am going to end it if you don't. I mean it. If I have to, I'll have a very revealing talk with your father."

"There's one more thing." At her grandmother's increasingly red face, she blurted out, "I need something for protection."

"Protection from what?"

Kristen swallowed hard but didn't answer. She couldn't tell her grandmother that she was afraid of Brittany. The well-meaning woman would lock them in the same room until they worked it out, which wasn't going to happen. "Uh, if there's a new witch in town, I need to protect myself. Right?"

"There's no sense in getting worked up over something that *might* happen." Grandma Noah shrugged. "I have something you can use, but it's in my safe-deposit box at the bank. I'll get it for you sometime this week, and you can come back for it." Her eyes narrowed. "Unless there's a reason I need to retrieve it now."

If she showed her grandmother how freaked out she was, the woman would insist on hearing the whole story. Kristen knew she had to keep her mouth shut. Hopefully, Brittany (or the new witch, if one existed) would wait for a while before attacking her again.

On the drive back to Sol Moreno, Kristen blasted rock music in the car's dark interior. Led Zepplin played one of her favorites. She sang along while navigating the winding road. There was a hill to the right and a deep plunge to the ocean on the left. Every time the singer got to the best line in the whole song, she added her voice to his.

"And she's buying the stairway to heaven."

Kristen shifted gears like a racecar driver, enjoying the feel of all that power at her fingertips. Her dad's car handled better than hers. An expensive sports car, it had three times the power under the hood. She loved driving at night, just her and the open road. As she drove, she replayed the long conversation with her grandmother. If they didn't drop the game by the next time she spoke to them, she was going to have a talk with their father.

Their dad had no idea they were witches. He didn't know about his mother, either. She had kept it from him because there was no sense in upsetting him when he didn't need to know. Daniel Noah was a hardline, by-the-numbers guy. He didn't have time for foolish fantasy. Hearing that not only were witches real but also that he was related to four of them would give the poor guy heart failure.

Lost in thought, Kristen didn't notice the owl until it struck her windshield, cracking the glass on impact. She screamed and wrenched the steering wheel to the right without thinking. Lines stretched across the windshield from the center point of impact, forming a spiderweb design. Brakes squealed, and the car started to skid out of control.

Her car zoomed off the road and just missed a tree. She stomped on the brake, desperate, and jerked the wheel in the other direction. There were too many trees to avoid. Everything moved past the windshield in a dizzying blur. It happened too fast for her to think logically, too fast for her to figure out the best way to save her life and her dad's car.

That was her last coherent thought for a while.

She slammed into a thick tree trunk.

An explosion of noise deafened her. Twisted metal, breaking glass, and a loud scream filled her ears. The airbag deployed, smacking her in the face with the force of a speeding train. It knocked all thoughts from her head but one. She was going to die.

After things settled, she sat there, stunned, unable to think or move. She tasted blood. A few pieces of glass fell with soft, clinking sounds. She took a couple whiffs of air, paranoid that the car was about to explode, but she didn't smell gas or smoke. That was a good sign. When she moved, it was slow and cautious, an inch at a time. She wiggled her fingers. They seemed to be okay. She slid a hand from her throat to her legs, checking for broken bones.

Bruises and cuts, but nothing broken. Later she would be in a lot of pain, but for now the adrenaline from the near-death experience had her feeling she could get out and walk without any trouble.

Her entire body quaked in the aftermath of the crash, and she felt like she was going to throw up. She lowered her head against the steering wheel for a moment. Her shoulders shook as she sobbed uncontrollably. She didn't know what to do. Then, she remembered her cell phone. It was in her purse.

But where was her purse?

It had fallen under the seat. Kristen leaned forward, holding her breath as sharp pain stabbed through her core. Her hand caught the strap, and she raised the purse back up to the seat. She opened it with one hand, rummaged around, and pulled the phone out. Another problem hit her.

Who was she going to call?

Feeling like she might puke at any second, she pushed the door open and fell out of the car. She hit the dirt with a hard thud. Her cell phone landed next to her hand.

Pebbles embedded themselves into her flesh. The ground was covered in broken sticks, small rocks, and dried leaves. Her arms scraped against the stuff as she tried to push herself up. The adrenaline was wearing off now, and she experienced the first wave of true pain.

She sat on her knees and looked at the car. It was a total wreck. The champagne-colored hood was bent in half. The thick tree trunk was almost in the center of the engine. There was a ton of damage. Her father was going to kill her.

What if the cell phone didn't get reception out here? She picked it up and checked for bars. There were five. She kissed the phone but didn't use it. Not right away. She had no clue who she should call for help. She could call one of her sisters, but they were both super pissed off at her. What if they didn't want to come get her?

She could try Zach, but it was a little early in their relationship to be calling him for favors in the dead of night.

Of course, she couldn't hide the damage to the car from her dad for long. He was going to eventually find out. Maybe she should tell him while he was out of town, give him some time to get over his homicidal feelings. She needed to call him. Mind made up, she pushed a button.

A shriek from above alerted her to danger.

The owl had returned.

It dove down and knocked the phone from her hand. The owl gracefully turned in the sky and came back for her. If it weren't for the danger it posed, the owl might have made a beautiful sight. It wasn't a regular owl. A witch was controlling that enormous bird. She was sure of it.

Did Brittany hate her enough to kill her?

Kristen took three steps backwards, then spun around and ran as fast as she could in the other direction. Fear made her legs pump harder than usual. She was going to beat the thing, reach safety somehow—if she couldn't outrun it, then she would grab a stick and knock the thing out of the air. Even if it had a witch controlling it, it was only an animal. If she could think clearly, she could come up with a spell to use against it.

Then, her trouble doubled.

A silver wolf came out of nowhere, blocking her path. With an angry snarl, it raced to meet her. There was nowhere for her to go. It leaped at her. She ducked, going down on hands and knees. The wolf leaped over her. She turned her head and watched in awe as the wolf jumped into the air a second time, paws raised, and struck the owl. The gigantic bird almost went down. Regaining balance, it flew away, disappearing in mere seconds. Kristen found herself alone with the wolf. It watched her through crystal blue eyes.

Kristen grasped the end of a large stick and lifted it high. She would need a weapon if it tried to attack her. Every inch of her body ached. Her neck hurt when she turned her head. She wasn't sure she could fend off the furry beast by herself, but she was sure going to try. Afraid to move, afraid to breathe, she stared at the wolf, waiting for it to make the first move.

It did.

The wolf turned and ran off as if a noise only it could hear had startled it. Relieved, she closed her eyes and lowered the stick. A familiar voice called her name. She climbed to her feet and yelled for Cyndi. She hadn't had the chance to call anyone, yet there her sisters were like a tiny miracle.

A tearful Cyndi ran to her and gave her a quick hug, saying, "I am so sorry. I hate it when we fight."

"Me too."

Cyndi sobbed. "I loved Jake, and I wanted to marry him."

"I know. That's why I couldn't tell you he was cheating."

"I understand why you crushed him. I just wish you hadn't. It makes me sick to my stomach that I kissed him after he'd already kissed Gina. You should have told me."

Tears pricked the backs of Kristen's eyes. "I'm sorry. He doesn't deserve you."

Cyndi wiped her damp face as she laughed. "Well, he's got what he deserves now. Gina is a bigger witch than all three of us put together.

She's going to drive him nuts. So, I guess you get your wish for prom this year."

"Wish?"

"Yeah, you know, you wanted the three of us to go together. No boys. We can do it now since we're all guy-free."

Kristen nodded. "That's right. I wanted to go to the prom with my sisters."

A flash of Zach's smiling face nearly blinded her mental eye. Until Cyndi spoke of going to the prom together, Kristen hadn't realized she was hoping to go with Zach. They hadn't talked about it, but she desperately wanted to go with him. Now what was she going to do? Brittany would kill her for even suggesting it, and poor Cyndi would stay home, missing the prom completely.

"How did you know I was here?" Kristen asked, changing the subject so that maybe they could both stop crying.

"Grandma Noah called," Cyndi said. "She was worried about you."

"How did *she* know I was out here?"

"She had a vision after you left, and she told us exactly where we could find you. Grandma's never wrong."

"We?" Kristen looked past Cyndi to find Brittany standing in the background, hands in pockets.

Brittany casually closed the gap between them. She playfully punched Kristen in the arm. "Glad to see you're still breathing."

"Thank you."

Cyndi beamed at them both. "Are you two making up? Please tell me you're making up."

"I don't know." Brittany shrugged. "I wanted to kill you earlier, but then when I thought you were actually dead, I felt kind of bad about it. So we'll wait and see how I feel tomorrow."

Coming from Brittany, it was practically an apology.

Kristen hugged her with one arm and raised the other for Cyndi. Cyndi stepped into the embrace. The three of them shared a rare group hug. They usually kept mushy moments to special occasions, but Kristen remained shaken by her experience. Thrilled to be alive, she didn't care if her sisters thought she was a crybaby.

Brittany ordered, "Fix the car so we can go."

Cyndi went to the damaged vehicle and did her thing. With a wave of her hands, she fixed the smashed car, and Kristen felt like kicking herself for not remembering her sister's ability to un-break things. She should have called on Cyndi first thing. Instead, she had been planning to call their dad. That was a confrontation she was glad to have missed.

"Thank you." Kristen hugged her sister again.

"What happened?" Cyndi asked. "Did someone run you off the road?"

She shook her head. "It was that owl again. That thing is being controlled by a powerful witch, someone who wants to seriously hurt me."

Her eyes went to Brittany.

Brittany shrugged. "Guess you should watch who you piss off."

Both Kristen and Cyndi did a double take. A moment ago, Brittany had waved the white flag. Now she was doling out veiled threats. What was happening to her? She was back and forth, hot and cold, calm and dangerous. Kristen had the feeling she was looking at the powerful witch behind the owl.

Cyndi took a step in her twin's direction. Her brows drew together over stunned eyes, and her face paled. When she spoke, her voice quivered. "Britt? Your aura is black."

10

Un-Crushed

Later that night, when the girls were safely at home, they gathered in Kristen's bedroom for a family meeting. Brittany joined them with obvious reluctance. She plopped down on Kristen's bed with a heavy sigh, and Cyndi sat next to her.

Kristen paced over the red area rug in bare feet while trying to explain her fears about Zach. When she gave them the list of possible reasons why he might not be under her spell, Cyndi gasped at the title of vampire, but Brittany seemed more concerned about a powerful witch being in town.

Kristen finished her story and stood off to the side, waiting for the consensus. She twisted her fingers in nervous agitation. When neither of her sisters spoke, she added, "The spell obviously didn't work on Zach. One minute he's doing everything I ask, and the next, he's ignoring me."

Brittany snickered. "Did you actually think he would be easy to control?"

"I gave him a very simple request. He's done a lot bigger things than lick a sidewalk. He carried my books and gave me his jacket, and you saw him hop on one foot, rub his stomach, and pat his head in front of everybody. There was resentment in his eyes a few times, but he followed every single command except that one."

Cyndi made a face. "You asked him to lick a sidewalk? Why would you do that?"

"Maybe you pushed him too far and broke the spell," Brittany said. "I warned you."

Kristen shook her head. "If the spell had been broken, the dust would have returned to my bottle, and it's empty." She removed the glass vial from her dresser drawer and showed it to her sisters. "Anyway, Grandma is always right. She told me to remove the spell because if it affected him at all, it's messed up now. It needs to be undone. I need to un-crush him tonight."

Brittany picked up a pillow and absently pulled on a tiny, red bow. "Why? Isn't this exactly what you wanted? You wanted him, and you got him. Is he a good kisser?"

Cyndi gasped. "You kissed him?"

Before Kristen could say anything, Brittany went into painful detail over Kristen's date with Titan High's rebel. Every word carried an ounce of bitterness with it. Although they had fought many times over the years, Kristen hadn't felt like her sister hated her until now.

"Something is really, really wrong here." Kristen tore the pillow from Brittany's grasp and set it out of her reach so she would stop pulling on the bows. "I need to remove the spell."

"Forfeit the game, then."

"This isn't about a stupid game!" Kristen shouted. "This isn't about winning some money or a car. It's over, Britt. There's something off about Zach, and Grandma is going to tell Dad everything if we don't stop. Game over."

"You are such a little drama queen."

"Someone has tried to kill me. *Twice!*"

"OMG!" Brittany leaped to her feet. "You are so overreacting. Grandma Noah won't tell Dad a damn thing. She doesn't want him to know any more than we do. Less, in fact, since she's lied to him his whole life; and there's nothing going on with Bevian except for the fact that you shouldn't have crushed him in the first place. He's way too strong for you.

"If there were something magical about Bevian, I would know. I've been paying special attention to him for over a year now, and you're wrong about him. You just can't control him because your powers aren't strong enough."

Kristen noticed Brittany didn't have anything to say about the fact that someone had tried to kill her twice now. She wondered if that meant Brittany already knew about it or simply didn't care.

"What if I'm not wrong?" She hadn't wanted to tell them the next part, but it seemed to be the only way to grab their attention. "I had the dream again when I fell asleep in the car on the way home."

Brittany rolled her eyes.

Cyndi gasped. "Three times."

"Actually, this was the sixth time." Kristen cringed as she recalled the dream in vivid detail. It had been the worst nightmare she'd ever had. "I saw my accuser's face."

"Who was it?" Cyndi asked.

"Zach. It was Zach. He accused me."

Cyndi covered her mouth with both hands.

Brittany snickered. "If he does, it's only what you deserve for crushing him in the first place. By the way, I don't see why we have to stop the game just because you have a personal problem and can't handle it on your own."

Kristen stared at her sister, incredulous at Brittany's attitude. True, the girl could be a little self-absorbed at times and was angry with her at the moment, but they were sisters. Blood was more important than lust. Wasn't it?

"What is wrong with you?" Kristen asked. "Just because I fell for someone you thought you wanted, you're mad enough to let me get killed? You don't even know him."

"You did it on purpose. You crushed the guy I liked, stole him out from under my nose, and now you have to live with the consequences."

Kristen was shocked by Brittany's vehemence and her lack of memory. "You told me to crush him."

"I was joking."

Cyndi stood next to Kristen and said, "I vote she removes the spell."

The room went dead silent.

"You what?" Brittany glared at her twin. "You're actually taking her side against me?"

"She's my sister, too."

The statement filled Kristen's heart with a glowing warmth, but it was short-lived.

Brittany stormed out of the room without another word. A few seconds later, they heard her bedroom door slam shut. It was dangerous to make Brittany mad. Both girls would need to watch their backs until she calmed down.

No one could hold a grudge like Brittany.

Kristen said, "I hope you realize that if you don't stand up to her someday soon, you are going to be dressing like her when you're forty."

The bedroom door opened, and their father stuck his head in. "What's going on in here?"

"Nothing, Dad." Cyndi sighed.

"I heard a door slam."

"Brittany got mad at me."

He smiled. "Good. At least she's home." He handed Kristen an envelope. It didn't escape her notice that it was already open, which he made no apologies for. Winking, he said, "You got your first application in the mail. It's a good school, not the best, but we can use it as a backup plan."

She forced a smile, unsure if she would be alive long enough to attend college. "Great. Thanks."

He nodded his balding head as he backed out of the room. His parting words rang in her ears. "We'll fill it out together this weekend."

Once the girls were alone again, Kristen said, "We need to do something about Brittany before she loses it and kills one of us."

"She'll cool off," Cyndi said in a hopeful voice.

They smiled at each other in a reassuring manner, but neither of them actually believed it. Kristen added, "Maybe we should put some sort of protection spell over each other. Grandma told me about one."

Cyndi nodded eagerly. "Let's do it now."

"First, I need to call the Crushed spell back to me. Stand in front of the door in case Dad decides to come back."

Kristen stood in the center of her bedroom and waved a hand over the tube. It would be a lot easier to call back the spell if she were standing next to Zach, but she didn't want to wait for morning. "Zach Bevian, you are no longer crushed. I set you free."

The pink smoke instantly appeared inside the vial. She stared at it in silence as her time with Zach played in her brain like a cherished movie. A sigh parted her lips. She pulled the cork and released the smoke. Without another color to war against, it quickly faded.

She'd lost Zach forever.

Going to school the next day had Kristen feeling nauseated. Her hands were clammy. She wiped them on her cute, black-denim mini. Since putting the crushed spell on Zach, she'd found him at her locker every morning. One time he had even surprised her with her favorite brand of latté. She was used to starting her day off by gazing into his clear blue eyes while having short, inane conversations about stupid things neither of them actually cared about. Even though it had only been a short time since she'd placed the spell on him, she had come to look forward to his company.

He probably wouldn't even speak to her now. They would return to their old habit of ignoring each other. It would hurt, but she would have to learn to live with it. Maybe someday he would come around. Maybe someday he would talk to her again.

And maybe someday cows would learn to fly.

Kristen entered the school behind her sisters, her Gucci bag swinging from her shoulder. Head bent low, she walked without purpose. It was funny how much things had changed. The stuff that used to mean the world to her didn't matter now. Grades didn't even seem as important as they had last month.

As usual, the girls walked the hallway together with her in the middle, traveling to theme music only they could hear. It was nice to have at least part of her routine remain the same. Even though Brittany was pissed off at her, she continued to do the usual stuff with them. No one spoke until…

Brittany turned on her. "What the hell is going on? I thought you said you removed the spell last night."

"I did." She pushed her way passed Brittany to find Zach waiting at her locker with a big grin on his face. For a moment, she thought she might be dreaming. She would have asked her sisters to pinch her, but she knew for a fact that Brittany would do it, and she'd make it hurt as much as possible. "I don't get it."

"Either you don't know how to retract a simple spell, or you are a liar." Brittany shook her head. "I'm going with the second option. First, you lie and go out with him behind my back. Then you lie about removing the spell. You are a liar and a cheater. Now I know why they used to burn witches at the stake."

With a last, vicious glare, Brittany spun around and marched down the hallway alone. She frowned at Zach as she passed him, but he didn't seem to notice. His eyes were on Kristen, glued to her as if she were the only girl in the long, brightly lit hallway.

"I think he really likes you," Cyndi said with a smile. She gave Kristen a cheerful shove in Zach's direction. "Maybe you were right, and he was never under a spell. Enjoy."

A breath of light blew through Kristen, refreshing her soul. Was it possible? Giving up his jacket? The kiss? The motorcycle ride? Had it been just the usual boy-girl stuff? Did Zach Bevian like her enough to do those crazy things just because she had asked?

She flushed guiltily as she remembered asking him to rub his stomach, pat his head, and hop on one foot. He had to like her big-time to do something like that. Did he like her that much? Did he *love* her?

Her face infused with heat.

Kristen couldn't wait to find out. She hurried to her locker, to Zach, with a smile on her face. She was so glad she had put on the black-denim mini and two-layer top even though she hadn't cared what she wore that morning. The world around her took on a fresh, beautiful glow. "You got here early," she said.

He shrugged. "I hate being late."

"Me too." Another thing they had in common. She frowned. "If you hate being late, why are you always tardy to class?"

"I have a reputation to live down to." He touched his abdomen. "It isn't easy. Trust me. I have an ulcer coming."

"Then why don't you just go to class on time?"

He grinned. "I'm complicated. Don't try to figure me out."

A wave of shyness washed over her as she wondered what her next move should be. Knowing he wasn't under a spell put a lot of pressure on her. What if she said or did the wrong thing? She needed to carefully choose her words. She didn't want him to stop liking her.

She removed a blue notebook for science class and the textbook from her locker while he waited patiently behind her. She used the moment to take a few deep breaths and steady her nerves. The dragons returned to her stomach, and they brought friends along. She shut her locker. Turning around, she smiled at him.

"Do you want me to carry your books for you?" he asked.

White-hot shock pierced her soul. Her smile died a quick death with the memories his innocent statement brought with it. The times she'd ordered him to carry her books, among other things, came rushing back to smack her in the face. He probably thought she was the most self-centered, bossy girl on the planet.

"No, thank you," she mumbled. "I've got them."

"Are you sure?"

"Yes," she snapped at him. When a frown took up residence on his face, she pasted a smile on hers and said, "I have to apologize for the way I treated you since the day you saved me from humiliation in the parking lot. I just haven't been in my right mind lately. Lots of pressure, you know."

Was that her talking or the queen of England? She sounded like a complete moron. *Think, idiot!* There had to be a way to salvage the relationship she desperately wanted to build with Zach.

"I had a great time with you on our date," she said. "Maybe we can do it again."

"Sure." His eyes searched her face intently, and he asked, "You want to go clubbing tonight?"

"Yes." The word came out sounding airy, breathless.

"Are you okay?"

"Why wouldn't I be?"

"You crashed your dad's car yesterday."

She nearly choked on saliva. "N-no I didn't. What makes you think I crashed the car? It's sitting in the garage at home."

"I guess I heard wrong."

Kristen allowed Zach to walk her to class, but she kept her mouth shut. Everything she said to him came out wrong. Her head felt like it was filled with cotton balls. She wished she had a spell to turn time back. She would return to the day she'd blown the dust on him, and she would keep it in her purse this time.

When they reached the door, Zach opened it for her. She hesitated. There were so many things she wanted to say to him, but she didn't know where to start. Stepping in front of a nearby locker so she wouldn't be blocking the classroom door, she asked, "Will you have lunch with me?"

"I always do, don't I?" Zach rubbed the side of his neck and dropped his eyes. "We could go off-campus if you want and eat lunch without all the scrutiny." Then, she noticed the interested stares they were getting. Passing students watched them. Some of them wore smirks, while others frowned at the odd couple Zach and Kristen made—the bad boy and the good girl. They were a walking, talking cliché. Over the years, she had become immune to the attention, but poor Zach wasn't used to it yet.

"Ignore them," she said.

He shuffled from foot to foot. "I feel like a damn monkey in a zoo."

"Sorry."

"It's not your fault." His mouth eased into a smile. "You'd better get into class before the bell rings."

"Yeah, you'd better get going, or you won't make your class on time. I don't want you to get an ulcer just to save your rep. Shock them and be on time for a change."

He bent forward as if he were going to kiss her. Instead, he turned his face and put his mouth next to her ear. "Have a good day, and don't let the morons get to you." He took a couple of steps away from her. Walking backwards, he said, "I'll pick you up at the library at nine tonight."

An elbow caught Zach in the ribs, and he gritted his teeth. No apology this time. Earlier, a kid had hit him by accident, mumbled *sorry*, and quickly moved to another spot on the crowded dance floor. This one didn't even bother to glance his way. Zach faked a smile for Kristen's benefit. She seemed to be having a good time. He didn't want to spoil it.

Colored beams of light slashed through the crowd as if secret agents were looking for a dangerous fugitive.

Kristen swung her leather-clad hips like a professional dancer. She raised both arms high above her head and wiggled her upper body beneath the shimmering, silver-mesh top. She looked good, but Zach was disappointed in her choice of clothing. For some reason he'd pictured her in a short, red dress. That would have been phenomenal.

It was hot, there were too many people, and the music sucked. "Maybe this wasn't such a good idea," he yelled.

"What?" She cupped a hand around her ear. "I can't hear you! The music is too loud."

He shook his head to indicate it wasn't important. Satisfied, she shrugged and continued to dance. Sweat rolled down Zach's back. His discomfort grew. One drop slid all the way down to his boxers. What was wrong with the air conditioning? Did they purposely turn it off to keep people hot and thirsty so they would buy more drinks?

There was something he wanted to get off his chest, a confession, only he didn't want her to actually hear him. This seemed to be the perfect opportunity. Smiling at her, he said, "I think I'm falling for you. Hard."

"What?" She frowned again. Throwing up her hands, she yelled, "I can't hear you!"

Of course, he couldn't hear her either, but he was adept at reading lips as long as the person spoke slowly and didn't use big words. His grin broadened. "I wanted to hurt you for what you did to me, but now I just want to kiss you."

Kristen shouted something. He couldn't decipher it this time. Grabbing him by the front of his shirt, she pulled him close and talked directly into his ear. "I didn't catch any of that! What did you say?"

Instead of answering her verbally, he tried a little experiment. Drawing back from her, he stared deep into her eyes. He pushed a visual at her, a mental picture of the two of them locked in a passionate embrace, but she continued to frown. The experiment failed.

Her eyes rolled heavenward. She returned her mouth to his ear and asked, "What is up with you? Do you want to ditch this place? You don't look like you're having any fun."

He only drew back a few inches, just far enough. His mouth found hers. He kissed her hard at first, half-afraid she might resist. Her arms went up and wound themselves around his neck instead. The kiss softened. His hands went to her shoulders. He grasped them and kneaded them gently as she melted against him.

Zach opened his eyes for a second. He wanted to check her expression. Knowing Kristen, she wouldn't admit to her true feelings if she were falling for him. He would have to read it in her eyes. Unfortunately, something else captured his attention. His peripheral vision caught a familiar shape threading its way through the crowd.

His head snapped to the left in time to see a dark-haired girl disappear behind some tall guys who were playfully shoving each other. Morgan? His heart stopped. Morgan couldn't possibly be inside the club. The lights, the noise, and the crowd would send her over the edge. Worried, he walked away from Kristen without a word of explanation.

Kristen called after him, shocked by his abrupt departure.

He hurried through the crowd, pushing his way to the rear of the building. He would have to tell Kristen about Morgan when he got back. The dark-haired girl had vanished. He searched in vain, finally stepping outside into the alleyway in case she'd left. Still nothing.

Zach stood in the dark alley and growled in frustration. A rat scurried into a mountainous pile of trash. He strained his ears to pick up retreating footsteps but only came up with the buzzing of distant cars. He made a mental note to check Morgan's notebook later. If she'd followed him to the club, they were going to have a long talk about privacy.

Kristen stared after Zach, mouth open. *Unbelievable!* The jerk plants an incredible kiss on her, and then he runs off. What in the hell was wrong with him? She reached for her cell, intending to call her grandmother. Before she could find her grandmother's number in her list, she saw Zach's head as he moved in her direction. He was coming back.

She wasn't going to let him think his disappearance had rattled her. Kristen Noah didn't need a guy to make her happy. She looked around for another dance partner. A lot of people danced in groups of three or four. Some were by themselves and danced with everyone at once. She found a boy, kind of cute, looking at her. He didn't seem to be with anyone.

Kristen danced over to where he was and began to dance with him.

He smiled at her. The two of them showed each other their best moves. It took Zach a while to find her. For a moment, she forgot about him and started to enjoy herself. Then, he was there like a dark shadow blocking out the warm sunlight.

"Oh," she said, feigning surprise. "You're back."

Mouth tight, he glared at the other guy and scared him away.

The coward abandoned her to her fate. She had no choice but to face Zach, but she continued to dance. His grim expression darkened. She pretended not to notice.

He leaned in, put his mouth next to her ear, and said, "I thought I saw someone I know, someone who shouldn't be here. I didn't have time to tell you. I had to try to catch her."

Her? Kristen's heart sank. He'd been looking for another girl? The situation was worse than she'd thought. First, he talked to her even though he knew she couldn't understand a word of it. Then he ran off, chasing after another girl. Maybe he didn't like her as much as she'd hoped.

Kristen turned and stormed off in the direction of the nearest exit. She left the club with the full knowledge that Zach would be hot on her heels. At least they'd be able to talk outside. She walked fast when she hit the sidewalk. She didn't want anyone to overhear the argument that was about to explode between them.

Zach grabbed her arm when she reached the corner. "What's wrong? Why did you walk away like that?"

"Are you kidding me?" She knocked his hand off her arm. "You walked away first."

"And I told you I was sorry. I thought I saw…"

"Yeah, I know. You thought you saw some random girl that you know. Whatever. I'm tired. Goodnight."

Laughter rumbled in his chest. "Kristen Noah is jealous."

"I am not jealous, you jerk!"

He didn't stop laughing, so she hit him. Hand balled into a fist, she swung it hard and struck him in the jaw. Neither of them had seen it coming. She hadn't meant to hit him so hard. Tears flooded her eyes.

She wasn't sure if she was crying because she'd hurt him or out of frustration because his hard face had hurt her first.

Instead of getting mad, he rubbed his jaw and asked, "Do you feel better now?"

"I hate you."

"No, you don't."

"I do too hate you." She started walking again, and he fell into step right beside her. She added, "Go away. I don't ever want to see you again."

"If that were true, you wouldn't care that I was looking for a girl. You like me way too much. That's the problem."

"Go to hell."

Zach moved fast, cut in front of her, and turned. He blocked her way. His hands grabbed her by the shoulders. Holding her still, he said, "It's okay. I know how you feel."

"You have no clue how I feel, and if you don't let me go right now, I'm going to hit you again. This time I'll put all my weight behind it."

"I know how you feel because I feel the same way. You're mad and scared and a little freaked out. You don't want to fall for me, but you can't stop yourself. It's okay." He pushed errant strands of hair off her hot cheek. "I'm falling for you, too."

And then he kissed her.

She tried to resist.

His mouth went soft on top of hers, coaxing her to kiss him back. The tip of his tongue snaked out to lick her closed lips. Just a flick. Shockwaves shot through her entire body. Her emotions went from zero to sixty in half a second. In the end, fear won out.

Her eyes popped wide open, and she pushed Zach away, determined to make a run for it. What scared her the most was the realization that he was right. This wasn't a case of simple attraction. She was falling in love with Zach Bevian.

She'd been wrong. Love did exist. It was more powerful than attraction, and if she allowed it to have its way with her, she'd die. Somehow, loving Zach would kill her.

Before she could flee, Zach took her hand. He walked side-by-side with her. They went to his motorcycle, and he drove her to the library in silence. For a moment, she'd thought he was going to let her go without saying another word. But that wouldn't be Zach. He waited for her to open her car door.

He kissed the tip of her nose and said, "We'll take things slow from now on. I promise. We'll get to know each other, take our time. We should probably take a step back and just be friends for a while."

Relief flooded her system. "Really? You don't think I'm a big baby for wanting to run away from this, whatever this is?"

"You aren't the only one scared to death right now." He whistled between his teeth before saying, "I hate the idea of falling for someone as much as you do. My life is far too complicated to let you all the way in. So let's agree not to fall. Just be my friend for now. Deal?"

He stuck his hand out, and she took it. "Deal."

11

Out of Control

Over the next four weeks, Kristen's life began to unravel. Brittany was on a roll. She had enlisted Gina into some weird kind of partnership, and they were trying to ruin Kristen's life. The brunette twit had won the coveted position of class president, and she'd taken Kristen's place on the cheerleading squad. Somehow, she'd convinced the coach to get rid of Kristen, kicking her off the team forever.

Kristen was sure magic had been involved. No way could that stupid girl win the job on her own merits. Gina's popularity was on the rise, while Kristen's declined day by day. In just one month, she'd watched everything she'd worked so hard for slowly fade away, and there didn't seem to be anything she could do to stop it. It was one thing after another. She was on a long, crazy descent into nothingness.

It didn't make any sense. Brittany's revenge spells in the past had been mean, sure, but she hadn't dared mess with the important things in Kristen's life. She hadn't tried to destroy her before. How could her sister be this angry over a boy she didn't know?

Picking clothes out the night before school and wearing trendy fashions had lost its luster. Still, Kristen was determined not to give up without a fight. She put on sleek, white pants and a lime-green, striped top that looked like it was made in two matching pieces, a sweater over a shirt, but was a single item. The short, puffy sleeves with scalloped edges created a girlish look that Kristen usually avoided in favor of being powerful, but on this particular day she felt like playing up her feminine side.

It was Wednesday morning. The girls were sitting at the round kitchen table, eating breakfast. Cyndi and Brittany dug into neat stacks of pancakes that were drenched in maple syrup. They could eat anything and not gain an ounce. Kristen, on the other hand, had to be careful. Sometimes it seemed like all she had to do was look at a piece of chocolate cake and her weight fluctuated up a couple of pounds.

With that in mind, she chose fruit and a slice of dry toast. She peeled the banana while staring at the sliding-glass door that led to the garden. Since the house was located on a private beach, they didn't have a normal backyard with a lawn or a swing, so their father had paid some guys to build a little yard on the side of the house.

Brittany had been on her cell when Kristen entered the kitchen. After a few indistinct, monosyllabic answers, Brittany disconnected the call. An awkward silence filled the room.

Kristen didn't realize how quiet it was until Cyndi threw up her hands and raised her voice for the first time in what seemed like eons. "Would you two talk to each other? Please! This is getting ridiculous."

"I apologized already," Kristen said while glaring at Brittany. "It's not my fault someone is acting like a child."

"You're not sorry," Brittany said, "but you will be. You deserve everything you have coming your way."

"And what do you deserve besides a punch in the mouth?"

"Bring it on!"

Kristen tilted her head to the side as if she had a nervous tick and pictured what she wanted to happen. Sticky syrup squirted up into Brittany's face and got on her Black Metal T-shirt.

She screamed, "You bitch!"

Brittany flung her hand out, and Kristen's chair toppled backwards, dumping her on the floor before she had the chance to grab onto something. The back of her head cracked against the faux-brick linoleum. For a second, she saw stars. Wooden legs scraped against the floor as Cyndi's chair shot out. She was at Kristen's side in an instant, hunched over her.

"Are you okay?" Cyndi asked while helping her to her feet.

Kristen ignored her, eyes on Brittany. "You are so dead."

Brittany smirked. "You think you can take me? Do you really think you're man enough? Go for it."

Cyndi cried, "Please stop fighting before someone gets hurt!"

Kristen thought back to how this all began the first day of school, over a boy she'd crushed on a whim. Impulsive moves weren't usually her thing. She believed in detailed planning. Making a list of pros and cons had kept her out of trouble in the past. She wished she had made a list before crushing Zach. It would have saved them all a great deal of trouble.

Zach hadn't been kidding about taking things slow. They spent time with each other in school, ate lunch together sometimes, and walked down the hallways while talking about meaningless issues. She didn't see him anywhere else. Part of her was relieved, while the other part desperately wanted to kiss him again. Maybe things would have gone smoother between them if she had given him a chance instead of crushing him. She should have gotten to know him in a normal boy-girl way instead of using her powers.

After a few slow breaths, Kristen said, "I don't know why you're so angry with me. Zach isn't even crushed."

"That's what you say." Brittany folded her arms over her chest, a pinched look to her mouth. "I think you lied about retracting the spell. I've seen him staring at you like you're the only girl on the planet."

"I honestly didn't know you liked him this much. How many times do I have to repeat myself? If I had known, I would have stayed away from him."

"Whatever."

With a sigh, Kristen tried to reach the logical side of her sister's brain. "Look. You dared me to crush him, and I did. Later, you told me you were kidding and that you liked him, and I said I was sorry. I removed the spell. We should call a truce."

"Too late." Brittany grabbed a paper towel, ran it under the faucet, and dabbed her top with it to remove the syrup. "Someone needs to take you down, and I'm just the girl to do it."

"Give it your best shot, and then start running. There won't be a safe place for you to hide."

Brittany shook her head. "You think you have more power than I do, that you're better than me, but I'm going to prove you wrong this year. I'm the strongest, most powerful witch in this family. So hang on to your hat, sis, because you're in over your head this time."

Kristen and Cyndi stared at each other in disbelief while Brittany stormed out of the room. It was like they didn't even know their own sister anymore, like she'd been replaced by a pod person. None of it made any sense. Brittany had overreacted once or twice in the past, but this was beyond anything they'd seen her do before. It was almost as if she hated the very sight of Kristen now.

Things only got worse when they reached school.

Brittany made Kristen trip over an invisible rock as they crossed the parking lot.

Kristen turned the gum in Brittany's mouth to dirt.

Brittany ran to the restroom and spit the dirt into the sink. She turned a faucet on and put her head under the running water to rinse her mouth out. Kristen watched from the sidelines. A few girls gave them weird looks before walking out. That left them alone. Just to be sure, Kristen bent over and peeked under the six stalls, searching for feet, before she spoke openly to her sister.

"I've had enough, Britt. Seriously. I am so over this. Say 'uncle,' or I'm going to make you wish you were never born."

Brittany spat a few more times before turning her blazing-hot gaze on Kristen. She wiped her wet mouth with the back of one hand and said, “I’m not afraid of you. You have no idea who you’re messing with.”

“Oooh, I’m so scared.”

“If you were smart, you would be. By the time I get through with you, you’re going to be a bigger loser than the freshman who chases pennies.”

The other kids loved to make fun of Stan Paddington. They threw pennies on the ground as he walked by, and the kid chased after them like they were worth a million dollars each. Poor kid had no idea they were even making fun of him. He was an oddball.

She was not going to wind up as the school joke. Angry at the mere thought of it, she flung both hands in Brittany’s direction. Her punk-rocker sister went through a stunning transformation. Instantly, her hair was shiny and combed with a bright red bow holding some back from her squeaky-clean face. Her hardcore clothes had been replaced with a pretty, white-with-red-polka-dots dress with a huge bow at the waist and ruffled sleeves.

Brittany caught sight of her reflection in the mirror and screamed like she’d seen a bloody body on the floor. “Change me back!”

Kristen opened the door and shoved Brittany into the crowded hallway before the girl could run and hide. Students openly gaped at her, including a speechless Cyndi. Kristen smiled and waited for Brittany to try to wiggle her way out of this one.

Brittany straightened her spine and smiled. She spoke with a sweet and shy voice. “I’m tired of dressing like Britt, so I thought I would try something new. Do you like it?”

So that was it. She was going to ruin her twin’s reputation to save her own. Kristen silently urged Cyndi to call Brittany out on it, expose her for a liar, but Cyndi didn’t do a thing. She went along with it and pretended to be Brittany. Apparently, there wasn’t anything Cyndi wouldn’t do for her twin.

Kristen went to her locker, annoyed and a little disappointed at the non-climactic end to all the drama. As soon as the other students heard it was Cyndi dressed like a walking, talking doll from generations past, they returned to their own business.

Cyndi walked over to Kristen and said, “I’m out of the game. Brittany told me to get out now because I might get caught in the crossfire. Something’s wrong with her. I’ve seen her mad before, but she’s totally out of control.”

Kristen wholeheartedly agreed, but she didn’t want Cyndi to leave the competition. Then the game would be down to the two of them—Brittany and Kristen. It would get dangerous for sure without vulnerable Cyndi standing between them. Kristen didn’t understand why Brittany was off-the-grid angry. She’d agreed to let Kristen enchant someone else to stay in the game. Why would she do that? Unless she wanted Kristen to remain in the game so she’d have an excuse to attack her.

“It’s not that bad,” Kristen said. She dialed her locker combination and opened the metal door. Her locker exploded, a small blast sending papers, folders, and books flying everywhere. A startled scream burst from Cyndi’s lips, while Kristen almost had a coronary.

Students laughed at the prank, but Kristen shook with barely restrained anger. Her lungs constricted until she couldn’t breathe normally. Her eyes went to the mess on the hallway floor. Not only were they scattered, the notebooks weren’t color coded anymore. Everything had been turned solid white.

Cyndi sighed before drifting away.

“Brittany!” Kristen shouted.

The girl stood a few feet down the hallway, wearing a nasty smirk along with the frilly dress.

That was *it*! Kristen was going to kill her sister, literally. She was going to release her anger and knock the whole building down on the stupid girl’s head. White-hot rage like she’d never known before drove out every reasonable thought, leaving only the urge to commit homicide.

She started to move in Brittany’s direction, purpose in each step, but Zach appeared out of nowhere and grabbed her from behind. He pressed her against her locker with gentle hands and stood close as if they were going to slow dance. His hands moved to her face. He leaned forward and rested his forehead against hers.

"Close your eyes," he said. Once she complied, he spoke to her softly. "It's okay. Everything is okay. Just breathe. In and out. Relax. Everything is fine."

Zach's voice soothed her and calmed her bubbling anger. She leaned back, following his instructions to the letter. He kept talking, repeating the phrases. Every once in a while, his lips brushed against her cheek, cooling her anger more. In seconds, she returned to a good and peaceful frame of mind. She couldn't believe she'd almost gone homicidal in front of half the school.

"Thank you," she said.

"You okay?"

"I have it together now. Thank you."

He released her and took a step back. Damn, he looked good. It seemed like ages since she'd seen him. Just looking at him made her feel a hundred times better. Her gaze went to his full lips. She wanted to kiss him right there in front of everyone.

"Do you like me?" she asked, feeling a bit insecure. "As more than a friend?"

The out-of-the-blue question seemed to startle him. "I… uh… of course I like you." His smile turned genuine as he brushed strands of hair from her face. "I like you way too much."

"What does that mean?"

He sighed, and his warm, coffee-scented breath caressed her face. "Let's just say that getting involved with you would really complicate my life. I've been trying hard to keep from falling for you."

Her lips slowly formed the word, "Oh."

"On the other hand, a little complication could be fun. I am finding it very hard to just be friends with you." He leaned forward and brushed his mouth against hers in a teasing kiss.

A few catcalls disturbed the air around them. The warning bell rang, and for a moment, she thought it was the alarm going off in her head.

He added, “I guess we need to get to class, unless you want to ditch school with me and take another ride.”

It was tempting.

She had promised herself to have more fun this year.

She shrugged and smiled. “I guess we could do that.”

Zach stroked a hand down her bare arm, sending shivers up her spine. “I’ve tried so hard to stay away from you, but I just can’t do it anymore. Maybe you should come to my house and meet my sister.”

Sister! Her heart nearly leaped out of her chest. That was the big secret he’d been hiding? He had a sister? Relief weakened Kristen’s knees. Her legs turned to jelly, and she held onto his arm. With a big smile, she said, “Sounds great.”

“Let’s go before someone stops us.”

He took her hand and pulled her through the glass doors. They walked across the parking lot together. Fortunately, it was empty. Everyone was inside, hurrying to their first class. She just hoped no one spotted them from a window. The last thing she needed at this point was to get kicked out of school.

Zach asked, “Do you want to drive?

She shook her head.

She climbed on the back of the bike and wrapped her arms around his waist. Relaxed now, she rested her cheek against his spine. Being with Zach felt incredible. All her problems melted away, and she temporarily forgot Brittany. She was going to meet Zach’s sister. He was allowing her into his life. What could go wrong?

Zach lived in a house that brought every scary movie Kristen had ever watched to the forefront of her mind. It was a huge, Tudor-style home with white stucco, dark brown trim, and a rock foundation. Add to that the diamond-cut windows and ivy crawling up the sides, and you had a place that made you shudder just to look at it. It answered at least one of Kristen's questions—Zach definitely came from money.

He opened the massive front door and waved her inside. She stepped past him into the foyer and forgot how to breathe. It was beautiful. A crystal chandelier glowed with golden light above their heads. A hand-carved staircase traveled up one wall. There were expensive paintings and pricey antiques along the other walls. She was almost afraid to move for fear she might break something.

"Wow," she said.

He grinned. "Glad you like it."

"Will you give me the tour?"

"Sure. But first, I'd better introduce you to my sister. She'll freak out if she hears voices." His expression and mood sobered as he explained, "My sister is handicapped. She may look twenty, but she's got the mind of a child. That's why I didn't want anyone to know about her. She doesn't like strangers, and I don't want her to get upset."

Kristen slid her hand into his and gave it a reassuring squeeze. The trust he had in her filled her with awe. Meeting his sister was an honor he hadn't bestowed on anyone else. "One of my cousins has a handicap, too."

"She doesn't like to be touched, so be careful about that. I'll go get her. Stay here. I need a few minutes to prepare her to meet you."

Kristen nodded.

Zach walked away, allowing the house to devour him.

While he was gone, Kristen drifted into the room on the left. It was being used as a study. There was a huge stone fireplace, and the pictures on the mantle caught her attention. She inspected each one closely, even though it made her feel somewhat snoopy. There was one of Zach's parents—at least, that's who she assumed they were. They looked like nice, regular people, big smiles and warm eyes. There was a picture of him and his sister. The girl had dark hair and dark eyes, no smile. There was something missing from those eyes, something vitally essential.

Between the pictures were angels carved out of wood. They

were so lifelike that her breath caught in her throat. She lifted one and examined it. Amazing. The angel had such a serene expression, half-closed eyes with a dreamy smile. She wondered where Zach had found them.

Maybe they had belonged to his mother.

"Who are you?" a cold, mechanical voice asked from somewhere behind her.

Startled, Kristen gasped and dropped the angel. Fortunately, it was made out of wood, not glass, so it bounced on the floor without breaking. She swung around to find the dark-haired girl from the photos standing there, teddy bear dangling from one hand. The neutral expression on her face mirrored the one in the photograph.

Kristen looked to the open doorway, hoping Zach would appear, but he didn't. Clearly, he hadn't been able to talk to his sister.

"I… I'm Kristen Noah, a friend of Zach's. He's looking for you so he can introduce us."

"Zach doesn't have friends. He keeps to himself. He told me he has to lay low. He keeps to himself. Talking to people is dangerous. Who are you? Why are you here?"

There was a definite challenge in the tone of voice. Kristen looked at the doorway again, desperate to see Zach's face. She didn't want to upset the girl. Zach might not forgive her.

Taking a deep breath, she said, "Zach and I are brand-new friends."

"Zach doesn't bring people home with him." Suspicious, the sister moved closer to Kristen. "He doesn't have friends. Zach doesn't bring people home with him." Her dark eyes raked Kristen from head to toe. "And he doesn't like it when people touch his stuff. Are you a burglar? If you are, I have the right to defend myself. Zach told me we're allowed to defend ourselves."

"I'm not a burglar."

"Burglars break into people's homes. They get shot because people have the right to defend themselves. Zach says we aren't supposed to hurt people, but we have to defend ourselves. I wrote it down in my notebook."

Kristen forced a smile. "That's good. It's good to write things down so you'll remember."

Morgan stared at Kristen in silence.

Kristen shifted from one foot to the other, uncomfortable.

"There you are," Zach said from the doorway. He moved to stand next to Morgan. "Have you met Kristen? This is my sister Morgan, and this is Kristen Noah. I hope you two will become good friends."

"You're home early again. You aren't supposed to be home until a few minutes after three. It's only nine o'clock now. Are you going to have snack with me at ten?"

"Well, I'll stay for a snack if Kristen wants to join us."

"I don't want her here," Morgan said, body rigid. Her voice started cold and flat, but by the time she reached the last word it had steadily grown louder. "Make her go."

"That isn't very nice, Morgan."

She glared at Kristen while hugging her brother close, a possessive flare in her eyes. "I don't care. I don't like her. Bear doesn't like her, either. Make her go away. Then we can have a snack together."

She ran out of the room and up the stairs. The door slammed shut above them a few seconds later. Zach gave Kristen an apologetic smile. "That actually went better than I thought it would. I'm going to talk to her. I'll be back in a second."

Kristen waited alone in the expensively furnished room. She found the girl's notebook and flipped through it, reading a few of the entries. Apparently, Morgan felt like she had to write everything down. There were lists of things to do, stuff that Zach had told her, and a few detailed entries on what Zach did when he left the house.

Did Zach know his sister liked to spy on him?

She had followed him to the club and seen him with Kristen on their second date. The girl wasn't as helpless or as clueless as she pretended to be. She'd known who Kristen was when she'd questioned her. Two sets of footsteps tromped down the stairs. They were coming back. Kristen tossed the notebook back on the table and went to stand by the fireplace again.

Morgan entered the room ahead of her brother. In a robotic voice, she said, "Kristen, we want you to have snack with us at ten."

Zach gestured for Kristen to respond to his sister's forced invitation.

"Thank you," she said. "I would love to have snack with you."

Morgan's smile changed, becoming slightly malicious. "Then maybe you and I can play a game."

Game? A shiver raced up Kristen's spine. There was knowledge glittering in the cold depths of the other girl's eyes. This girl wasn't just ill, she was off her rocker. Kristen had no doubt that if Morgan could kill her and get away with it, she would.

Zach stood there smiling, completely oblivious.

12

Exposed

"I don't think your sister likes me very much," Kristen said as they took a walk through the woods behind Zach's house. There wasn't another person for miles. He owned two-hundred-plus acres. It was weird to think everything in sight belonged to him. There wasn't another person for miles. Little Morgan didn't like visitors.

Kristen tried to keep her tone light. They weren't at the point in their relationship yet where she could tell him the truth about a close relative, especially not the sister he obviously adored. She peeked at him from beneath lowered lashes, checking his expression.

He shook his head and smiled. "You just aren't used to how she acts. She doesn't like or dislike anyone. Remember the movie *Rain Man*? That's Morgan, except for the freaky number thing. She can't do that."

The trees parted on a clearing overgrown with weeds and wildflowers. There was an old, red barn in the center. It looked like one of those picture-perfect calendar photos. For a moment, Kristen forgot about the crazy sister. She felt like an explorer making an amazing discovery. Her lips parted on a soft gasp. "I wish I had my camera."

Zach gave her a doubtful look. "Are you kidding me? You'd want a picture of that?"

"It's beautiful."

"It's old and falling apart."

She smiled and took him by the hand, pulling him towards the building. "Where is your sense of adventure? Let's have a closer look."

"Are you sure? The guy who sold me the land said no one has used it for over a decade. It might not be safe."

"Hey, I thought I was the one who worried over nothing." She grinned before ushering him closer. Walking behind him, she pushed him to the large opening while laughing. "You're big and strong. I trust you to protect me."

He returned her smile. In a quick role-reversal, he spun around, wrapped his arms around her, and put her in front of him. They stepped into the old building together. "It stinks in here," he grumbled, his smile evaporating.

Kristen tried hard not to wrinkle her nose. Yes, it did smell, but it was nice to have Zach alone. She wanted to share her fears and frustrations with him. So much had happened since the last time they'd spoken. "Everything has been crashing down around me for the last few weeks."

"I noticed. Gina has been working overtime to get to you. I don't know what her problem is, and I can't believe your sister is helping her. I think siblings should have each other's backs, no matter what."

Kristen wished she could tell him the truth about Brittany, the game, and her powers. If he knew what she was dealing with, how her sister was a dangerous witch, he would finally understand what was truly going on. Maybe he could help her think of a way out of it.

But she couldn't tell him. He would either think she was insane or lying. Then there were the dreams to consider. He was going to accuse her someday and steal her powers away. As much as she wanted to trust him, she couldn't.

"Brittany will come around eventually. She always does."

Zach rubbed his hands down the length of both of her arms in a comforting gesture. "We can't choose our relatives."

"What about you and Morgan? You seem to get along."

He made a face. "She's the only family I have left, and she needs me. But sometimes, honestly, I just want to put her in a box and ship her as far away from me as I possibly can."

Changing the subject to a happier one, she asked, "Where did you find those amazing angels on the fireplace?"

With a laugh, he pulled Kristen into a tight embrace. "Let's not talk about that right now. We should take advantage of this rare moment."

"What do you mean?"

His voice fell to a whisper. "We're alone."

"Yeah. I noticed that."

"Scared?"

"Of you?" She laughed, thinking about how silly she'd been to ever believe he was horrible or dangerous. Now when she gazed into those blue eyes, she only saw the good in him. "Of course not."

"You never have to be afraid of me. I will always take care of you." His eyes dropped to her mouth while his fingers caressed her face. "Do you have any idea how much I've been wanting to kiss you?"

She blushed. "Me too."

"All through snack time, while Morgan was going on and on about nothing, I just kept thinking how I wanted to reach over the table and take your face between my hands like this." He demonstrated. "And kiss you breathless, like this."

His mouth covered hers in a kiss that seared what was left of her brain. She couldn't think; she could only feel. Her lips parted beneath his on a blissful sigh, and she marveled at the tenderness of his touch. It was hard to believe this was the same guy she'd recently hated.

A groaning sound filled her ears. For a moment, she thought the sound was coming from Zach, but it grew louder, more insistent. It was a bad sound, the sound of impending doom. Fear coursed through her veins.

They broke apart in confusion.

As if by mutual consent, their eyes traveled upward. The terrible noise magnified a hundredfold. A large, single beam directly over their heads seemed to be the only thing holding the barn up. It snapped while Kristen was staring up at it. The decrepit roof was going to fall on them. There wasn't time to move, wasn't time to run. It was over. They were going to be crushed.

Kristen's eyes went to Zach's. There wasn't time for her to tell him how important he was to her. She thought she might actually be in love with him. Now he would never know.

Zach grabbed her.

He couldn't possibly protect her from the collapsing barn, but the fact that he was willing to try made her love him even more. The words stuck in her throat. Instead of getting hit by something, she felt as if she were playing that silly kid game where you twirled around and around until you almost passed out. It was like she was flying through the air with nothing to hold on to except for Zach's warm body.

Then she was falling, and Zach's comforting presence was gone.

She screamed. The ground rushed up to meet her, and her body slammed against it. A cloud of dust momentarily distorted her vision. Eyes open, she scrambled to her feet and found herself no longer inside the barn. They were back in the woods. Her mind headed for a total meltdown. She yelled, "What the hell! What's going on? How did we get out here?"

Zach was on his knees a few feet from her. His eyes were glued to her as if he were afraid to look away. He stood up slowly, hands out like he was trying to calm a frightened animal. "It's okay. Don't be upset. I can explain."

"Explain what? *You* did this? How?"

"Let's just say you aren't the only one in Sol Moreno with powers."

A dark fear, worse than anything she'd experienced before, seeped into her bones and clouded her judgment. She had *trusted* him. Total betrayal rocked her senses. Unable to breathe, she just stood there, staring at him in shock. His words rolled over her a second time.

"Wait a second," she said. "How long have you known about me?"

His gaze dropped to the ground.

"How long?" she shouted.

With a frown, he admitted, "I figured it out a few weeks after starting at Titan. I saw Cyndi blow colorful dust into a boy's face. Then that kid started following her around, doing everything she asked him to. It was obvious to me, at least."

"Why didn't you say something?"

"Because then you would have known that I was like you. I'm hiding from the witches' council because of Morgan. I couldn't afford for you to notice me. And anyway, I thought you were a psychotic, stuck-up witch with delusions of grandeur. So I avoided you for as long as I could."

"Until I blew the dust into *your* face." Her skin crawled at the memory of how he'd behaved after she'd crushed him. That whole time he'd been playing a game with her. "You lied to me."

He gawked at her, disbelief written all over his face. "*Excuse me*? You lied to me first! And you tried to use me, make me into your little puppet boy. I was going to blow your butt out of the water and accuse you in front of the whole damn school that day, but…"

The blood drained from her face. "Why didn't you?"

"I went home to vent so my anger wouldn't explode and destroy the whole block. After I got myself under control, I realized I couldn't do it. I don't want the council to know Morgan is with me. Then, when I got back to school, I found you fighting with Gina. You were so strong, so determined to beat her down.

"When you turned those beautiful eyes in my direction and demanded my jacket, I couldn't resist. For a while, I thought I might actually be enchanted. It took time to figure out I just wanted to be near you. I was under a different sort of spell."

On any other day, his words would have filled her with such unimaginable joy she would have been floating ten feet in the air, but she couldn't get past the lies and the betrayal. Then, there was the crazy power he had. She had never seen anything like it.

"How did you do it?" she asked. "I've never even heard of someone who could do what you just did. My grandmother is the most powerful witch I know, and she can't do anything close."

"I can explain." He took a step in her direction.

Kristen automatically backed away, arms raised and fists clenched. She spread her legs in a fighting stance as she thought of a spell, something that would knock him off balance so she could get away. He was dangerous—that was crystal clear. Anyone who could pop from one place to another was capable of anything. He might be able to make the ground open and swallow her. Maybe he could even wipe her memory clean so she wouldn't remember this conversation.

"Stay away from me," she said. "I mean it."

"You don't have to be afraid of me."

"Right. So says the boy with the wicked power."

"I would never do anything to hurt you."

She didn't believe him. The Zach she'd thought she knew didn't exist. He had been playing a part the entire time, laughing at her behind her back because she had believed she was in control. Memories surfaced one after another, all the times she'd spent with him. None of it had been real.

"What was the plan?" she asked. "Were you going to play games with me, make me fall for you, and then accuse me in front of half the school?"

His dark brows drew together. When he answered her, his voice was quiet. "No. I was going to get you to fall for me so you would remove the spell and I could return to my normal life. But that was before I got to know you. You aren't like any other girl I've ever met."

"What is the big master plan now?"

"There is no plan." He moved another step closer. "You have to listen to me. I think I might be in love with you."

Claiming to love her was the last straw. Without warning she took off through the woods as fast as she could, legs and arms pumping, fear adding to her speed. She wasn't running from Zach; she was running from a stranger with a familiar face. He had lied and manipulated her. As far as she was concerned, he was worse than Jake.

"Kristen, stop!" His feet pounded the hard earth behind her.

He was chasing her.

In a full-on panic, she pushed herself to run faster. Kristen looked over her shoulder as she tore through the woods. She didn't hear him anymore, and she didn't see him, either. There were only trees. She tripped over an exposed root and went down hard, scraping her knees and the palms of her hands. The fall knocked the breath out of her. Around her, the woods got deathly quiet. No birds chirped. No insects buzzed. She glanced up and saw the reason why.

There, a few short yards from her face, was the wolf from the other night. She was almost certain it was the same animal, although that didn't make any sense. They were miles from the place she'd last come across it, and how could it possibly know where to find her?

Every muscle in her body froze. She didn't dare breathe as their eyes connected and held. Her mind tried to work quickly and find a way out of this mess. She searched her brain for a good spell, but before she could come up with anything, the wolf changed. It transformed in front of her eyes, going from wolf to boy in mere seconds.

Zach stared down at her, his gaze mirroring the wariness in her heart.

"You." She stood on shaking legs and shouted, on the verge of hysterics, "You can change into a wolf? Are you kidding me? What else can you do? Just how powerful are you?"

He approached her slowly, hands in pockets. "I don't think you're ready to hear anything I have to say right now."

A jumble of emotions brought her to the edge of a mental breakdown. Fear, sadness, and confusion—each grew at a rapid rate until she thought she would collapse under the weight of them. He was right about one thing though.

She didn't want to hear his explanation.

"I'll take you back to school," he said while reaching for her arm.

She stepped to the side, avoiding him easily. "I'm not getting on that motorcycle with you again. Forget it. Point me to the road, and I'm out of here."

"You can't walk back to school. It's too far."

"I'll call Cyndi. I have my phone."

"I have a car, too. Remember?" His tone was flat and lifeless, a good match for his eyes. "I can take you to school in it."

"I am not going anywhere with you, not ever again."

Digging a hand into the pocket of his faded jeans, he pulled out a set of keys. While she watched, still shaking, he removed a gold one from the ring and held it out to her, saying, "You can take the car. Leave it in the school parking lot with the key under the seat. I'll get it later."

She reached out slowly, afraid it was a trick. Snatching the key from his hand, she held it tightly and took a few steps backwards. "Where is it?"

"In the garage."

"Where is the garage?"

"Next to the house."

She swallowed her rising anger. Getting answers out of him was like undergoing a root canal without anesthesia. If he was trying to be cute, she wasn't in the mood for it. "Where is the house?"

"Follow me."

She walked several yards behind him. Her eyes floated in a puddle of tears over losing the boy she'd loved. It was almost like he'd died. Almost. Only in truth, he had never really existed. An occasional rock made her stumble. She wanted to run to catch up with him, snuggle close, and pretend the last ten minutes had just been a dream. His shoulders were slumped in defeat, and he looked as sad as she felt. She wanted to tell him she loved him, too, but she couldn't. Even if he was who he claimed to be, even if he weren't a threat, she couldn't be with a boy she didn't trust.

Zach had not only lied to her, he'd also pretended to be something he wasn't.

A small voice deep inside reminded her that she'd done the same thing.

She told the voice to shut up.

It was over.

Although the day had started with promise, it was going to end in frustration and pain. Another loss. The last time Zach had been this miserable, he had just lost his parents. Maybe he should resign himself to the fact that this was how his life would always be. Maybe he'd been born under an unlucky star. He always lost the people he loved, no exceptions.

Someday soon, he was going to lose Morgan, too. He could feel it. Maybe that was why he let her get away with acting like a brat sometimes.

He stood on the dirt drive in front of his home, choking on a cloud of dust as he watched Kristen leave in his car. Fists clenched, he turned away and wandered back to the garage. Kristen was gone. She wasn't coming back. Somehow, he was going to have to find a way to deal with the loss. He should have known better than to fall in love. Thanks to the situation with Morgan, he was doomed to spend his life alone. Nothing anyone could do to change that little fact.

"Zach!" Morgan tore across the yard screaming his name. She didn't see him in the garage. Her eyes were focused on the now-empty road. The dust hadn't quite settled yet. Fists clenched, she screamed, "Zach! Come back!"

It was the first time in years she'd shown any real emotion. He wasn't sure if it was a step toward full recovery or a momentary lapse. Half the time he was convinced she wouldn't notice if he were replaced by a talking hamster. Stunned speechless, he watched his sister kick the gravel in fury.

He found his voice and said, "I'm right here, Morgan."

She spun around, and relief flooded her eyes. She whimpered. "I saw the car go, and I thought you were leaving without saying goodbye."

"I wouldn't do that."

"Promise me!" Morgan threw herself against him and clung to him. Her fingers dug into the flesh of his arms. The thin shirt he was wearing proved no protection against her claws. Part of him, a small part that he tried to keep buried, resented her.

"Promise me you won't let her take you away from me."

"Who? Kristen?" He started to pat her on the back to comfort her but stopped himself in time. For a moment, he'd forgotten she didn't like to be touched. "You don't have to worry about her. After what happened today, I doubt she'll ever speak to me again."

The way Morgan had her head tilted against his chest allowed him only a partial view of her mouth. For a second he could swear her lips lifted at the ends just slightly as if she were inwardly rejoicing over the fact that he'd lost the only girl he'd ever loved.

His resentment grew an inch.

A new suspicion came to mind. "Where were you thirty minutes ago?"

"In the house."

"You weren't playing around with magic again, were you?"

"No!" She stopped embracing him and took a step back. "You told me not to use spells. I wrote it down, but I remember, too. You told me not to use my powers, and I don't. Are you mad at me?"

"I'm not mad." With a harsh sigh, he turned away from Morgan. He didn't want her to see the rage building inside him. He was mad but not at her. "There's an evil witch in town, but I don't know who it is. I'm going to have to find him or her before they seriously hurt someone."

The two of them walked back to the house. Morgan searched for Bear while he went upstairs to his bedroom. The second he crossed the threshold he saw the secret drawer in his headboard was open. He jumped on the king-sized bed, scrambled to the top, and reached inside. His hand closed around the glass vial of magical dust. Relief flooded his system.

It was short-lived. He brought the empty vial up to his face and felt the bottom drop out of his world. The love-spell dust was gone.

"Morgan!"

He ran downstairs, found her in the family room, and confronted her as gently as he could under the circumstances. Holding the empty glass vial up, he asked, "Did you go into my bedroom and take this out of my headboard?"

Morgan stared at him in silence, eyes huge.

Lowering his voice, he stepped closer to her. "You aren't going to be in trouble. I just need to know what you did with the dust that used to be inside of this."

"The sand," she said, correcting him. "It was sand. Sand belongs on the beach. Mom told us not to take sand off the beach. I wanted to fill a bottle and take it home. She told me sand stays on the beach. You had sand in there. I took it to the beach. It belongs on the beach."

Morgan was the only person he knew who would think it was sand. At least she hadn't used it on some poor unsuspecting boy. Zach couldn't even imagine how bad a disaster that would be, his mentally ill sister and a hormonal boy drunk on love.

"Are you mad at me?" she asked.

"No, but you need to leave my stuff alone. Okay? Stay out of my bedroom from now on."

She nodded in agreement. "I will. I promise. I'll go write it down in my notebook. Don't go in Zach's room. I'll write it down and underline it three times."

She left, and Zach let out his pent-up breath. He was so thankful she hadn't used a spell on anyone. Someday it would happen, though. He knew it. Someday she would go too far, use her powers, and he would be forced to say goodbye to her forever. The thought was an arrow in his heart. He had hoped, after spending months on end with her, it would be easier to let her go. It wasn't.

Destroying her was going to destroy him.

13

Alone

"Where'd you get the cool new ride?" Brittany asked. She circled the black sports car, dragging her fingertips over the gleaming body with a deep yearning in her eyes. Somehow, she had managed to ditch the girly dress, trading it for jeans and a tee. She cast a wide smile in Kristen's direction. It was like their fight had never happened. That was how Brittany handled things. No apology—just pretend it didn't happen and wait for the other person to forget. Too bad for her, Kristen was tired of her cold-and-hot routine. The girl was in serious need of medication.

As her sisters stared at the borrowed car in awe, Kristen realized she'd never felt so incredibly alone. They were standing in the center of the school parking lot, surrounded by her peers, people she'd desperately tried to impress over the years, but she didn't see them. She didn't hear them. Her heart ached for something she couldn't have. Oh, why couldn't Zach have told her he loved her yesterday?

She might have believed him then.

Despite the things she'd seen him do, a big part of her wanted to race back to him. She wanted to jump into his arms, squeeze him tight, and never let him go. She missed him already. How was she going to get through the rest of the school year without him?

Forget that. How was she going to get through the rest of her life?

Since Brittany had settled down, Kristen didn't want to say the Z-word and start another war. "I borrowed it."

"From who?" Brittany's eyes narrowed. A flicker of intelligence sparkled in the girl's eyes. She knew exactly where the car had come from. Letting it go, she smiled and wound an arm around Kristen's neck, sounding almost proud. "Ditching school now? Be careful. You're going to lose your halo."

Afraid to go into school earlier with only a couple hours left, she had sat in the car and waited for the twins. She had chosen to sit in Zach's car instead of her own because of the tinted black windows. If a teacher gazed outside during class, they wouldn't see her inside of it. It had seemed like an eternity before she saw the first of the students emerge from the main entrance. She had wanted to tell her sisters everything on sight, but she hadn't managed more than two words before Brittany had interrupted her.

A group of kids walked past them, whispering and giggling. Their expressions said they thought Kristen was the punchline of some dumb joke now. No longer the girl everyone envied, she had become an outcast, a notch above the girl who didn't bathe on a regular basis. She dropped her eyes, pretending not to notice her waning popularity.

"Ignore them," Cyndi said.

Kristen was only half-listening as she tried to figure out how to deliver the bad news about Zach. There didn't seem to be any way to soften the blow. Finally, she just blurted it out. "Zach is one of us."

Cyndi gasped. "No way."

"He admitted it after I saw him do some pretty incredible stuff."

"I don't think so." Brittany shook her head. "There is no way that Zach Bevian is a witch, warlock, wizard, whatever you want to call them." She rolled her eyes. "He just isn't. I can smell someone with power clear from the other side of town."

Kristen didn't bother to point out that she'd been the one dating

Zach. If anyone should have known, it should have been her. Instead she said, "He can change into a wolf, and he can vanish and reappear in a place miles from where he started."

"Now I *know* you're lying." Brittany folded arms over her chest. "No one can do crap like that, not even Grandma Noah."

Wide-eyed, Cyndi asked, "Did you see him do it? Seriously?"

"He made me disappear and reappear with him, so yeah, I'm pretty sure he can do it." His passionate words returned to the front of her mind. He had told her he loved her. Every sour turn of the day came back with the subtlety of a nuclear bomb. She bit the inside of her cheek to keep the tears at bay.

She climbed back into Zach's car, and Cyndi followed.

"Is it over between you and Zach?" Cyndi asked.

"Yes." Kristen faked a smile. "I'm fine with it. In fact, it's great. I almost threw my future away because of him. I should have listened to Dad, kept my eyes on the prize, and not let a boy get to me. At least it's not too late. I can start studying hard again and fix the damage Brittany has done to my life."

Cyndi put a hand on her arm. "I'm sorry it didn't work out."

"I can't go home tonight," Kristen said. "I don't want to see Dad. He wants me to start filling out college apps and writing essays, and I feel like my whole world has turned to mush. I can't even think right now."

"Okay. Relax. We won't go home." For a few minutes, the car's interior was quiet. Then, Cyndi snapped her fingers. "I know—we'll spend the night with Grandma Noah. Give me a second and I'll call her, let her know we're coming."

Brittany beat her to it. Before Cyndi could dig her phone out of her purse, Brittany pushed her way into the front seat on Cyndi's side because the compact thing didn't have a backseat. Cyndi wound up sitting on the hard hump in the middle. Of course, being Cyndi meant she didn't complain about it.

"Grandma told me to give you a warning," Brittany said. "So here it is. She told me only extremely evil witches have the powers you described. She wants us to get down to San Diego as soon as possible so she can help us figure out what tall, dark, and scary is really up to."

Kristen put the car key under the seat and grabbed the door handle. "Let's go, then."

"Can't we take Zach's car?" Brittany asked.

"No, we can't. He's coming after it. Let's go."

Brittany mumbled under her breath about some sisters not being any fun at all, but Kristen pretended not to hear it.

Kristen dug her hands into the soft soil. Grandma Noah was right about gardening. It *was* therapeutic. Stress dripped off her like tiny beads of sweat as she made a hole in the rich dirt. She placed a tiny plant into the hole and pushed the soil around it. Then, she patted the dirt down to make sure the thing would stay in place. Just a little water, and the plant would be ready to grow.

She lifted her head and watched the twins work on the other side of the yard. Cyndi was having a blast. Her smile was almost as big as the floppy straw hat she'd borrowed from their grandmother. Brittany, on the other hand, wore a sour expression. She hated anything remotely connected to work.

Grandma Noah bent over and pulled a few weeds away from her favorite rosebushes. She looked up and smiled. Although her face and hands were dirty, her eyes sparkled. Still, something beneath the cheerfulness worried Kristen. Grandma Noah didn't seem quite herself today. She was distracted, but she hadn't said a word to Kristen about Zach yet.

"How much longer do we have to stay out here?" Brittany whined. "It's hot."

"Hard work is good for you. Puts things into perspective." A few minutes later, Grandma Noah moved closer to Kristen. She hunched down next to her and spoke in a low voice the other girls couldn't hear. "I need you to tell me everything there is to know about the boy. What did the wolf look like? How fast did he change? I want every detail."

Kristen whispered the whole story to her grandmother and watched with a growing feeling of dread as her grandmother's calm demeanor underwent a metamorphosis. Her mouth tightened. The normally sparkling, pale blue eyes darkened. In a matter of seconds, the woman seemed to age ten years.

Grandma Noah dropped her head, and her shoulders sagged beneath the white cotton blouse. "Oh, sweetheart, you have gotten yourself into a mess this time. I'm not sure I can help you out of it."

"What is it, Grandma? How bad is it? What can I do?"

"With a warlock that powerful, I'm afraid there isn't anything you *can* do. I don't have a spell good enough to protect you. I don't think one exists. The medallion I have for you will boost your power, but not enough."

"Should I leave town? Change schools? What?"

Grandma Noah patted her hand. "Let's not go to extremes just yet. First, I want to approach the witches' council and find out more about this boy. They must know about him. They would have to know about him and the powers he has. Let me talk to them. In the meantime, you keep your distance."

Kristen looked away, not wanting her grandmother to see the regret in her gaze. Truthfully, she didn't want to stay away from Zach. Even though part of her remained deathly afraid of him, a bigger part longed to be with him. She said, "He told me there's someone after me, but that it's not him. He claims he's been trying to use his powers to protect me. Maybe we're wrong about him. Maybe he's telling the truth."

Grandma Noah shook her head decisively. "No. I'm sorry, sweetheart, but there isn't any possible way for that boy to be anything other than trouble."

"But, Grandma—"

"Do you have any idea how someone goes about possessing the powers this boy has?" After Kristen shook her head, her grandmother said, "They have to sacrifice somebody. 'Innocent blood', they call it."

Kristen shivered as an icy finger touched her spine.

Her grandmother added, “They have to kill another person, usually more than one. Only an evil witch or warlock can acquire the power to transform into an animal, not to mention the power to teleport.”

Kristen clamped her lips firmly shut and replayed each damning word in her mind. How could Zach be evil? He had saved her from falling off the cliff and from being crushed by the barn, and he had the most amazing blue eyes she’d ever seen. In the past she had thought them to be cold and calculating. Lately, she only saw warmth in them.

“Stay away from him,” her grandmother repeated in a firm voice.

Kristen didn’t know if she could do that.

14

Spying

"Didn't you finish your homework at Grandma's house?" Cyndi asked from the doorway of Kristen's bedroom.

It was late Sunday afternoon. They had returned from San Diego that morning, bright and early. Instinctively knowing what had to be done, Kristen had gone straight to work. Now she glanced up from the dozen or so open books on her bed and explained, "This isn't homework. I'm trying to find some powerful spells that I can use in case Brittany doesn't stop attacking me."

She was also desperately trying to find a reasonable explanation for Zach's abilities other than the one her grandmother had suggested. Zach couldn't have killed another person just to become a stronger witch. He wouldn't do that. She would bet her last dime on it. He was a good person, and she was going to prove it. Unfortunately, she hadn't found a thing to prove his innocence. According to the books she'd thumbed through, only human sacrifice could give a witch or wizard the ability to transform. Somehow, the books had to be wrong.

"I'll help you." Cyndi sat on the opposite edge of the bed and picked up the volume closest to her. "What did I see Grandma Noah shove into your hand before we left the house? I didn't say anything because I didn't want Brittany to find out about it, but you can trust me. What was it?"

"This." Kristen reached into her blouse and pulled out a gold chain with a medallion on the end.

"Is it for protection?"

"Kind of. It's supposed to enhance my abilities and make them stronger. I should be able to do bigger and better spells now."

"Don't let Brittany see it. She'll want it."

"That's why it's under my shirt. It would defeat the purpose if Britt got her hands on it. I'd be dead within the week."

Cyndi didn't argue the point. "Have you tried it out yet?"

"No." She was actually afraid to use a spell with the magical charm hanging around her neck. What if it fueled her power to the point she couldn't control it? What if she became more dangerous than Brittany?

Cyndi's face took on a light of excitement. "Well, do something. Come on. I want to see if it works."

"Where is Brittany? I don't want her to walk in and—"

"Don't worry about her. She left a few minutes after we got home. When I asked where she was going, I got this—" Cyndi stood up straight, changed her expression to one of barely veiled hostility, and did her best Brittany impression. "—FYI, I do have a life outside of you."

"Stop it. I hate it when you talk like her. You're too good at it."

"Thank you. Thank you very much. Now quit stalling and do some magic."

"Like what? What do you want me to do?"

Cyndi tapped a finger against her chin and gave it some serious thought. A light popped into her eyes. "Well, since you obviously aren't over Zach, let's see what he's doing. Spy on him."

"That's impossible."

"No. It used to be impossible because you didn't have enough power. Grandma Noah does it sometimes. Go ahead. Try."

Kristen inhaled deeply. She summoned all of her power into one place and concentrated on Zach. Nothing happened.

She clenched her hands into fists. Straining with the effort, she forgot to breathe this time. Her head began to ache. She released her breath in a frustrated hiss and said, "It isn't working."

"Maybe you should hold the charm in your hand."

Kristen removed the necklace from her throat. She held it like Cyndi told her and tried to do the spell again. It still didn't work. Her head was beginning to throb painfully, worse with every try. "Oh, forget it. Nothing is going to happen."

"Do it once more. Please. I think I know what might help."

Kristen almost told Cyndi to get out of her room and let her rest. Instead, she closed her eyes and forced the image of Zach to the front of her mind. Cyndi reached out and grabbed her hand at the last second. The extra magical connection brought the sound of rushing wind with it. Kristen's eyes popped open, and she gasped.

There, on her wall, was the most amazing sight. It was almost like watching a giant television. The color was good, brilliant even, and there was incredible sound, as if Zach were in the room with her. Her heart ached, and fresh pain hit her hard at the sight of him, knowing she'd lost him forever.

On the other side of town, Zach bent under the hood of his car. He was inside the garage, dismantling the engine. The garage door was up, allowing the bright sunlight to invade even the darkest corners. Too bad it couldn't drive the darkness from his soul. An image of Kristen came to mind, but he banished it the second it appeared. He would go nuts if he kept thinking about her. It was over. Nothing he could do about it.

"Why are you sad?" Morgan asked from somewhere over his shoulder.

He jumped and struck his head on the hood. His hand went to the wound to check for blood. Turning with a grimace on his face, he bit back the curse words floating around in his mouth. The girl moved like a panther in the jungle. He really should replace the locket around her neck with a bell.

"I'm not sad," he said.

"You only work on your car when you're sad. You completely rebuilt the engine when Mom and Dad died. I remember, but I wrote it down, too. I could show you. You only work on your car when you're sad."

"Fine. I'm sad. I don't want to talk about it, okay?"

Morgan's expression remained impassive. "When I'm sad, you tell me it helps to talk. You make me tell you about it even when I don't want to. You should talk if you're sad. It will make you feel better. You make me talk when I'm sad."

"That's because when you get sad, you lose control of your powers, and you could hurt somebody."

Her head tilted to the side, reminding him of a dog upon hearing a strange noise. "Are you sad because you're stuck taking care of me?"

"No." Setting the wrench in the open toolbox, he went to his sister. His first response hadn't sounded a hundred percent positive, so he tried again. It was partly to convince her and partly to convince himself. Sometimes dealing with her was like pushing a giant boulder up a steep incline. Sometimes he resented her, but in the end it came down to one thing—she was his sister, and he loved her.

"Of course I'm not sad because of you." Hands on hips, he stood directly in front of her. "Why would you ask me something like that?"

"You get sad sometimes because you can't be normal. You want to do normal things with other kids. You can't do what they're doing. It's because of me. I can't control my powers. You have to take care of me. I'm sorry I make you sad."

Guilt and remorse piled on top of the grief at losing Kristen. What was he thinking choosing a girl he'd known only a short time over his sister? First love hurt like hell, but it always ended. If he hadn't lost her this week, it would have happened at some point down the road. It was probably better to let her go now.

"Don't worry about me. I couldn't be normal if I tried. Believe me, me being sad has nothing to do with you."

Morgan stiffened, and her eyes darkened. "Are you sad because of her? Are you sad because of that girl?"

"Drop it." He walked back to the car, picked up his wrench, and returned to the engine. Determined to forget Kristen Noah existed, he concentrated every brain cell he had on fixing the car. After he finished this project, he'd find another. Maybe he would take up with a girl at school, someone hot. A few kisses with a pretty girl would help him forget all about Kristen.

Was he sad over her?

Kristen tried to memorize everything about him from the way he looked in faded blue jeans to the way he moved his hips while turning the wrench. Her tongue darted out and licked her dry lips. There was no way he could be evil. She didn't believe it, not for a second. There had to be a reasonable explanation for his dark powers.

Morgan turned cold eyes in their direction as if she'd heard Kristen's thoughts. She looked straight at Kristen. Those dark eyes, almost black now, pinned her in place. Kristen gasped and stepped backwards. Morgan lifted her hands and flung them in Kristen's direction. Two things happened simultaneously—the picture died, and the lights went out.

Cyndi shrieked.

It was a good thing it was still light outside or they would have been plunged into darkness.

Kristen put the chain back around her neck and returned to her books, more determined than ever. She had to find a way to prove Zach innocent. But how? There didn't seem to be anything in the books other than what her grandmother had told her.

"Wow," Cyndi said. "That was intense. That girl is seriously damaged. If I were you, I'd stay away from her."

"Morgan has power, too, so it has to be a family thing, right? Even though Grandma Noah said dark powers aren't inherited, that has to be it. How else would Morgan have them?"

Cyndi shook her head in wonder. "You are completely gaga over this guy. Never thought I'd see the day when Kristen Noah couldn't think straight over some boy."

Kristen took a deep breath and admitted it aloud. She needed to tell somebody, and Cyndi was the only one who *might* understand. "I love him."

"What? Are you crazy? The guy turns into a wolf. I mean, that is kind of cool, and it was ultra-romantic the way he saved you from the owl, but you need to listen to Grandma Noah. He has bad powers for a reason."

"I can't help it." She hugged the book she'd been reading to her chest and stared off into space, daydreaming about a possible future with Zach. "I really, really love him, and I can't imagine living life without him."

"Why aren't you with him, then?" Cyndi asked.

She wanted to call him, ask him to swing by and take her somewhere far, far away where they could be alone without sisters or school or anything else getting in the way. However, there was another problem to consider. She'd seen him accuse her in several dreams. It was bound to happen sooner or later.

Maybe if she stayed away from him she'd be safe.

On the other hand, maybe he was going to 'out' her because she'd dumped him. What was she supposed to do when she didn't know what would lead up to the accusation? No matter what path she chose, it could be the wrong one.

"Did you hear me?" Cyndi asked. "If you love him, why don't you go get him?"

"It's not that simple," she said with a heavy sigh. She returned to her book, saying, "First, I need to find out why he has these powers. Then I'll work on the other problem."

With a shrug, Cyndi left, closing the door quietly.

Kristen's eyes drifted to the phone, and her fingers itched to pick it up. It would be so nice to hear Zach's voice. How could it possibly hurt just to call him long enough to tell him she wasn't afraid of him?

The only thing that stopped her from calling was that he might tell her he loved her again. Then what? She couldn't say it back, not now. Her grandmother insisted Zach was dangerous. She had to stay away from him. A phone call would just invite trouble.

Kristen went to her desk and opened the notebook with her homework inside. She'd finished another essay, three pages of math, and a ten-page research paper at her grandmother's house. She stared at the blank paper on top and frowned. Hadn't she set her essay on top? She lifted the first page, the second page, and the third. They were all blank.

Panicking, she tore through the stack. Every single page was blank. Grabbing her workbook, she opened it to the pages she'd completed. They were clean, no flowing cursive in pencil. There was only one explanation.

Someone had used magic to erase her work. *Brittany*? Who else could it be? Kristen had hoped they'd reached a truce, but Brittany was on the war path again. True to form, the girl had lost her mind.

Clutching blank papers in her hands, she screamed.

15

Twisted

Monday morning, Kristen decided to take the bus so she wouldn't have to be in the same car as Brittany. They hadn't spoken about the homework incident yet. Kristen had fought the urge to confront her sister at home, not wanting to risk their dad overhearing. No doubt, it was going to be a loud conversation. Once the twins had left the house, she hurried down the sidewalk, heading for the bus stop.

Public transportation got a bad rap sometimes, but it sure came in handy when you lost the use of your car. Unfortunately, she'd picked a bad day to walk to the bus stop. When she'd told Cyndi that she and Britt could take the car, she hadn't considered how much she was going to have to carry. There were two textbooks, three notebooks, and a couple of library books, not to mention her large purse.

If she didn't move fast, she was going to miss the bus. She stumbled down the sidewalk while trying to juggle everything. The bus was going to show any minute, and she wasn't even halfway there yet. Then she'd have to wait several minutes for the next one. She'd be late to class.

While groaning over her current plight, she lost her grip on a couple of items. When one thing fell, everything began to fall. She gave up and let them go. The stuff landed on the sidewalk in a messy heap. At least she hadn't been carrying anything breakable—she was grateful for that small concession. She hunched down to retrieve her belongings. Focused on her task, she didn't hear the soft footsteps approaching.

She recognized the boots on sight. Keeping her eyes lowered, she continued to retrieve her things as she wondered what in the world she was going to say to him.

Zach spoke first. "Cyndi told me you were taking the bus."

Good old Cyndi. Kristen silently fumed. Her sister was trying to play matchmaker even though she knew how badly Kristen wanted to avoid Zach. Now he was hovering over her on a near-empty street. Before she could stop him, he hunched down and started picking her books up for her.

"I've got it," she said, but he continued to grab stuff. With a louder voice and more force, she repeated, "I've got it!"

"I need to talk to you."

The sound of his voice brought her gaze up to meet his. His blue eyes locked on hers. They pleaded for her to listen and understand even before he verbalized the desire. The actual words were lost on her because she was busy trying to think of a clever way to avoid the conversation.

"I'm going to miss the bus," she said.

"I'm driving you to school today."

It was a statement, not a question. He gestured to the car she hadn't seen pull up to the curb. The black sports car brought back a bad memory, the last time she'd talked to him, the day she'd discovered he wasn't an innocent boy under her spell.

"No, thank you," she mumbled.

"I know you don't want to be late for class. Stop being so stubborn, and let me give you a ride."

Giving in was easier than she'd imagined. In truth, she wanted to be with him for as long as possible before the inevitable separation.

She allowed him to carry her books to the car and open the door for her so she could slide into the warm interior. He handed her stuff to her before shutting the door and running around the front to get in beside her. He moved fast, as if afraid she might bolt the second he turned his back.

Without saying another word to her, he whipped out onto the road. She twisted her fingers while searching for something to say. Her brain refused to cooperate. How could she talk when she could barely breathe?

Zach spoke first. "You do know that I wouldn't hurt you, right? Tell me you've learned that much about me?"

"Yes."

"Good. At least that's something."

They pulled into the parking lot, and Zach picked the furthest spot from the school. He did it on purpose, and they both knew it. He was trying to fix it so she would have to talk to him. She reached for the door handle, but he intercepted her hand. His skin was hot, slightly rough.

She forgot to breathe again.

One word from him, the right word, and she would be in his arms in a flash. She wasn't sure what that word was, but she had a bad feeling it existed. Imagining her insides were made of steel, she sat quietly and listened to him. Her hands clutched the books until her fingers were sore. In her head, she repeated two phrases—*I am strong. I will not give into him. I am strong. I will not give into him.*

"Sorry," he said, moving his hand as if the contact had burned him as well. "Even though you may not care anymore, and it might not make a difference to you now, I want to tell you the truth about Morgan."

"You don't have to do that."

"I know. I want to, but not here. There's not enough time. It's kind of complicated—my life story, I mean. Meet me out here at lunch."

"Can't we talk in the cafeteria?"

"Sure, and have everyone hear the details of my life as a witch? I don't think that would be a very good idea."

She gave in because she just wanted to put some distance between them before she jumped into his arms and kissed him like there wasn't going to be a tomorrow. She blurted out, "Okay. I'll see you later."

He let her get out of the car, but his eyes remained glued to her backside. She felt his gaze burning holes through her thin cotton blouse. Apparently, he wasn't going to attend classes today. Either that or he wanted to be late. He could probably smile and charm the teacher, whoever it was, into letting him slide.

Zach Bevian could talk anyone into anything.

That's why she needed to be careful.

Since they made it to school a few minutes before classes were scheduled to start, Kristen went to the gymnasium. She had a hunch about whom she would find there.

Sure enough, Brittany was throwing basketballs into the hoop while twelve boys pretended they were trying to block her. She laughed as she darted around two of them and tried to make a basket. The ball hit the rim and bounced off. One of the boys leaped up and hit it into the basket for her.

Kristen went straight up to Brittany and pushed her with two flat hands against her chest. Brittany tossed the ball to the side. She pushed back.

The boys surrounded them in a large circle, watching in silence. Not one of them attempted to intervene. Barely paying attention to them, Kristen didn't notice they were acting strange.

"What is your trauma now?" Brittany shouted.

"Did you do it?"

"OMG! You need a shrink." Brittany lifted her hands up in mock surrender. "What is it you think I did this time?"

Hands on hips, Kristen fought the headache that was threatening to override her other senses. "My homework disappeared."

"Your homework is gone?" Brittany laughed as if she'd heard the funniest joke of her life. "Wish I'd thought of it."

"So it's just a coincidence that you keep threatening me and now my homework is blank?"

Brittany shrugged. One of the boys handed her the discarded basketball, and she took it. Passing it back and forth between her hands, she said, "I guess Grandma Noah was right. There's a new witch in town. Leave it to you to piss the girl off before we're even introduced."

"I don't believe you." Kristen shook her head slowly and took a step in her sister's direction. "You're lying."

"I always take credit for my work. Anyway, maybe it was your idiot boyfriend. If he can change into a wolf, he can certainly make homework go bye-bye."

Kristen gasped, taken by surprise at Brittany's blatantly open comment in front of the twelve boys. Was the girl trying to get them accused of being witches?

"Boys," Brittany said to the guys around her, "show my sister how to play dodgeball."

Kristen frowned. "What?"

Basketballs flew at her from every direction. One struck her in the knee and another caught her on the shoulder. Fierce scowls focused on her. Without an ounce of compassion or a strand of hesitation, the boys continued to fire balls at her. They threw them hard, using all of their strength and determination to hurt her while Brittany watched with a satisfied smirk.

"Enough!" Kristen roared.

The twelve boys flew backwards along with Brittany. They landed hard several feet from where they'd been standing. A few of them slid on the slippery gymnasium floor. The balls shot in the other direction, too, as if fired from a cannon.

Stunned, Kristen swallowed while staring at the prone bodies.

She hadn't meant to launch an attack.

The boys jumped to their feet, and a few of them helped Brittany up. Every single boy asked her if she was okay. No longer smirking, she stared at Kristen with wide eyes and a slack mouth.

Before her sister could start asking questions, Kristen ran out. She hurried to her locker, her entire body shaking in the aftermath of what could have been a disaster. Two truths hit her at the same time—those boys had been crushed, and the medallion had to go.

It was far too powerful. Someone could have been seriously hurt. Protecting herself wasn't worth the risk to the people around her. She hadn't even been thinking of a spell when she'd knocked everyone down. Imagine what could have happened if she'd actually mumbled something.

She opened her locker and threw the medallion inside. As soon as she could, she'd return it to her grandmother. Until then, it would be safe in her locker. The last thing the world needed was for Brittany to get her hands on it. That girl was already totally out of control.

Kristen and Zach were in the parking lot at lunchtime when the car windows exploded around them. It had started out like any other normal afternoon, kids going to their cars, leaving school grounds in favor of local fast food places. No one had any idea what was about to happen.

Against her better judgment, Kristen had gone outside to meet with him. His car was gone. She didn't have to ask him what he'd been doing while she was in her classes. He'd driven home and exchanged the car for the bike. Possible reasons sprang to mind. The one that worried her the most was that he knew how irresistible he looked on the bike—the rebellious boy mothers always warned their daughters about, the untamed heart of a wild boy with a good streak deep down.

He was sitting sideways on his motorcycle, legs crossed at the ankles. If the bike tipped in the other direction, he would fall, but he didn't seem worried. An easy grin appeared on his gorgeous face when he saw her. She had to work hard not to return it.

"Okay," she said, "I'm here. What did you want to say to me?"

His smile faltered, and his eyes darted around the parking lot. "Maybe we should take this conversation somewhere more private."

"I am not going anywhere with you. Say what you have to say, or I'm going back inside."

"You aren't going to make this easy on me, are you?" His shoulders slumped. Standing, he leaned close and whispered, "My sister and I come from Maine. We were born with powers, just like you, but unlike you, my sister was ill and couldn't control them. She was easy prey for a strong hand and a flattering voice.

"There was this guy who used to work for my parents, a gardener. We didn't know he was actually a warlock. He'd heard about my sister and figured he could talk her into anything. He gave her a book with powerful dark magic inside, a book that had been hidden from generations of witches."

With a heavy sigh, Zach turned and took a few steps away from her.

Kristen walked up behind him, wanting to hear the rest. "What did she do?"

"She killed our parents."

The words were softly spoken, and Kristen wondered if she'd heard him right. Before she could ask him to repeat it, all hell broke loose.

Several car windows exploded simultaneously. Kristen screamed. Glass flew in all directions like sharp rain in a violent thunderstorm. It happened so fast that neither Kristen nor Zach knew what was going on. She tried to duck, but Zach spun around and grabbed her by the shoulders. Before she could guess what he was up to, they were spinning in dizzy circles again, flying through a black universe.

He had made them disappear again.

Kristen clung to him, scared to death of where they would wind up. Even if there was time for her to ask if he had a plan, if he knew where they were going, she didn't have the breath left in her body to force the words out. She squeezed her eyes shut and prayed they wouldn't land in a worse situation than the one he'd rescued them from.

16

Clueless

Her second trip was only slightly easier than the first. At least she knew what to expect this time. She tensed, prepared for impact. Zach's hands vanished from her arms just seconds before she hit the ground with a resounding thud. A painful grunt burst through her parted lips. The hard landing jarred her down to the marrow in her bones, and the breath left her body. Near panic, she struggled to fill her lungs.

Everything hurt, every single inch of her.

Not totally surprised to find the familiar, leaf-covered soil beneath her, she sat up and glared at Zach. Apparently, he was going to make a habit out of abducting her. She turned her head the other way and saw his house. At least she knew where they were this time.

Zach hurried over to her. "Are you okay?"

"Do I look like I'm okay?" She took the time to brush dirt off her expensive jeans. There was a crunchy leaf hanging from her hair, halfway blocking her peripheral view of Zach. She pulled it loose and let it drift back to the ground. "Why did you do that? Why did you bring me here?"

"Are you kidding me? It was like a war zone. I didn't want you to get hurt."

"I don't need your protection. I would have been fine on my own. If things got too hairy, I could have used a spell."

He grinned. "Oh really? So you could have popped yourself out of there like I did, huh?"

She dropped her eyes, not wanting him to see the shadow of fear and doubt in them. His words reminded her of her grandmother's warning. According to the books she'd read, he had to have done some bad stuff to have such power. "You shouldn't have brought me here."

"I didn't have time to think. You were there. You saw what happened. I had to act fast, so I just picked the first place that came to mind. It wouldn't have been a good idea for us to pop up somewhere public since that would have been kind of hard to explain."

"I should go back to school. Since you can just pop back there, why don't you let me borrow the car again?"

He held his hand out and she took it, allowing him to pull her to her feet. His hand was too warm, and it gave her a tingly feeling in the pit of her stomach. Disturbing didn't come close to how he made her feel. She wanted to put as much distance between them as she possibly could.

He shook his head. "Not yet. First, I need to tell you everything. Then you'll understand. You still might not want to be with me, but at least you'll have the facts."

She wasn't sure she wanted them.

He led her into the house via the front door. They went to the study and closed themselves inside. He twisted the lock into place.

"We need to be quiet," he said. "I don't want Morgan to know we're here. She freaks out when plans change. She should be in the kitchen having lunch right now. If you just give me a few minutes, I can explain everything."

Part of her desperately wanted the information. She sat in a wingback chair near the desk while he took a seat in the big, rotating chair behind the sturdy piece of office furniture. He looked unsure of where to begin. Lacing his fingers together on the wood surface, he took a deep breath before launching into his life story.

"Like I said before, I was born with powers. When I was five, I got mad, and before I knew it, my toys were flying around the room. One of them broke the window. My mother had to grab me to calm me down. I'm sure you have similar stories."

She nodded but didn't say a word.

He continued. "Morgan did stuff like that, too, only she was more powerful than most and more dangerous because she didn't understand she was doing it. The autism or whatever it is kept her from developing empathy or compassion. When she killed our parents, she actually expected them to show up at some point. Sometimes she still asks me when they're coming home. She doesn't understand death."

He hesitated.

Kristen leaned forward in her seat.

"I was out that night," he said. "I was having fun with my buddies when my house blew up with my parents and sister inside. They were all killed."

Kristen blinked at him. "You had another sister?"

"No. I'm saying Morgan died in the explosion with our parents."

Okay. He was either lying or crazy or both. "Morgan is in the kitchen eating lunch."

"Before Morgan caused the explosion, she used a spell long forgotten by the elders. She sacrificed herself and our mom and dad because the gardener convinced her to do it. Too bad for him, she didn't stick to the plan, and he died in the blast, too. She was supposed to put a lock of his hair inside her locket so she'd be connected with him. He would be like a sponge, taking on her powers, but he wouldn't have to risk or sacrifice to do it. Only, she used my hair instead. She was used to me taking care of her and wanted that to continue."

Was he saying Morgan was a zombie?

Kristen jumped to her feet. "I really need to get back to school."

Zach stood, too.

She headed for the door, but he got there first. Her hand enclosed the doorknob. His hand covered hers as he stopped her from turning the knob. His touch was tender, nothing scary about it, but his words terrified the life out of her.

"Morgan is a familiar," Zach said. "She isn't human anymore."

"How is that even possible? I've never heard of anything like that happening before."

"It's black magic—the worst kind." He let her hand go and turned away. While pacing the room, he finished explaining. "The gardener gave her the book and told her what to do. It's got quite a few dangerous spells in it, including the spell to become a familiar.

"Familiars have amazing powers. You've only seen a couple of the things we can do. When the council figures out she's still with me, that she's a familiar, her life will end. They'll kill her after they torture her. That's why I have to protect her. She's still my sister."

"How did you find out she was still alive after the explosion?"

"I buried my family—all of them—and about a week later, Morgan showed up in my bedroom like a ghost, only she wasn't a ghost. She was a familiar. She had attached herself to me before dying, so I became her master in a way."

The truth dawned in Kristen's mind with the brilliance of the rising sun. "That's why you have dark powers. It's because of her."

He hadn't sacrificed innocent blood, but Morgan had.

"Yeah. Lucky me."

"I don't know that much about familiars. Grandma Noah mentioned them once, but she told me they were a thing of the past."

"Exactly. Black magic. No one has used it for decades." He shoved his hands deep into the pockets of his jeans. "Anyway, Morgan hasn't changed much. She still thinks and behaves like a child."

"A dangerous child."

"I can handle her." Zach walked over to Kristen. He brushed hair away from her face. He seemed to have a difficult time not touching her when they were standing this close, not that she minded. "I forbid her to use the simplest of spells. So far, she's obeyed me. Mentally, she's a little girl. She doesn't want me to be mad at her, so she won't use her powers. It's been so long since she's done anything, she probably doesn't even remember how."

Kristen had a feeling sweet little Morgan practiced magic behind her brother's back on a regular basis. An image of Morgan flinging her hands at Kristen while she was spying on them came to mind. Should she tell Zach?

"I'm not sure if I could forgive Brittany or Cyndi for killing my parents."

"It's hard even now if I think about it too much, but she didn't know what she was doing. It wasn't her fault. She's mentally challenged, and a deranged warlock tried to use her to gain power. Really, it was more my fault than hers. I should have watched out for her better. I should have protected her from people like Ethan." He smiled sheepishly and shrugged. "Besides, I love her."

There it was. She couldn't share her doubts about Morgan with him because it would tear his heart out.

"Do you understand now?" Zach asked with a hopeful expression.

"Yes."

"Do you still want to avoid me?"

"No." As he started to smile at her, Kristen added, "But I have to."

"Why?"

She couldn't tell him that she'd dreamed about him pointing an accusing finger at her. She'd had the dream seven times now. It was going to come true if she didn't find a way to stop it. Avoiding him seemed like a good start.

Changing the subject, she asked, "Is there a way to get rid of a familiar? If Morgan gets out of hand someday, tries to hurt someone else, is there something you can do to stop her?"

"If things ever get bad, really bad, I would have to have someone accuse me."

Kristen softly gasped.

"You don't have to worry about Morgan," he said, stroking the length of her arms. "I have her under control."

Kristen prayed he was right.

"Can I trust you to keep my deepest, darkest secret?" he asked. "Like I told you before, I've been keeping her from the witches' council. They have no idea she's alive, no idea she's a familiar. If they ever find out, they'll kill her. So I need you to keep this to yourself. Morgan's life depends on it."

"I won't tell anyone, but someday the council will find out. They have spies everywhere. Grandma used to have a seat on the council, so she would know. Someday they'll find out, and they'll come for Morgan."

They'd come for him, too, but Kristen didn't want to think about that.

He turned his face from her, blinking his eyes, but not before she saw they were damp. "I know. I plan to have someone accuse me of being a witch someday, so I can free her myself. She'll just disappear, no pain, no fear. She'll be dead, quick and simple. It's the best way to save her from them."

"I hope you don't have to do that."

"But I will," he said with certainty. "I know I will. That's why I've been spending as much time with her as I can, building memories and saying goodbye. I didn't get to have closure with my parents. Deep down, I knew from the second I heard her story that I would have to kill her someday."

Kristen placed a hand on his solid chest. "You won't be killing her. She's already dead. Remember that. None of this is your fault, and I don't want you to feel guilty over it."

He put his hand on top of hers and smiled, but it was tinged with sadness. "I'm going to lose my sister. I can't stop that from happening, but I can hold on to you. I won't lose you, Kristen, not you, too."

"I don't want to lose you either, but…"

His hands moved to her face. Holding it gently between his palms, he lifted it for a kiss. His movements were slow and deliberate, giving her a chance to say no. She could evade his mouth if she wanted to. She could tell him to stop. But did she want him to stop?

Decision made, she grabbed a handful of T-shirt and pulled him closer. Their mouths met in a heated rush. For the first time in her life, she didn't worry about the future, didn't try to plan it out. Her nightmares of being accused by him were momentarily forgotten. She was destined to be with this boy. Nothing else mattered.

Taking a step back, she slid fingers beneath the short sleeve of his shirt and pushed it up to reveal the tattoo. "What does it say?" she asked, breathless. "What is the tattoo?"

His gaze refused to meet hers as he replied, "Remember to laugh. Don't forget to love."

"I'm serious."

"So am I. It was one of my mother's favorite sayings." He lifted his gaze to take in her expression. "What?"

"Everyone at school is afraid of you, so I figured it was a quote from *The Godfather* or a bunch of swear words. If they could read it, your reputation would be ruined forever."

He grinned. "Why do you think it's in Italian?"

A few minutes later, they exited the study hand-in-hand. A burst of energy had Zach feeling like he could fly. Instead of walking Kristen out the front door, he pulled her down the darkened hallway to the kitchen. He was hoping Morgan would be around for at least another year, and he wanted Kristen to be in his life forever, so he decided the two of them needed to get to know each other better.

"She's probably finishing lunch now," he said.

"She doesn't like me. This isn't a good idea."

The last time Kristen had voiced her concern that Morgan disliked her, Zach had blown it off, saying she didn't understand his sister. Back then, he'd believed Morgan wasn't capable of those types of feelings. Now he wasn't so sure. A couple times in the past few weeks he'd seen Morgan react in ways he hadn't thought were possible. Maybe becoming a familiar was slowly changing her and making her better.

Maybe he wouldn't have to kill her. If she got better and learned to control her powers, it was possible he could hide her from the council indefinitely.

"She doesn't know you," he said. "She isn't good with change. Once the two of you get better acquainted, she'll love you as much as I do."

The sound of a chair scraping the floor was followed by running feet and the slamming of the back door.

Zach frowned at Kristen before racing down the hall to the kitchen. He dashed inside with Kristen right behind him. "What's going on?" he asked. "Was someone in here with you?"

Morgan glanced up from her half-eaten sandwich, eyes wide. Bear was in the chair next to hers. She had a glass of milk in front of her and a glass of apple juice in front of the stuffed animal. Both glasses were nearly empty. Morgan shook her head. "No one was here."

He stood over her and stared down at the evidence. "Since when does Bear drink apple juice?"

"I give him juice when you aren't here."

"Who ran out the back door, Morgan? I heard it slam shut."

She shrugged, and her eyes dropped to the plate in front of her. She played with her food, picking the corner of the bread apart.

Morgan was lying to him. It made him wonder how many times she'd lied to him in the past. Zach went to the door and opened it. He stuck his head out and looked around, but saw nothing. Something gritty crunched beneath his boot, and he knelt down for a closer look. There was sand on the floor.

Anger building, he asked, "Did you go to the beach again, Morgan, or did your company bring sand in with them?"

Before he could ask her more questions, Kristen pointed at the window and shouted, "Did you see that?"

"What?"

"Long, blonde hair. I'll be right back."

Kristen raced by him and out the door. In a few seconds he saw her sprint by the window, chasing whoever it was who'd been visiting Morgan. He thought about running out the front door and trying to trap the visitor between them, but he decided to stick with Morgan and get the answers straight from her.

He left her alone long enough to get her notebook out of the family room. He returned with it and sat in the vacated chair across from his sister. Opening the notebook, he checked every page. There wasn't anything about visitors or going to the beach or doing anything she shouldn't be doing. She was using her notebook to lie to him.

"Do you write down everything in here?" He shook the notebook at her.

"Are you mad at me?" she asked, lips trembling.

"Just answer the question. Do you write everything down in here? Everything you do? Everyone you see?"

She shook her head. "I don't want you to be mad at me, so I write stuff in my other notebook, too."

He stared at his sister in total disbelief. She was keeping two sets of notebooks, like some bookie laundering money for the mob. Tossing the useless notebook on the table, he said, "Get the other one. I want to see it."

"Don't be mad."

He sighed and rubbed the place between his eyes. "Just get the other notebook. Now."

Morgan leaped out of her chair. It rocked backwards, ready to fall, but he caught it with one hand as she raced from the room.

Kristen entered a few seconds later, looking confused. Walking over to the table, she sat in Morgan's empty chair. "Did you get anything out of Morgan?"

He explained about the dummy notebook before asking, "Did you find the intruder?"

"No, but I'm pretty sure I know who it was."

Brittany. She didn't have to say the name. Burning acid churned in his stomach at the thought of Kristen's deranged sister getting her claws into Morgan. It was like the gardener incident all over again. There was no telling what crazy things Brittany was trying to get Morgan to do.

Morgan returned with the notebook. She handed it to him, eyes on the floor, and mumbled, "I'm sorry. Don't be mad."

He flipped through the notebook as fast as he could, scanning the pages. When he found what he'd been dreading, he read it aloud to Kristen. "Went for a walk on the beach. Met a nice girl named Cyndi. She has power, too. Her sister doesn't want her to use her power. Zach doesn't want me to use mine. We're friends now. Cyndi told me we're going to be best friends."

The entry ended.

"It couldn't be Cyndi," Kristen said, her body numb with shock. "Cyndi wouldn't lie about meeting Morgan. It has to be Brittany using Cyndi's name."

He nodded in agreement as he found another damning entry. "Cyndi and I played games using magic today. She is better than me. She told me I need practice. She says I can be as good as her."

Zach slammed the notebook on the table.

Morgan jumped. "I'm sorry."

He reached out to touch her, remembered it wasn't allowed, and drew back his hand. "You need to stay away from *Cyndi.* Promise me you won't see that girl again. She's dangerous."

Kristen glared at him. "My sister isn't the dangerous one here. You really need to open your eyes before it's too late. Morgan is deceitful and crazy, and if she has autism, then I'm a frog."

17

Breathless

Hand on her arm, Zach led her from his house like a party crasher being ejected. Once her foot touched the sidewalk, she jerked her arm from his grasp. She understood he was protecting his sister, but he needed to see that girl for the dangerous psychopath she was instead of blaming it on Brittany.

"I think you should leave," he said, jaw tight.

"Not before I say something." She confronted him in a head-on collision, an irresistible force meeting an immovable object. "I know you think history is repeating itself and another powerful witch is trying to take advantage of poor, defenseless little Morgan, but that is not what's happening here. Brittany is not an evil warlock bent on ruling the universe."

"No. She's an out-of-control teen without morals, and she wants to use my sister for… what? Revenge? Power? I don't even want to know. You just keep your crazy sister away from mine. Take care of her, or I will."

Her mouth dropped open. "What does *that* mean?"

In a deadly serious voice, he said, "I'll accuse her in public if she doesn't leave Morgan alone."

Kristen shook her head, shocked by his attitude. He wouldn't even listen to her. How was she supposed to get through to him? "Does a familiar have powers over the witch they serve?"

"Not even close. Why?"

"You believe everything that girl says. She lied straight to your face when you asked who was visiting her. Then, once she sees she's been caught and gives up her second notebook, you believe everything that comes out of her mouth. Does she have power to blind you, or is it guilt because you didn't stop her from killing your parents?"

"Morgan has the mental capacity of a child. She doesn't understand things the way we do. Yes, she occasionally tells a lie to save her own butt, just like any kid would, but she doesn't have it in her to be that deceitful."

"She's smart enough to use a fake notebook."

Zach turned away from her. He walked along the concrete path only to return to her side. His hardened expression didn't soften in the slightest. Shaking his head at her, he said, "Morgan is my responsibility, and Brittany is yours. Keep that nutcase away from my sister, or I will."

Kristen's voice rose in frustration. "Morgan has already killed three people! My sister could steal presents from an orphan on Christmas Eve and still not be as bad as yours. Brittany might be a bitch at times, but she's not homicidal."

He pulled a key from his pocket and handed it to her. "Take my car and go. I need to get back to my sister."

"Yeah, good idea. You'd better keep an eye on that crazy witch before she kills someone else."

"Don't worry. I'm going to pack up and leave, and I'll take Morgan with me. The council could figure out where we are any second. Brittany might even tell them. We'll be gone in a day or two. Just keep your sister away from her until then."

The bottom dropped out of her stomach. For a moment, she thought she must have imagined him saying he was leaving. He was going to run away with his sister, no hesitation. Leaving Kristen behind didn't seem to bother him in the slightest. If he didn't care, why should she?

She started to leave, but something stopped her. A solitary thought. This might be the last time she ever saw Zach, and she didn't want to leave things this way. Unshed tears glistened in her eyes. She blinked them away while pushing hard on the metal key's sharp points until her fingers hurt. Turning slowly, she faced him again.

"So I guess this is it."

He rocked back on his heels, hands thrust deep into his pockets. "Looks that way."

"Do you have to leave town? Isn't there something else you can do?"

"If you're suggesting I destroy Morgan now, forget about it. I'm not going to kill my sister just so I can hook up."

"Is that what I am to you? A hookup?"

Zach covered his face with both hands and groaned in frustration. Lowering his hands, he said, "You know I didn't mean it like that. I don't want our last conversation to be a fight."

Last conversation? Kristen could hardly breathe. She was on the verge of losing him forever unless she could convince him to return for her. Forcing a sad little smile, she said, "I'll miss you."

He nodded, lips compressed into a single line.

"Will you come back someday?" she asked. "After you have someone accuse you, will you come back?"

"I don't know."

A thousand things floated through her mind, things she could say to him, but there wasn't any point. Words wouldn't stop him from leaving. She took a step backwards and turned to go.

"Kristen." He spoke in such a low, soft tone she almost missed it.

She faced him again. "Yes?"

He didn't say anything, didn't even look at her. Shoulders slumped, he kicked at an invisible rock with the toe of his boot.

Not one to give up easily, Kristen went to him and stood directly in front of him. She bent her knees a fraction so she could see his downcast eyes. They glistened just like hers. He *did* care. The idea of leaving her was killing him, too.

In a soft voice, she asked, "What is it? What do you want to say?"

He removed his hands from his pockets and slid them around her, pulling her close. Burying his face in her neck, he shuddered. "I love you."

Oh sure. He loved her, just not enough to believe her over his sister.

She shoved at him until he released her. His arms dropped to his sides, and she put distance between them. The plan was to race to the garage, jump into his sports car, and drive away without a single glance back. Her mind told her to be strong and walk away, but her body refused.

Choking on a sob, Kristen dropped the key on the ground and ran back to him. She jumped into his arms, and he caught her without hesitation. Arms wound tightly around his neck, she squeezed her damp eyes shut and tried to burn everything about the moment into her memory. She didn't want to forget a single second.

"I love you," she said. "I want you to know that, even though you're leaving. No matter how many boys come and go, I will never forget you, and I will never stop loving you."

"Gee, that makes me feel better." He set her back down on her feet and looked at her through narrowed eyes. "Boys, huh? Already thinking ahead? You really know how to make a guy feel special."

The sarcasm in his voice made her laugh. Once. Then another wave of sadness overwhelmed her. "I promise to compare every date to the one I had with you."

"And find them lacking," he added in monotone.

"Of course."

She bent over and picked up the key. She started to leave again, but this time he caught her hand with his and gently pulled her back in his direction. Hope blossomed in her heart. Maybe he was going to tell her he'd changed his mind about running away.

"There's one thing I want to know before you go," he said. "You can be totally honest now, since I'm not going to be here for much longer. Tell me why you kept pushing me away. Why did you say you couldn't be with me?"

She couldn't think of a reason not to tell him now, so she did. "My sisters and I all have our specialties. Cyndi fixes things, and Brittany is brilliant with revenge spells. Mine is prophetic dreams. When I have a dream three times, it comes true, and I've been having these horrible nightmares."

"Why do I have the feeling I played a part in them?"

"You were the star." She took a deep breath and blurted out, "You accused me of being a witch and took away my powers."

There. She'd told him. Now he knew why she'd been acting strange around him lately, why she was so dead-set against them reuniting as a couple. Losing her powers was on the top of her 'things that would kill me' list. She couldn't function without them. Not much scared her, but becoming a normal girl and having to learn to live without magic terrified the life out of her.

"I wouldn't do that," he said.

"I know."

"Do you?" He took possession of her chin between his thumb and finger and lifted it high, forcing her wary gaze to lock with his. He repeated, "I would never do that to you, not in a million years. I wouldn't hurt you like that, no matter what."

He was saying all the right things, but there was still a cutting shard of doubt in her heart. "I've had the dream seven times now. It's going to happen. There's nothing either of us can do to stop it. I've tried to keep my dreams from coming true before, but no matter what I do, the dreams become reality."

Zach shook his head emphatically. "This one won't. I don't care how many times you have the dream. I am in control of my mouth, and I won't do that to you."

"I believe you." She lifted a hand and waved as she backed away.

This time his voice stopped her. A quiet desperation drowned each word like brandy poured over ice. "Meet me tonight."

Her heartbeat quickened, and her face flushed. "What?"

"Come back at midnight. Morgan will be in bed. We'll forget everything else, everything keeping us apart. It'll just be you and me, the way it should have been all along."

"Okay."

"And wear a red dress if you have one."

She frowned and laughed at the same time. "Red dress?"

"Yeah." He rubbed the back of his neck and looked away, unable to meet her eyes. "It's kind of a fantasy I have of you."

Lucky for him, she had the perfect dress hanging in her closet. With a spring in her step, she hurried to the garage and left in his car, promising herself she was going to knock his socks off tonight. It was her last chance to make him love her enough to change his mind and stay.

When she arrived at his house later that night, she stood at the end of the sidewalk, unable to move, unable to breathe. Zach had outlined the walk with candles. They burned bright, amazing. She smoothed sweaty palms on the red silk material that covered her upper thighs. Shockingly short, the dress ended just below her fingertips.

She'd spent the entire afternoon getting ready. Her feet were scrubbed clean, encased in her red stilettos with toenails painted to match. For an extra-special touch, she'd put on a shiny, gold anklet. It gleamed against her tanned skin. She couldn't wait to see the look on Zach's face.

The dress had a modest front but dropped low in back. Her mom had bought it for her over the summer, telling her it was an original and some famous actress had wanted to wear it to an awards show, but the designer was a friend and owed her a favor.

Kristen hadn't worn it before, thinking it too sexy and not at all her style, but now she silently thanked her mom for it. It was perfect. She felt prettier than any movie star on the red carpet. Her hair hung down in loose, golden waves, and she'd had her makeup done at a salon.

Lucky for her, her dad was out of town on business again. Instead of sneaking out of the house or coming up with a convincing lie, she'd gone out the front door while Cyndi gushed about it being the most romantic thing ever—romantic and sad—two star-crossed lovers who were meant to be but just couldn't catch a break.

Music floated around the side of Zach's house to her—"Lady in Red" by Simply Red. The male singer's haunting voice sang about her, about her relationship with Zach. She followed the music, knowing it would lead her to him.

She rounded the corner and gasped. Zach waited for her next to the empty swimming pool. He had turned the patio into a dance floor surrounded by flowers and candlelight. Zach had a dark suit on. It looked good on him, incredible even. He started the song over again and walked to her, carrying a red rose.

His steps were agonizingly slow.

Kristen couldn't catch her breath. She stood statue-still, afraid to move and break the fantasy. Zach circled her once. His eyes didn't miss a thing. When he made it to the front again, he handed her the rose. An arm slid around her waist, and his cheek rested against hers as they began to move to the music. Zach sang part of the song next to her ear.

"…is dancing with me… cheek to cheek…"

"Is this a dream?" she asked, breathless. She was floating on air and praying she wouldn't wake to discover she was in her own bed, alone.

"If it were, I couldn't do this." With quick feet, he slid to the side and dipped her backwards.

She giggled with delight.

He pulled her back up and held her tightly as they continued to dance. The boy had some nice moves. It was hard to believe this was the same guy she'd watched swagger down the hallway at school.

"You're graceful," she said.

He put a finger to his lips. “Shh. Don’t tell anyone.”

“Your secret is safe with me. I wouldn’t want any other girl to expect this kind of treatment from you. Seriously. How did you learn to dance like this?”

“My mom insisted I try everything at least once. Dance, sports, art—you name it, and I at least gave it a chance.”

They danced in silence to the end of the song. He spun her around before drawing her close again. Her arms wrapped around his neck at the elbows. She went down slowly, legs sliding apart until she performed the perfect splits. She almost touched the ground with her inner thighs.

He bent with her, still holding her close. Then, he stood straight again, taking her with him in slow inches.

She didn’t want this night to end.

He stopped dancing and stared into her eyes for what seemed to be an eternity.

She found herself lost in those incredible eyes, on the verge of drowning in them. No matter how long she lived, how many men she knew, she was certain Zach was it for her. She wouldn’t love anyone else. Funny thought coming from a girl who hadn’t believed in love just a couple of months ago.

His head lowered, and he kissed the tip of her nose. “I made a late-night snack for us.”

Her stomach revolted at the idea. It was on high alert, nervous and twisted into so many knots it wouldn’t have a place for food. She smiled up at Zach, not wanting to spoil a single moment of their last time together. “Sounds good.”

They walked to the round table in the corner. He pulled a chair out for her. His hand stroked her bare arm before he moved to the other side and sat down. There were three platters of cheese, crackers, and strawberries. A small bowl in the center held melted chocolate.

“I should have brought you here on our first date,” he said.

But at the time, he hadn’t wanted her to know about Morgan. Kristen understood the implications of what he was saying. If it weren't for his sister, they could have a happy life together.

Zach scooted his chair closer to hers and said, "I hate being that far away from you."

It was an ironic statement considering he was ditching town. "Where will you go when you leave?"

He rested his arm along the back of her chair. Instead of answering the question, he picked a strawberry, dipped it in the melted chocolate, and held it up to her mouth. She took a bite, crushing the sweet fruit against her tongue. He popped the rest of it into his own mouth.

He asked her, "Are you going ahead with your plans? College? Job in Hong Kong?"

"I honestly don't know. I feel like I've changed so much since school started." She gazed into his eyes, wanting him to feel the sincerity in her words. "I changed because of you. You've taught me what love is… real, that I don't have to be perfect to be happy, and that I have a lot to learn about life. I want to explore everything, try everything. Your mom was a smart woman."

"Thank you. I think so, too."

"I just wish we could explore new things together."

A loaded silence closed in around them. She wanted to ask him to stay, but the words got stuck in her throat. She leaned closer to him and rested her head on his shoulder. Neither of them ate anything else after that. They let the food go to waste, content to enjoy each other's company. Tears dampened her eyes again. She wanted to shake him and scream and beg him not to leave her; she wanted to wrap her arms around him and refuse to let go.

Zach picked up the two champagne flutes, handed one to her, and lifted the other to make a toast. "To us."

She sniffed the golden, bubbly contents.

"It's non-alcoholic champagne," he said with a wry smile. "What can I say? I'm a wild man."

She giggled.

They each took a sip while staring into each other's eyes. Possible arguments for him to stay entered her mind, but she kept her mouth shut. Nothing was going to sway him. If he would just promise to return, she could handle his departure better.

She mentioned it to him again, the possibility of him coming back.

"I don't want to make any promises," he said.

"Tell me you *want* to come back, at least, and I'll be satisfied."

"You know I want to." He sighed. "And someday I probably will, but you might not want to be with me by then."

She frowned.

He added, "You could be married."

"I won't get married. You don't have to worry about that. My mother would kidnap me 'cause she thinks a girl should play the field, not tie herself down to one guy, and my father would ship me to a non-English-speaking country if I even thought about getting married before I'm thirty. They've been crystal clear on their feelings on that subject."

"Don't put your life on hold because of me."

"Too late. You can't change my mind. I'll wait forever if I have to."

He cleared his throat and got up. In seconds, he returned with a small box. It was gold with a red ribbon expertly tied around it. He handed it to her with a soft smile in place. As if embarrassed, he sat next to her and took another drink instead of watching her open it. She tore the wrapping with shaking fingers. What could it possibly be?

Kristen reached inside and pulled out a small, wooden angel. "It's like the ones on your mantel."

"My mom collected angels. Some were made out of glass, and some were crafted from metal. Her favorites were made of wood like this one." He paused for a second before admitting, "My father made them for her."

"Your father made this?" Kristen lifted her gift to eye-level.

Zach slowly shook his head, refusing to meet her gaze. "I made this one."

The confession blew her mind. She brought the tiny angel closer to her face and took in the detail. It was the most amazing thing she'd ever seen. Winking, the angel held a hand to his mouth as he blew a kiss. “How? How did you learn to do something so incredible? Did your father teach you?”

He nodded. Obviously pleased at her response, he sat up straighter. “You really like it?”

“I love it.” She held it gently between both hands. “I will always treasure it. Thank you.”

She placed cool lips on his warm cheek.

As Zach leaned over and set his glass down, her peripheral vision picked up movement. She turned her head to the right and looked to see what it could be. Upstairs, standing at a window, his psycho sister watched them. Kristen lifted her champagne glass in mock salute, hoping to piss the girl off. Maybe his familiar would race down the stairs and let them have it, dropping the charade. Then Zach wouldn’t have to leave.

18

Missing

Following her late-night date—she'd crawled into bed at five that morning—Kristen slept in. Lucky for her, it was Saturday. In her dreams, she'd been back in Zach's arms. It was so incredibly real she'd been able to smell his cologne and feel his cheek next to hers. She had woken with tears streaming down her face, her pillow wet. A blanket of grief covered her, suffocating her. How was she supposed to go on without Zach?

She stayed in bed for over an hour after waking up. Eyes on the ceiling, she drowned in the sorrow that permeated every pore. Zach was leaving town, and she'd never see him again. Her mind went in circles, trying to find a convincing argument to get him to stay, but she couldn't come up with a single one. Zach had made up his mind to go. There wasn't anything she could do about it.

Later in the day, her bedroom door opened and Cyndi stuck her head in. Kristen was sitting on the bed, still in her pajamas, looking at the precious mementoes from her time with Zach. They included the angel and rose from last night, a movie ticket, pictures of them taken by her friend on the yearbook committee, and a couple of notes he'd left sticking out of her locker.

There was half a box of tissues beside her and several used, discarded ones scattered around the floor. Hair pulled back in a tight ponytail, her face had tearstains, her nose was red, and her eyes were swollen. Across the room, the stereo played Simply Red, the song about the woman wearing a dress similar to hers. Zach had given her the CD at the end of their date. Every time the song ended, she started it again.

It was their song.

Cyndi gasped at the sight of her. "What happened to you?"

"H-he's l-l-leaving," she sobbed, sprouting fresh tears.

"I'm sorry." Cyndi hurried over to her and sat beside her, arms wrapping around her in a big hug. "Do you want to talk about it?"

"No." Kristen grabbed a fresh tissue and wiped her face. She took a deep breath and forced the tears to stop flowing. "I'm g-going to be f-fine."

"Of course you are."

Kristen almost started crying again as she pictured the grief in Zach's eyes when she'd left him standing on the sidewalk in front of his house. Shaking off the memory, she quickly changed the subject to something that didn't make her feel like she was dying inside. Taking another deep breath to steady her voice, she asked, "Do you know why the car windows exploded at school yesterday?"

"Brittany."

"Big surprise. Why did she lose her temper this time?"

"Well, I didn't want to tell you last night and ruin your big date, so I kept my mouth shut, but Brittany has been suspended from school for two whole weeks."

Kristen squinted at her sister. She must have heard wrong. As bad as Brittany could sometimes be, she wouldn't get herself suspended. She wasn't that stupid. "What?"

While twisting her fingers, Cyndi explained the whole thing in an overly-excited voice. She hardly took a breath between sentences. "A girl went to the principal and told him Brittany had beaten her up.

Her face was a bloody mess. I saw it. Brittany totally denied it, of course, but there were witnesses. They all said the same exact thing. So, Brittany went nuts and the windshields blew up. Funny thing is, I believe her, and it's not because she's my twin and I'm sticking up for her, either. I can tell when she's lying. She didn't beat that girl up."

"Then why would the girl say she did?"

Cyndi hesitated. "Well, Brittany thinks the girl lied because you crushed her and made her say those things."

"*What?*" Forgetting about her problems with Zach and her broken heart, Kristen stood on the mattress. With Cyndi in her way, she had to walk a few steps before she could jump off the side of the bed. She began to pace as soon as her feet hit the floor. "I don't crush girls. I don't think it's even possible for one girl to crush another."

"Well, someone used magic to make all those people lie, because Brittany was telling the truth. I know she was."

Kristen decided she needed to ask Brittany about it herself. She'd be able to tell if the girl were lying or not. Unlike Cyndi, she wasn't easily fooled. Kristen asked, "Where is she?"

"I don't know. That's what scares me. She didn't come home last night, and she hasn't called or anything. It's a good thing for her that Dad is gone for the week or she'd be toast. Of course, she'll still be suspended when he gets back, so I guess she's going to get into trouble no matter what. But I swear she didn't do this. I just wish I could prove it."

Hopefully Brittany wasn't with Morgan Bevian again. Zach hadn't been playing around when he'd threatened to accuse her. He would do it without a single regret if he thought his nutty sister was in jeopardy. Kristen's gaze swung to her landline phone in the shape of red lips. Should she call him and ask him if he had Morgan in his sight?

Kristen's imagination ran wild. She stared at Cyndi for a moment and thought about all the times the girl had done her Brittany impression. Morgan's notebook had clearly named Cyndi as her new friend. Was it possible? Could Cyndi be the crazy one and not Brittany?

"Have you met Morgan?" she asked Cyndi in a casual tone.

"Zach's sister? No."

"Are you sure? She might have given you a different name."

Cyndi shook her head emphatically. "I know what she looks like, remember? She made the lights go out with a freaky wave of her hands when we spied on Zach. If I'd met her, I would know it. Why?"

A wave of relief rolled over Kristen. Inwardly, she laughed at herself for being such an idiot. Of course it wasn't Cyndi sneaking around with Morgan. No one could possibly keep up a sweet act like that for years on end. Eventually, they would slip up and unknowingly reveal their black heart.

Kristen sighed. "I think Brittany is using your identity again."

"Great. Is she going to get me thrown into jail, suspended, or killed?"

It was a reasonable question. Kristen paced faster and contemplated the situation. What should she do? She couldn't call Zach. He would go hunting for Brittany, ready to accuse her on the spot. Brittany most certainly couldn't live without her powers. The girl used at least five spells a day on average. She couldn't boil water without using powers. She would be even more lost than Kristen would be if it happened to her.

Cyndi frowned. "Have you noticed anything weird about her lately?"

"You'll have to be more specific. This is Britt we're talking about, and you know that doing weird stuff is kind of her hobby."

"Well, one second she hates you and wants to kill you. The next second, she's talking about you as if the two of you haven't been fighting at all. Britt and I used to be chained at the hip, remember? She wanted me with her everywhere she went, but now I hardly see her. She says she has other friends and she's doing things I wouldn't enjoy, but since when does she care about what I want or what I would enjoy?"

That did sound weird.

"She hasn't been acting like herself for a long time," Kristen said. "I guess she was hung up on Zach more than we realized."

Cyndi frowned. "I don't think that's it. I mean, she always thought he was hot, but she was just playing with the idea of hooking up with him. It wasn't serious."

"But she told me she wanted him. You were there. She's pissed off at me because she wanted him and I crushed him."

"She wasn't serious about that."

"Then why is she mad? Why is she out to get me?"

Cyndi shrugged. "I don't know. I used to be so close to Britt that I knew what she was thinking before she did, but I don't have a clue what's going on in her head anymore."

Now it was Kristen's turn to frown. She went to her bed, sank down on the edge, and tried to recall Brittany's exact words. Kristen was sure her sister had told her again and again that she'd wanted Zach for herself. If she wasn't head over heels for him, then why was she so adamant about taking Kristen down?

They spent the day searching for Brittany, calling her friends and going to all the places Brittany enjoyed. When darkness fell, Brittany was still missing. Kristen's concern multiplied with each passing hour. She and Cyndi decided to check the basketball game at school. Since Brittany had been kicked out, it was possible she'd be there. Suspending Brittany from school was like daring her to show up.

Cyndi checked the gymnasium while Kristen stayed outside. She didn't want to see her old cheerleading squad doing their thing without her. It would be a painful reminder of everything she'd lost, thanks to that nasty Gina girl. Although she was almost certain she'd outgrown her former hobbies, she was afraid the sight of her ex-squad would bring up some bad memories.

Rain poured from a black sky. Beneath the hood of her yellow slicker, Kristen crossed the parking lot. Every time another person came into view, she looked at them expectantly and asked if they'd seen her sister. No one had. A couple of people suggested Brittany might have left town, run away. Deep down, Kristen hoped that was the case. Running away would be preferable to making trouble with Morgan Bevian.

When Zach appeared in front of her, she thought she was imagining him. He wasn't wearing a coat, and his white T-shirt was plastered to his strong chest, molding to the muscles like a second skin. He looked incredible, breathing deeply as if he'd been running, and her eyes devoured him. For a second she forgot about Brittany, forgot everything except for the fact that she was in Zach's presence again.

With a desperate look in his eyes, he shouted, "Where is your sister?"

She didn't have to ask which sister he meant. "That's why we're here. Cyndi and I are looking for her."

"Morgan is gone, too."

Great. That was all they needed—Brittany and Morgan teaming up against them. Kristen closed the distance between them. "I assume you searched your house?"

He nodded. "I checked the garage and the beach, too, but I own too many acres to search the property from one end to the other. I've been going crazy. Where could they have gone? Do you have any idea where Brittany would have taken my sister?"

She bristled. "Brittany didn't *take* your sister anywhere. It was probably the other way around."

"Don't start defending that witch to me again! Brittany is vicious and manipulative, and Morgan is a child who goes along with other people because she doesn't know any better."

"Morgan is not the sweet, defenseless little girl you think she is!"

He threw up his hands. "I don't have time to argue with you about this right now. I have to find my sister before your sister hurts her."

Kristen breathed through her open mouth as rain hit her in the face. She was too cold and tired to argue with him. It was no use. He wasn't going to listen to her, especially not when he was freaking out over his missing sibling. "It doesn't matter which one is doing what right now.

We need to find them both. Agreed?"

"*Yes*," he hissed.

"The three of us should work together until we find them. Agreed?"

He nodded.

"I think we need to start at your house," Kristen said. "We can split up and look in the woods. That's probably where they are. Did you check your sister's notebook for a clue?"

Sighing, he tilted his head back for a moment and allowed the rain to beat down on his face. "She didn't write anything in it today. Nothing. Which doesn't make sense because I told her we were moving. There should have been an entry about it, but there wasn't a single word."

Simple explanation for that. Morgan had been playing games with her brother, pretending to be handicapped. Of course the girl didn't write in her notebook today—the notebook wasn't an essential part of her cover anymore. "Did you check her back-up notebook?"

"Yes."

Kristen pulled out her cell and called Cyndi. She filled the girl in as quickly as she could. By the time she finished the story, Cyndi had exited the gymnasium and was walking toward them. She nodded at Zach. Then the three of them started across the parking lot. They were going to take Kristen's car because Zach's didn't have a backseat for Cyndi.

Kristen removed her hood when the hard rain turned into a light sprinkle.

Zach turned to Cyndi as they were walking and said, "Feels weird that we've never talked. You're Kristen's sister, and I've been dating her, but I haven't even met you."

Cyndi giggled. "I feel like I already know you. Kristen has told me a lot about you. I guess you know stuff about me, too."

Before Zach could respond, the sound of an accelerating car reached their ears. The three of them turned their heads at the same time. The car was coming straight at them. The driver hit the accelerator, and the car zoomed across the parking lot. It was going to hit them head-on. Kristen froze in the headlights.

Zach's strong arms wrapped around her from behind and swung her off her feet. He threw her. With a painful grunt, she landed on the hood of a parked car and rolled across it. Cyndi's frightened shriek filled Kristen's ears. Fear caused Kristen's entire body to go numb as she imagined Cyndi getting hit by the car. What if Zach hadn't had time to save her, too?

Kristen tried to grab onto the car's hood so she wouldn't continue over the side, but it happened too fast. As she tumbled off the edge, the hard tarmac rushed up to meet her. *Bam*! She hit the ground. The impact rattled her bones and her teeth.

Metal crunched against metal. A car alarm went off. Kristen raised her head slowly. The car that had almost killed them had barreled into a parked vehicle in the next row. Groaning, she placed her scraped palms on the asphalt and pushed up. Every inch of her body ached. It was then she glanced under the parked car and saw her sister on the other side.

Eyes closed, head bleeding, Cyndi wasn't moving.

Kristen forced her body to obey the command to move. Standing on shaking legs, her knees threatened to collapse. She wanted to run to her sister, but she had to take it one painful step at a time. Her body refused to cooperate and go faster. Holding onto her thighs with trembling hands, she pushed herself to keep going.

Zach was on the ground a few feet away, trying to sit up. He touched his side and winced as if he had a hurt rib. Kristen wanted to go to him and help him, but first she had to make sure her sister was okay. At least Zach was conscious. She hobbled around the car and knelt next to Cyndi.

There was blood on the side of Cyndi's head. The girl was breathing, but she was out cold. Tears flooded Kristen's gaze as a cold fear filled her heart. What if Cyndi died? She couldn't stand the thought of losing one of her sisters. She gently brushed hair from Cyndi's face and begged her to wake up. Her voice sounded strange to her own ears, raw with emotion and high-pitched with a slight quiver.

Legs moved past them. Kristen glanced up to see Zach heading for the crashed car. He pulled at the car door, struggling with it for several seconds before it popped open. Reaching in, he grabbed the driver by the arm and dragged them out.

Kristen expected to see a stranger… or Morgan. When she saw the driver's face, she lost every ounce of control that she had.

It was Brittany. Her own sister had tried to kill them.

Kristen leaped to her feet, oblivious of the pain, and ran at Brittany with clenched fists. This time her crazy, neurotic sister had gone too far, and she wasn't going to get away with it.

Brittany wobbled. Her dazed eyes looked around as if she had no idea what had just happened. Maybe she was stoned or drunk. Kristen didn't care. She was going to rip the other girl apart with her bare hands.

"You!" Kristen shouted, "You did this? What is *wrong* with you?"

Zach purposely stood between Kristen and Brittany. Hands up, he kept them away from each other. Brittany was screaming back, hysterical, but Kristen couldn't understand a word the girl was saying, not that she cared. There was no excuse for what she'd done.

Kristen screamed, "You killed Cyndi! Are you happy now?"

Loud sobs shook Brittany's entire body. "*No!* I didn't. It wasn't me!"

"You were driving the car."

"No!" Brittany tried to run to her twin.

Kristen shoved Brittany backwards. She hadn't meant to hit Brittany so hard, but the other girl fell back against the car. Kristen struggled to control her temper. She saw herself hit Brittany and heard the horrible things that came out of her mouth, but she couldn't stop it. It was like she was watching the whole ordeal from above.

"Stay away from her! If she dies, I hope you die, too."

Streetlights exploded, sending a shower of sparks down on their heads. Kristen tried hard to control her raging fury, but there wasn't much she could do about it. She wanted to rip Brittany's head off. The stupid, manipulative, insane girl had probably killed their other sister.

She deserved to die.

Kristen reached for the screaming Brittany again, but Zach pushed her back.

"Enough!" he shouted.

Brittany turned away and started beating the top of the car with her fists, sobbing uncontrollably. She yelled unintelligible words.

"You were right," Kristen told Zach, throwing up her arms in surrender. She could barely speak through the tears. "I guess I owe you an apology. My sister is the crazy one."

He sighed wearily. "No. I don't think she is." He took Brittany gently by the shoulders as if he cared about her and turned her in his direction before saying, "Pat yourself on the head and rub your stomach."

With one hand on her stomach and one on the top of her head, Brittany performed the kid game, no questions asked. Her tears stopped instantly. She performed the task in robotic fashion.

Kristen gasped. "She's been crushed? You? Did you crush my sister?"

He shook his head and told Brittany to stop what she was doing. Then he asked her a simple question. "How do you feel about Morgan?"

Brittany's expression immediately changed. A blissful smile stretched her lips, and her eyes took on an excited glow. "Morgan is soooo wonderful. We're going to be sisters as soon as Kristen and Cyndi are out of the way. I love her. She's my angel."

Head down and shoulders slumped, Zach admitted, "I made a vial of love potion last year. Morgan told me she'd dumped it at the beach, and I believed her. I am so stupid."

"You didn't want to lose her. I get it." Kristen's eyes drifted to the unconscious Cyndi, and she sobbed. "We need to get an ambulance. Cyndi won't wake up, and I need her to wake up. I can't lose her."

"I'm not going to let that happen." Zach waved a hand in Cyndi's direction.

She immediately sat up. Her head was healed, and there was a stunned expression on her face. "Hey, what's going on? Why is everyone staring at me? Brittany, where were you? We've been looking everywhere for you."

Zach asked Brittany for her cell phone. She handed it to him before running to her twin. The two girls hugged while Brittany cried, and Cyndi demanded to know what was going on.

"What are you thinking?" Kristen asked Zach.

"Morgan has to call Brittany to give her an order, and now we have the phone. When my sister calls, I'm going to talk to her. Now that I know she understands me, there are a few things I need to say to her. Then, I'm going to do what I should have done a long time ago. I'm going to destroy her."

19

Redeemed

Kristen gazed out the kitchen window as raindrops pelted the glass. It seemed like the storm would never pass. It was dark outside, but she could still see Zach pacing in front of her house. His rigid body passed from the light of one streetlamp to the next and back again. Hands shoved deep into his pockets, head down, and shoulders slumped, he looked defeated. It was all Morgan's fault. Kristen wanted to break the girl's neck for hurting Zach.

He had been outside, alone for over an hour, refusing to come inside. He'd said he was too upset to be decent company. Confusion and anger had him on the brink of murder. It was understandable. Kristen hoped he would focus that anger in the right direction, which was his sister.

With a sigh, she turned away from the window and returned to the living room.

"Here is another pillow for you," Brittany told her twin.

Kristen joined her sisters in the sitting area of the large room. She sat on the sofa and put her feet on the coffee table. It had been a long and terrible night, and she had the feeling it wasn't over yet. She was worried about Zach and her sisters. Morgan had an abundance of dark power, and she was smart enough to have fooled Zach into thinking she was a sweet innocent for years. What would she do next?

Brittany had been waiting on Cyndi like an indentured servant, taking care of her every need since they got home. Every five minutes, she issued another apology. At least she'd stopped crying; although, her eyes were still red-rimmed and puffy. After fluffing the pillow and pushing it behind Cyndi's back in the plush chair, she sat on the ottoman next to her twin's feet.

"I've been wondering about something," Cyndi said. Brittany sat up straighter, eyes wide and attentive. Cyndi asked, "I've always wondered what the boys we crush feel like. So what's it like? What is it like to be crushed?"

Kristen's gaze swung to Brittany. She had wondered the same thing more than once. She removed her feet from the table, set them on the floor, and leaned forward, eager to hear Brittany's response. It was probably something they should have considered years ago—what was going on in the boys' heads—but they had been too young when they'd started the game to even care. As they'd matured, they had been more concerned with winning and claiming their prizes than with the boys.

Brittany's eyes flooded with tears again. She grabbed another tissue and blew her nose before answering. "I don't know how to describe it. Morgan, she told me to do bad things, and I…"

"You didn't want—" Cyndi tried to finish the sentence.

"Wrong. I *did* want to. The way she talked about it, she made it seem logical. She wanted to be my sister, and I wanted that, too, more than anything. I wanted it more than anything I've ever wanted in my entire life."

"It's okay. That was just the spell."

"She told me I had to get rid of you to make room for her. She complained that Zach wouldn't let her be herself, wouldn't let her do magic, so we were going to get rid of him, too. She told me we would be better off without any of you."

Cyndi shivered. "That's awful."

"When I did something bad to Kristen, it felt good. I wanted to do it. I hated her for being with Zach, and I wanted to destroy her, but afterwards I always felt sick to my stomach. I tried to be nice and make up for it. Then that witch would give me another order, and I would follow it without even thinking."

Cyndi said, "Those poor guys we crushed will never know why they followed us around like puppies and carried our books and stuff. I feel so guilty now."

Kristen nodded in agreement. She thought back to the times she'd seen the boys after un-crushing them. One of the boys had given her dirty looks. Another had run in the opposite direction every time he saw her coming, and a third had watched her with longing. Their reactions made perfect sense now. She said, more to herself than to her sisters, "I am not going to crush anyone ever again."

"Me neither," Brittany said, ripping another tissue from the box. "Game over. Nobody wins this year."

Kristen asked, "When did it happen? Exactly when did Morgan get to you?"

"She found me right after I had that kid at school stand up and almost accuse you. I went out that night, walked on the beach, and that's where I met Morgan. She came straight up to me and asked if I was your sister. Before I could even think of a sarcastic comment, she blew dust into my face."

"Makes sense." Kristen nodded. "You were messing with me before then, but after that you started acting nuts. I even thought you sent the owl after me, but the owl was Morgan. Zach changes into a wolf, and she turns into an owl. That's why he was so freaked over the owl having yellow eyes—he suspected it was her."

Cyndi began to giggle, and once she started, she wasn't able to stop. Holding her stomach, she laughed and laughed until tears rolled down her face and she was gasping for breath. Kristen and Brittany exchanged amused, yet puzzled, glances.

"Are you okay over there?" Kristen finally asked.

Cyndi vacated the chair and crossed the room to plop down next to Kristen on the sofa. She hugged one of Kristen's arms and announced with glee, "I just realized something. Brittany was crushed by a girl."

"Shut up," Brittany said, lips twitching.

"Brittany is in love with a girl."

Brittany threw a pillow at Cyndi, but her twin easily smacked it out of the air. It landed near her feet. Brittany mumbled, "Bitch."

"You know I don't play that game." Cyndi tried to look stern but failed miserably. "Say you're sorry."

Kristen groaned. "No, please don't start her with the apologizing again. I'll blow my brains out and save Morgan the trouble."

Soft laughter followed the statement.

The door shut behind them, and instant silence filled the room. Three sets of eyes snapped up to find Zach in the entryway, dripping wet. Grief-stricken, he looked like a man returning from a long war after watching his best friend die. Had he heard Kristen's insensitive comment about his sister?

She jumped off the sofa and hurried to his side, while Brittany rushed upstairs to get some towels. "Are you okay?" Kristen asked.

It was a dumb question, and she regretted it the second it left her mouth. He must have thought it was a dumb question, too, because he didn't bother to reply. She stepped closer, wrapped her arms around him, and held him tight. The side of her face pressed against his soaked shirt. For a second, he didn't return the embrace. His indifference scared her more than a flash of anger would have. She hugged him tighter.

After a short time, his hands came up to rest on her back.

Brittany returned with three towels. She gave the smallest one to Zach and used the other two to mop the floor. She didn't even complain about doing manual labor, leaving Kristen to think the girl was feeling ultra-guilty. Kristen opened her mouth to reassure Brittany, but then she clamped her lips shut. Until Morgan was dead, it would probably be good to have Brittany quietly compliant.

Zach dried himself off with slow movements, sleepwalking

through the task. His eyes were blank and almost as cold as Morgan's. It sent a shiver up Kristen's spine. She hoped he'd never get that angry at her. If looks could kill, Morgan would already be dead.

He shook his head. "I can't figure out how she did it. How did she fool me for so long?"

"You wanted to believe her," Kristen said. "Your parents were gone, and she was all you had left, so naturally you put your faith in her."

"She goofed up once in a while, dropped the act for just a second, but I didn't want to see it."

"She was your sister, and you loved her."

"I don't understand how she did it. I made the love-spell dust, not her. Brittany should have been under my control." He made a face at Brittany who was still pushing towels around the wet floor. "No offense."

"None taken." Brittany glanced up with a strained smile.

"Maybe it has something to do with her being a familiar," Kristen suggested.

He groaned and rubbed the spot between his eyes while squeezing them shut. "I don't understand any of this. I want to know how she did it and why. I want the answers now. If I don't get them soon, I think I'll go insane."

Cyndi piped in. "Ask Grandma. She knows everything."

Brittany finished what she was doing, strolled over to the sofa, and wrapped her arms around Cyndi from behind. "That is genius. Pure genius. Of course Grandma will know."

Kristen nodded at Zach. "If anyone can explain it to us, Grandma Noah can, but it's so far away, and Cyndi needs to rest."

"I'll stay with her," Brittany said. "You two go ahead."

"It's a long drive," Kristen repeated.

Zach grinned, almost looking like his old self again. "Close your eyes and picture your grandmother's house."

"Why?"

"Trust me."

Kristen shut her eyes and concentrated on the inside of Grandma Noah's house.

Before anyone could guess his intentions, he grabbed Kristen's wrist and they disappeared. They were gone before Cyndi gasped, gone before Brittany shook her head in wonder.

This was Kristen's third trip, so she knew what to expect and steeled herself for impact. She managed to spread her legs wide while in transition, arms out for balance. When she reappeared in her grandmother's living room, she landed on her feet for a change, but she forgot to bend her knees. Pain shot up her legs. She winced while turning to look at Zach, but he wasn't there. She was alone.

Grandma Noah let out a surprised shriek and dropped the pot of tea she'd been carrying to the coffee table. The ancient pot broke, smashing into a million pieces against the brown carpet. Her hands went to her chest, and she shouted, "Oh! Where did you come from?"

Kristen was still trying to figure out why Zach wasn't with her. Panicking, she raced to her grandmother and grabbed the elderly woman by both arms. "Where is Zach? He was with me, and now he isn't."

"Zach?" Her grandmother's shrewd eyes narrowed. "Are you talking about the boy with the dark power, the one I warned you to stay away from? Well, if he tried to pop into my house, then he's caught between this place and that, wherever it was he came from. He's in limbo.

"As a security precaution, I installed a protective spell around this house years ago. The only reason you managed to pop in is because the house knows you are my granddaughter, but an intruder gets stuck between times. We won't have to worry about him again."

Kristen shook her head hard. "Grandma, no! You have to help him."

"And why would I do that when the world is better off with him right where he is?" She bent over and waved a hand over the broken pot. The pieces reunited instantly. "I spoke to the council about him, and they had no idea about his powers. They're investigating it."

"Grandma, you don't understand. It wasn't him."

As fast as she could, because she was worried about Zach, she explained everything. She explained about Morgan, told her about Brittany being crushed, and counted the number of times Zach had come through for her. She ended with, "I love him."

"You what?"

"*I love him!*" she shouted, and the walls shook. Taking a deep breath to calm down the way Zach had taught her, she lowered her voice and said, "I didn't think it would ever happen to me, not after the way Mom and Dad talked about it, but I love him. Please bring him back."

Grandma Noah shook her head. "This goes against my grain." She waved her arms in the air and said, "This is Evelyn Noah speaking, and I command the protection spell over this house to be lifted as of fifteen minutes ago."

Zach appeared.

Kristen rushed forward, jumped on him, and squeezed his neck. She knocked him back a few inches, but he managed to stay on his feet.

Confused, he put his hands on her back and said, "Uh… I'm happy to see you, too."

She cried, "You were stuck in limbo because Grandma put a protection spell on her house. I didn't know about it, and I had to tell her everything before she would release you."

"And I'm warning you," Grandma Noah said, wagging a finger at him, "you might be powerful, but I know a trick or two. Don't make me regret bringing you back. You do anything to harm my granddaughter, and I'll turn you into something nasty, like a dog with a bad case of worms."

Zach stiffened with a grim expression on his face. "Okay."

Grandma Noah gestured for them to join her at the kitchen table.

She loved to play hostess, especially to a newcomer. After waving a hand over the pot, she poured fresh tea for them. It was hot and sweet, better than the store-bought stuff. Then, Grandma Noah waved a hand over an empty plate, and cookies appeared.

With a grin, she offered the treat to them, saying, "Chocolate chip. I made them myself. Try one."

They each took a cookie and bit into them, making the appropriate 'yum' noises. Zach looked to Kristen as if to reassure himself that he was acting the right way and wasn't going to be turned into an animal.

Once Grandma Noah was satisfied, she took a seat across from them and said, "I assume you have a good reason for popping in and scaring the life out of an old woman, so spit it out. What brings you both here?"

Kristen and Zach exchanged wary looks, not knowing where to begin. He gestured for her to do the talking, so she did. "Why is Brittany under Morgan's spell when it was Zach who brewed the potion in the first place?"

"Easy." Grandma Noah smiled. "If Morgan is a familiar, she is linked to Zach. They are almost the same person. Brittany would have followed his orders, too, if he had given her any. Next question."

"How can you destroy a familiar?"

Grandma Noah made a face. "Now that's a tough one."

"I already told you," Zach said. "I have to be accused, lose my powers, and then she'll die."

Ignoring him, Kristen turned desperate eyes back to her grandmother. "Is there another way? Any other way?"

"There is, but it will be difficult."

"We'll do anything." Kristen reached across the table and rested a hand on top of Zach's. "Won't we?"

He shrugged. "I'm willing to give up my powers. That's the fastest way to do it."

"You need the locket from around her neck," Grandma Noah said. "The locket is the source of her power. Get it, burn the hair inside, and destroy the locket using a spell that I happen to have."

While her grandmother went to the desk and wrote the spell down, Kristen bent close to Zach and whispered in his ear, "Give this a chance. Please. We can get the locket."

"Accusing me would be a lot simpler and a lot safer. I don't want you to get hurt because of me."

"Why are you so determined to get rid of your powers?"

"Why are you so determined to see me keep them? Are you afraid your feelings for me will change if I'm not powerful anymore?"

It was ridiculous for him to even suggest such a thing. Sure, she'd been shallow in the past, but she was a different person now. She loved him for him, not for his powers. Nothing was going to change. She was almost a hundred-percent positive. "I liked you before I knew you had powers. Remember?"

He shrugged. "Then what's the problem? If you accuse me, Morgan will die, and we won't have to risk injury by taking the locket from her. She sleeps and showers with that thing, you know. It isn't going to be easy to take it."

Brittany's cell phone began to play a loud song from her favorite band. Zach pulled it out of his pocket and stared at the caller ID. With a scowl on his face, he said, "It's her. It's Morgan." He stared at the phone as if it were a deadly cobra.

"Are you going to answer it?" Kristen asked.

"I want to," he said. "This would be the first time I've ever spoken to my sister—to the real her, anyway. I want to hear what she has to say, but if we're going to get a hand on that locket, we need to see her in person. If I answer, she'll know we're onto her."

Zach pushed the phone at Kristen and said, "Pretend to be Brittany."

"I can't."

"Try."

"I can't do a good Brittany impression. We need Cyndi."

"There's no time for that."

Grandma Noah snatched the phone out of Zach's hand. She waved a hand in front of her throat before answering it. Her voice changed. If Kristen closed her eyes, she would swear it was Brittany talking.

"What do you want?"

It was Brittany's usual way of answering a call.

Grandma Noah's eyes grew wide. Pretending to be crushed, she laid it on thick. "Please let me do that for you. I can do it. I want to do something for you. I love you. Please let me do it."

With a heavy sigh, Grandma Noah put the cell down on the table. "That girl is nuttier than my special peanut butter cookies. I've never heard such a crazy laugh."

"What did she say?" Zach asked.

"She figured out Brittany failed to kill Kristen, and now she wants to do it herself."

An icy finger touched Kristen's spine. She shuddered. Having Brittany try to kill her was one thing, but Morgan wouldn't hesitate.

"That's it," Zach said, turning to Kristen. "We aren't going to try to get the locket and risk your life. You need to accuse me."

20

Powerless

Kristen and Zach were sitting on the hood of his car, his arms wrapped around her and his chin resting possessively on her shoulder as she reclined back against him. Instead of pulling away, she snuggled closer, not wanting the moment to end. For two days, Zach had given in and searched for his sister so they could destroy the locket, but Morgan had vanished without a trace. There was no other way to handle the situation. She was going to have to publicly accuse Zach.

They couldn't keep Brittany from using her phone or from leaving the house for much longer. The girl was going stir-crazy. There was a party coming up, and no matter how bad Brittany felt about what she'd done, Kristen knew she would be at that party, regardless of the danger.

With a sigh, Zach released his tight hold on Kristen. "We'd better go inside and get it over with."

"I don't want to," she groaned. "I just want to stay like this with you forever."

"We'd starve to death."

"You could pop in some cheeseburgers." She laughed, only half-kidding.

He climbed off the car and held a hand out for her. She slid her palm across his skin, taking her time. The skin-to-skin contact made her flesh tingle. He pulled her off the hood, and her feet landed next to his on the tarmac. Cupping her face between both hands, his eyes became deadly serious. "We have to do this. I promise you it won't be that bad."

Her gaze drifted to the school. "I just wish there was another way."

"I know. Me too." With a sigh, he said, "I can ask Brittany to do it if it's too hard for you. I'm sure she won't mind."

"No. If someone is going to publicly accuse you, it's going to be me. I want to do this for you. I just hate it."

He pulled her close again and kissed the side of her head. Together, they turned and walked to the brick building. They held onto each other the whole way. Kristen felt a little like a prisoner on death row taking a last walk, the one leading to the hangman's noose. Letting him go, she entered the building a step ahead of Zach and took in familiar faces. These kids were going to think she'd lost her mind.

They went to Kristen's locker first. She stalled, removing a notebook and a pencil with trembling fingers. The loud chatter behind her didn't even register. Her mind was focused on Zach and the terrible thing she was about to do to him. She asked, hopeful, "Can we wait till lunch? Do it in the cafeteria?"

"No." He grinned at her. "Treat it like a bandage and rip that sucker off."

"How can you be so calm? You're about to lose part of who you are. You won't be the same guy anymore."

The grin died. "Are you afraid you won't want to be with me anymore?"

"Stop asking me that. You know I love you for you and not for what you can do. I'm just saying that you've lived one way, and now you're going to have to learn how to live another way. It's going to be hard. Don't you get that?"

He bent close and talked low so no one would overhear him. “It’s okay. Really. I told you before. I don’t even use my powers except when I’m rescuing you from my sister, and after today, I won’t need to do that anymore. I’ve had to lay low for over a year now. I’m used to doing things the normal way. I’ll be fine.”

Kristen believed him, and she wished she could be as strong about it. The mere mention of losing powers scared her speechless. She didn’t think she could handle it. Taking a deep breath, she said, “Okay. Here we go.”

He nodded, a sober expression on his face.

She stepped into the center of the crowded hallway, turned, and pointed a finger at his chest. If it weren’t for the graveness of the situation, she wouldn’t be able to keep a straight face. She felt incredibly stupid. Loud and clear, she shouted over the chaotic noise. “Zach Bevian is a wizard!”

Zach fell back against the lockers, and the blood drained from his face.

A few of the kids laughed, but most of them stared as if they were waiting for the punchline, so she gave them one. “Zach Bevian is the wizard who enchanted me and stole my heart.”

Eye rolls met her statement. The other students returned to what they’d been doing before she’d interrupted them with her ‘show.’ She hurried over to Zach, asking in a low voice, “Are you okay?”

Bent over with hands on knees, he seemed to be trying to catch his breath. Slowly, he stood straight up and leaned against the lockers again. A smile stretched his lips. He reached out a hand and caressed her cheek. “I’m okay. I had the breath knocked out of me for a second. That’s all.”

Wrapping an arm around his lean waist, she led him back to the glass doors. “You aren’t in any shape to be in school today. We need to get you home.”

They went to his car at the rear of the parking lot. He rested against the driver-side door. Arm still around her, he held her close for a moment. His face pressed against her neck, seeking solace. “I don’t want you to take this the wrong way, but I have to go home alone."

"Why?"

His eyes glistened, and he looked away. "This will be the first time I've gone home since Morgan… she's gone, and I need to face it on my own. This is something that I have to do on my own."

Kristen understood, but a new worry nibbled at the edges of her mind. Could Zach forgive her for killing his sister? Because that was exactly what she'd done when she'd accused him. She'd killed Morgan, and he wouldn't have even had to get rid of his sister if it hadn't been for her sister getting herself crushed by the girl.

"Will you call me later?" Her voice sounded weak to her own ears.

"If you don't call me first," he said.

Guilt weighed heavily on Kristen's shoulders. She took a few steps away from the car as he got into the vehicle. She stood there alone, waving at him until the car vanished from view. Her heart sank. She wished there were something she could do for him, some way she could make him feel better, but he was going to have to grieve for his sister before he could move on.

It didn't matter that Morgan had been a monster. He'd still loved her.

Zach stood in the foyer for several minutes, reluctant to travel further because each step would take him closer to the truth. Morgan was gone. Dead. He wouldn't see his sister again. It didn't seem real. A few days ago, she'd been living with him, pretending to be helpless, and now she was gone. For years, he'd taken care of her. Now what was he supposed to do?

He dropped his keys on the nearby table before going to the study. The fireplace was his first stop. He stared at the pictures on the mantel, especially the ones with Morgan in them. After taking one into his hands, he walked down the hallway to the family room. The first thing he saw was Morgan's notebook on the coffee table where she'd left it. A deep sadness washed over him. It didn't seem right that her belongings were still in the house when she wasn't coming back. He wished her things had gone with her. A new wave of pain washed over him.

Zach dropped to the sofa, set the picture on the cushion beside him, and picked up the notebook. Curious, he started at the beginning. His eyes scanned each entry. This was her dummy notebook, the one created to keep him from knowing what she was truly up to. He flipped through the pages slowly, but it was the last one that caught him off guard. Unlike the previous entries, this one was not neatly written. It had been scrawled in haste.

Look at the doorway. Cold, wet fear, the kind that comes when you're alone in a house at night and hear a strange noise, crept up his spine and seeped into his bones. He silently prayed he was dreaming as he turned to face the open doorway. Somehow, he knew what he would find—the stuff nightmares were made of.

Morgan stood just outside the doorway with arms folded and pinched facial features. He rose off the sofa, thinking he had to be imagining things. Or perhaps a familiar's ghost hung around for a while after it died. He walked towards her with cautious steps, all the while reassuring himself it couldn't be real, that Morgan was gone forever.

"What are you doing here?" His tongue felt three sizes too big for his mouth.

A new, intelligent light danced in her brown eyes. "At six this morning, a little bird told me something that blew me away. Did you have someone accuse you today? Did you give up your powers just to get rid of me?"

This wasn't a ghost. His gaze dropped to the locket around her neck. All he had to do was reach out and snatch it. Kristen's grandmother had insisted on giving them the spell to destroy it, just in case. He charged at Morgan. She didn't try to avoid the inevitable collision. Instead, her laughter rang in his ears, growing louder as he hit an invisible wall. The unexpected impact knocked him backwards, and he landed on the floor with a loud grunt. Zach got up and tried again with the same result.

His gut burned with an uncontrollable fury. Waving a hand in her direction, he tried to hit her with a spell before remembering he'd given up his powers. The bewildered look on his face made her laugh harder. He wanted to kill Morgan with his own hands, strangle the life out of her, but he couldn't get to her. He punched the invisible wall between them again and again. Nothing happened. It was no use. The spell was too strong.

Exhausted, Zach sat on the arm of the sofa and gasped for air. He needed a few minutes to regain his strength before finding a way to get his hands on her. Somehow, he was going to do it. He was going to get that locket and destroy it.

"How long were you faking your illness?" he asked.

"Since Mom and Dad died."

"How can you be so cold about it?" Standing up, he shouted, "They were your parents! They loved you."

"Who asked them to?" Morgan shrugged.

Zach wondered how much he actually knew about that night. What was fantasy, and what was reality? "Did the gardener actually give you the book of old spells, or did you lie about that, too? Did he encourage you to become a familiar, or was it your idea?"

She grinned. "I wasn't faking my mental issues back then, idiot. How could I possibly know about familiars or power? You have no idea what it was like for me."

"Tell me. You have my undivided attention."

"It was frustrating as hell. I know you probably thought I was brain-dead or something, but I understood a lot more than you think I did. I heard people talk and comprehended a great deal of it, but I couldn't communicate with them. I couldn't say what I wanted to say."

"Why did you use my hair instead of the gardener's?"

Morgan paced in front of the doorway, clearly agitated. "Mom told me over and over how my brother was going to watch over me. That night, I put a piece of your hair in the locket because I thought

I needed you. Then I blew the house up, and I learned the truth. It didn't hurt, in case you care. I didn't hear an explosion or anything. One second I was doing the spell, and the next I was standing outside with Ethan."

"Wait a second." Zach frowned. "Ethan died in that explosion. How could he be outside and inside at the same time?"

A sly smile stretched her lips. "He was standing next to me when I came back as a familiar. I could think straight for the first time. It was like someone had turned on a light. He knew I would be cured, but he figured I couldn't kill him. He told me that if I did, I would die, too. That's when I told him I was your familiar, not his."

She fell back against the wall, laughing. A hand went to her stomach as tears came to her eyes. She couldn't seem to stop laughing. After a few minutes, she managed to say, "Y-you should have seen the look on h-his face when I told him. It was the funniest thing ever. I wish you'd been there. Before he could even think, I used my brand-new powers to put him inside the house. So he *did* die there, but not in the explosion. I think the roof collapsing on his head did the job.

"Anyway, I was happy that night I made you my so-called master, but I've regretted it almost every day since. You are zero fun. You forbid me to use magic, forcing me to sneak around behind your back. I had to practice, you know. Then, to top all that off, you hook up with that hair-brained witch and decide to kill me just so you can be with her. What sort of brother are you?"

Mouth tight, he shook his head slowly. "I was not going to kill you to be with Kristen. I was going to kill you because you are a *psychopath!*"

Morgan placed her hands on the doorframe and leaned forward slightly, enough to drive him crazy, but not enough so he could grab her. She knew exactly what she was doing. She said, "I've been searching for another witch, someone fun to switch ownership to, and I finally found the perfect one. As of about seven this morning, I am no longer your familiar."

She had a new master? A new person to hold her invisible leash for her? That explained why she wasn't dead. They should have gone with plan number one and tried harder to get their hands on the locket. Zach had the spell written on a piece of paper in his pocket. If only he could get his hands on that necklace somehow.

"Who's your owner now?" he asked.

"That's for me to know."

"What are you planning to do?"

Her smile grew. "I am going to kill your stupid girlfriend."

Fists clenched, he tried to break through the invisible barrier again, but it was too solid, too strong.

Morgan laughed. Turning away, she began to walk down the hallway in the direction of the door.

Zach yelled her name. He didn't have any power, but there had to be something he could do. There had to be a way to stop her.

"Leave Kristen alone! I'm warning you, Morgan. I will hunt you down and kill you if you don't stay away from her."

Her voice called back to him with no emotion whatsoever. "That's not a very nice way to talk to your sister."

"I repeat, if you go near her, I'll…"

"What?" Morgan returned to the doorway, cheerful smile in place. "What will you do without your powers? Nothing. Absolutely nothing. That's what you'll do. Just so you know, I put a spell on this entire room. The windows are unbreakable. The chimney is blocked. You'll be stuck in here until someone finds your dead body. Ironic, isn't it? You kept me prisoner, and now you're the one trapped. Goodbye, Zachary."

He continued to shout at her, but she didn't return a second time.

She was going to kill Kristen, and there wasn't anything he could do to stop her.

21

Itch

The dream began.

Kristen walked with hesitant steps down Titan High's main hallway. The lights flickered. The building seemed to be empty, but she wasn't fooled by the lack of activity. She hugged her books to her chest, fearing what might happen next. Any second now, students would appear, and they would accuse her of being a witch. Usually, she was already surrounded at this point. The silence bothered her more than anything. Were they going to jump out and scare her?

Kristen trembled. This was the worst nightmare yet. She squeezed her eyes shut and scrunched up her face, concentrating on waking up. It didn't work. She opened her eyes to find she was no longer alone. The sight of an extra body startled her, and she nearly jumped out of her shoes. A closer look made her realize that she knew this person. Hope flared in her chest. She was safe.

Grandma Noah was at Kristen's locker with the door open, peering inside. She couldn't see her grandmother's face. It could be a trick. If this nightmare were anything like the other ones, Grandma Noah would be a bloody mess, or she'd be missing an important facial feature. The woman in question closed the metal door and turned, holding her hand out to Kristen. Relief flooded through Kristen when she saw her grandmother's face.

For a second, Kristen thought her grandmother wanted to touch her. She reached for her outstretched hand, but it wasn't empty. The gold medallion dangled from her grandmother's fingers. The elderly woman said, "Take this, and go to the gym. Go alone."

Kristen reluctantly took the necklace. She held it up high and glared at it. Her grandmother wouldn't offer it to her if she knew how dangerous it had turned out to be in Kristen's hands. She'd almost injured Brittany and several boys in the gym not that long ago. "But it's too powerful for me to control. I don't want anyone to get hurt."

"Take it and go to the gym," her grandmother repeated. She sounded like an automated response that people sometimes got when they called for show times or directions. "Go alone."

"I don't understand. What am I supposed to do in the gym?"

Grandma Noah looked to the side, and Brittany stepped out of the shadows. Their grandmother went to Brittany, handed her a crystal, and said, "You are going to need this if you're going to survive the night. Love is your most powerful weapon. Remember that."

Kristen waited for Brittany to mouth-off with some random complaint that she thought was funny even though no one else did.

Brittany simply nodded.

Zach stepped forward next. He approached with a grim expression on his handsome face. He put an arm around Kristen's shoulders, kissed her on the forehead, and said, "I'm sorry I can't help you. She's my sister, and I can't do a blasted thing to stop her. I shouldn't have given up my powers so easily."

Grandma Noah handed him a square piece of paper and said, "You have your part to play in this little drama. Don't let my granddaughters down. They need you. You are the *only* one who can stop your sister. It has to be you."

What could Zach possibly do without powers?

Her grandmother returned to stand directly in front of her. "Tell Cyndi that being an individual isn't all it's cracked up to be. I want her to keep dressing like Brittany. Do you understand?"

Kristen shook her head, totally confused by the statement. "Are you serious?" She looked around again and asked, "Where is Cyndi? Why isn't she here?" Hurricane-force wind whipped through the hallway. Kristen tried to grab on to something, but her hands closed on air. Zach was gone. She continued to reach out with both arms, eyes squinting. The wind blew harder, and she slid backwards on the shiny linoleum. Something loud that sounded like an invisible vacuum sucked up the wind. Total silence remained. For a moment, she wondered if she'd gone deaf.

Once again, she was alone in the hallway.

Her grandmother's voice echoed in her ears. "Cyndi is in Room 210."

Grandma Noah's face popped up in front of hers, so close she almost bumped noses with her. The woman shouted, "Wake up!"

Zach tried everything he could think of to escape Morgan's trap. He slammed heavy objects against the window, but the glass refused to crack. He started on the opposite side of the room, ran at the doorway full-force, and crashed into the invisible wall again and again. It didn't budge. He did it until he was out of breath, his body was bruised and battered, and he felt like one more hit would break some bones. It was no use. Nothing worked. He couldn't save Kristen.

Defeated, he sank onto the floor next to the doorway and buried his face in his hands. Since there wasn't anything else to do, he began to play the 'what if' game with himself. What if he'd paid closer attention to how Morgan was behaving? He could have stopped her. What if he'd killed her after realizing what she'd done to their parents? That would have been the best solution.

In hindsight, he could see things more clearly. Morgan had slipped up on occasion, momentarily dropping the act, but he hadn't wanted to know the truth about her. Deep inside, he'd fought to hold on to the illusion she was his sister, because the alternative had seemed worse to him at the time. The bad boy of Titan High had been afraid to be alone. What a joke.

He groaned. "I should have killed her. I should have killed her a long, long time ago."

A new voice followed his. "Does my sister know you talk to yourself?"

He lifted his head slowly, afraid he was imagining things. No way was he this lucky. But there she was, standing in the hallway outside the family room, his last hope. He leaped to his feet and shouted in desperation. "Brittany! Get me out of here! Morgan is going after Kristen, and we have to stop her."

"What?"

"We don't have time for long explanations. Morgan is going to kill Kristen if you don't get me out of here."

Brittany stepped into the room and stared at him with narrowed eyes. "What do you mean get you out of here? What is your problem? Can't you walk?"

"Morgan put a lockdown spell on this room. I need you to pop us out of here. It's the only way for me to escape. Grab on to my arm, and let's go."

"I can't pop," she said and sneered at him, "have you lost your mind?"

"I think you can. I'm willing to bet my life on it… and Kristen's life. Morgan transferred herself to someone else so I couldn't get rid of her. I think she's attached herself to you, and if I'm right about that, then you can pop in and out of places now."

"How would she even do that, transfer to me?"

"By taking a strand of your hair."

Brittany's face lost all color. "She popped into my room this morning and took my hairbrush."

"Let's go. Do it quickly, or we're going to be too late."

Brittany threw her hands up in the air. "OMG! I cannot pop. Read my lips. I'm telling you I can't do it. Even if I have that power now, which I don't, I don't know how to use it. If I tried, we'd probably end up in the Pacific Ocean, and I can't swim that good."

Zach took a deep breath and tried hard to calm down. He spoke to Brittany in the same voice he used to use with Morgan. "It's simple, okay? Listen to me. This isn't rocket science, you know. A monkey could do it. Take my hand, close your eyes, and concentrate on your home. Focus on being there. Convince yourself that you are already inside your house. It's that simple."

With an irritated expression on her face, she took his hand in a hard grip and closed her eyes. Zach squeezed his eyes shut and silently prayed that Morgan had chosen this girl to be her new master. Otherwise, they'd both be stuck in the family room forever.

Wake up!

Kristen bolted upright, surprised to find herself on the sofa. She lifted the hair off her hot, sweaty neck. The cool air felt good against her damp skin. Her memory slowly returned in confusing fragments. She'd stretched out on the sofa after Cyndi had gone upstairs to rest. Cyndi had had a headache since the accident. Kristen decided to check on her before going to her own room to finish the pile of homework that needed to be done before morning.

She glanced at the digital clock on the table near the stairs. The lit-up numbers told her it was only a few minutes after seven. The sun was almost gone, and the house was dark. No one had turned a light on while she slept. Careful not to run into the furniture, she went upstairs to peek inside Cyndi's room before heading to her own. Her sister was snoring softly beneath a sheet.

Once she got to her own room, Kristen sat on the mattress instead of at the desk. She reclined against the row of pillows and spread her books in front of her bent knees. It was hard to concentrate. She hadn't heard from Zach since he'd left her at school following the loss of his powers. She'd tried to call him, but he hadn't answered. His silence worried her. It was possible he blamed her for killing Morgan.

And why wouldn't he?

Kristen sighed and forced thoughts of Zach to the back of her mind. She had a ton of reading to do, and if she didn't get started, she'd be up all night.

A short hair tickled her forehead. She swiped at it. An itch brought her hand to her scalp again. She scratched. Another second and another itch. Something was crawling on her. It felt like tiny feet moving from her hairline to her eyebrow, probably an ant. She swatted at it. Then it happened again, only this time it was in a different area.

She hurried to her dresser and picked up the handheld mirror, hoping she didn't have lice. That would really be the topper of an already horrible year. She would have to transfer to another school.

There was a tiny, white spider on her forehead. She smacked it hard, smashing it against her skin. Before she could set the mirror down, another spider appeared.

What the hell?

She watched in horror as a few tiny, white spiders crawled out from her hairline. The few turned into several, then hundreds, then thousands. Kristen screamed and dropped the mirror. The glass broke, but she didn't care. She repeatedly smacked herself in the forehead, trying to kill them as she ran to the bathroom so she could drown them in the sink.

Cyndi came out of her bedroom to see what the noise was about. She blinked her sleepy eyes several times. "What's going on?"

"Spiders!" Kristen kept hitting herself and pulling at her hair, desperate to kill them.

"What are you talking about?" Cyndi grabbed at her hands, trying to stop her from hurting herself.

Kristen blasted past her and ran into the bathroom. There wasn't time to turn on the light. She had to kill them. She shoved the stopper into the sink and turned both faucets on full blast. Millions of tiny feet crawled over her face and neck. She screamed, hitting them with her hands again and hitting herself in the process while waiting for the sink to fill with enough water to drown them.

"There are no spiders!" Cyndi shouted.

"Get them off me!" Kristen crashed into the wall and almost knocked herself out.

Zach came out of nowhere. He grasped Kristen's wrists and pulled her hands away from her face. He tried to talk to her, but she couldn't hear what he was saying over the sound of her uncontrollable screams. He forcibly turned her around, wrapped a tight arm around her waist, and made her look into the mirror as Cyndi flicked on the overhead light.

From the doorway, Brittany said, "Wow, you have totally lost it."

The spiders were gone, but how? Kristen stared at her reflection in stunned silence. Her skin was red in several places where she'd almost beaten her brains out. She shook her head slowly, trying to understand what had just happened. "There were spiders everywhere. I saw them."

"They weren't real," Zach said. His grim eyes met hers in the mirror. "Morgan isn't gone. She did this. She's messing with you, torturing you, and she isn't going to stop until you're dead."

22

Kidnapped

Fifteen minutes later, Kristen was sitting on the sofa, wrapped in a blanket with a glass of warm milk between her hands and Zach beside her. He rubbed her shoulders with gentle, circular motions. Deep concern drew his brows together and tightened his facial features. She listened, limbs shaking, while he told her about his fight with Morgan and how she'd trapped him.

Brittany straddled the ottoman on the other side of the living room. Behind her, the wall of windows and the two glass doors looked solid black. Kristen hated to be in the living room at night with a light on because someone could be out there, watching, and she wouldn't know it. They could see her, but she couldn't see them. Their dad refused to cover the windows with curtains. He liked knowing the ocean was out there and thought she was being silly about it. They had a private beach, he often reminded her. Kristen didn't think it would be too hard for someone to climb the gate or walk down from another beach. She kept her gaze off the windows, but they stayed in the back of her mind, refusing to budge.

Once Zach finished his story, she told everyone about her dream.

Brittany scoffed. "Why do you get sent on a secret mission by

Grandma, while all I get is a bumper sticker about love and a stupid crystal?"

Ignoring her sister, she told Zach, "It's the first time I've had this dream, but I know it's important. That same feeling was there, the same feeling I get when I have premonition dreams. It's going to happen."

"Your grandmother already gave me the spell to destroy the locket." Zach pulled the piece of paper from his pocket. "And she gave you the medallion."

Kristen asked Brittany, "Has she given you a crystal?"

"Of course not. It was just a dream. You still have those, you know."

"You always say that."

"Why were you at Zach's house, anyway?"

Brittany shrugged defiantly. "I was going to take care of that evil witch by myself. No one puts a spell on me and gets away with it."

Zach's eyes narrowed. "I thought she popped in on you this morning."

"She did, but she caught me off guard. I didn't have the chance to fight the spell."

Kristen stared at Brittany in silence, freaked out over what could have happened. Sometimes Brittany didn't think before acting. She was way too impulsive for her own good.

"Don't try to take her on alone. She'll give you another order or turn you into a cricket or something. Anyway, I accused Zach at school to get rid of her so none of us would have to deal with her again."

"Well, no one told me that, so I figured she was at the house, and I guess I was right because she showed up to trap Zach. You should be grateful—Zach wouldn't be here if I hadn't rescued him."

Kristen shivered, and Zach pulled her closer to his warm body. His lips touched the side of her face. For a moment, he nuzzled against her, eyes closed. She drank some more of the heated milk, still shaking from the earlier ordeal. The fact that Morgan was out there somewhere, plotting to kill her, had her totally freaked out. How was she going to survive?

Zach shared an idea with them. "I want you girls to go to your grandmother's house. She can protect you while I take care of Morgan."

"How?"

"I'll get the locket from her somehow."

"No way." Kristen shook her head. "There is no way I am leaving you to deal with her on your own. You don't have powers anymore."

Zach shrugged. "I can be pretty resourceful."

"I don't care. There has to be something else we can do." An idea came to her. It was a great idea, only one problem—they needed Brittany's cooperation. Kristen set her half-empty glass on the coffee table, tossed off the blanket, and crossed the room to stand next to her sister. Out of desperation, she asked Brittany, "How sorry are you about the things you did?"

Brittany wore a grief-stricken expression. "You know how sorry I am. I almost killed Cyndi, and I did terrible things to you. I would do anything to make up for that."

"There *is* something you can do." Kristen took her sister's hands, squeezed them hard, and said, "If you sacrifice your powers, we can destroy Morgan."

Brittany jerked her hands out of Kristen's gasp. Her shocked expression quickly turned to anger. "Excuse me? I know I didn't just hear you ask me to give up my powers."

"You'd be saving lives. You have the opportunity to save Cyndi, Zach, and me. This is your chance to make up for the hell you put us through and redeem yourself. You'd be a hero."

"No!" Brittany kicked the ottoman out of her way before walking around Kristen. "There is no way in hell I am letting anyone accuse me."

Kristen looked to Zach for support. With her eyes, she silently told him they were going to accuse Brittany whether she liked it or not. Zach shook his head slowly, obviously against it, but she nodded her head firmly. They were doing it. End of discussion.

Brittany folded her arms over her chest. "I don't see anyone here for you to accuse me in front of, and I'm not going anywhere with you.

Think of something else."

"Zach gave up his powers to stop her."

"And look where it got him! She'd already transferred herself to me. What if she's done it again? Did it ever occur to you that maybe this is her plan? We go around accusing each other until no one has any powers left, and then she wipes us out one by one."

"She's got a point," Zach said. "You need my help, and I'm powerless to do anything. It would be a mistake to take Brittany's powers, too. You'd be even more helpless. That could be what she wants, a showdown between the two of you."

Kristen disagreed with both of them. The truth was that Brittany could be dangerous to them. Morgan had been controlling her for weeks. If Morgan found a way to get to her again, Brittany could turn around and kill them all. It would be a lot better for them if Brittany lost her magic.

Brittany said, "I don't see you giving up your powers. Why should I? It's your worst nightmare come to life, but you want me to live it. Right. Talk about selfish."

"I would do it in a heartbeat if it would protect someone I love."

"That's because you're little miss perfect."

"Don't start that crap with me, Britt."

A scream ripped through the night air. It came from upstairs. *Cyndi*! They looked at each other with wide eyes before darting up the stairs. Zach took the lead. He raced up the steps two at a time. Kristen was on his heels with Brittany taking up the rear.

They raced down the hallway to Cyndi's closed door. Zach thrust it open. There, inside the bedroom she shared with Brittany, was a terrifying visitor. Cyndi stood next to her bed with Morgan behind her. Morgan's hand was tangled in Cyndi's hair, holding her hostage. A nasty sneer twisted the evil familiar's mouth.

Zach shoved Kristen behind him to keep his sister from hitting her with a fatal spell, but that wasn't Morgan's plan. She laughed, her dark eyes flashing with malicious humor. In the blink of an eye, she and Cyndi disappeared together. There wasn't time for anyone to do anything. There wasn't even time for them to think about doing something. The two girls were gone in a flash.

Brittany shoved Zach and Kristen out of her way. She charged into the room, a startled cry fading on her lips. Standing where the girls had been half a second ago, she looked around. Her eyes widened. She lifted her hand and pointed at the wall. Zach and Kristen entered the room all the way to see the damage. Written on the wall, scratched into the paint by a magical finger, was a message.

School. Midnight. Cyndi for Kristen.

"Just like in my dream," Kristen said. "We have to go to the school."

"She took my sister!" Brittany yelled. "We have to stop that witch *now!*"

Zach shook his head. "We are not doing anything. You are going to stay out of this, and I'm going to take care of Morgan."

"You can't do it alone," Kristen said. "She's my sister, and I'm going with you. Don't try to stop me. I'm going, and that's final."

"Fine. Stick close to me."

"I'm going, too," Brittany said.

Both Zach and Kristen blocked the doorway. Brittany glared at them and tried to push past, but they held her back. Kristen said, "You can't go. You are still under Morgan's power. If you want to help, let us accuse you. We can go somewhere public right now and do it. Morgan will die, and Cyndi will be safe. How badly do you want to save Cyndi?"

"Forget it. I'll do it myself."

One second Brittany was standing there yelling, and the next, she was gone. Kristen stared at the empty space. For a moment, she thought Morgan had taken Brittany, too. Then she saw the unchanged expression on Zach's face. Brittany's vanishing act hadn't surprised him in the slightest.

Kristen gasped. "What the… how did she do that?"

Zach rubbed the back of his neck, looking sheepish. "I kind of told her how."

"What? Why?"

He quickly filled her in on the rest of his story, telling her how Brittany had rescued him from Morgan's trap by popping them back home. He told Kristen how desperate he had been to reach her, feeling helpless and certain Kristen would be dead before he got out of there, so he'd told Brittany how to pop. He finished with, "It was the only way for me to get to you."

"I hope she didn't go to the school. She'll wind up killing Cyndi instead of rescuing her."

"I don't think she's that stupid."

Kristen wasn't so sure.

They spent the next half hour preparing for their life-and-death mission. Zach waited at the bottom of the stairs for Kristen while she finished getting ready. When she finally descended, dressed entirely in black, his breath caught in his throat. She looked incredible in her snug pants, sleeveless shirt, and short boots. She could have been a sexy spy in a late-night movie.

She carried a dark gray bag. Tossing it to the sofa, she said, "It's my dad's. There are flashlights, extra batteries, rope, a knife, and a few other things we might need."

"Good deal." He grinned and tried to lighten the mood a little because he knew how worried she was about both of her sisters. "Have you done this before? Do you sneak out on secret missions in the middle of the night after doing your homework?"

"You bet." She tried not to look at him, probably wanting to hide the tears glistening in her eyes, but he saw them.

He pulled her into his arms and stroked her back. "It's going to be okay. I promise you. I won't let Morgan hurt Cyndi."

"How are you going to stop her without magic?" Her jaw tightened, and her hand went to her forehead. Lowering her voice, she added,

"I'm sorry. I know you're only trying to help."

"And you're only worried about your sister. I get that. It's okay. Even without powers, I am going to make sure you get Cyndi back safe."

"I don't know what I would do without you."

More than anything, Zach wanted to comfort Kristen, wanted to make sure she was in the right frame of mind to do this. If she were too worried, she might make a mistake. Morgan would take advantage of that, and Kristen could get hurt. The mere thought nearly drove him to his knees. How was he going to protect her?

Putting on a brave face, he pushed hair out of her eyes. "We can do this. Together. We have something Morgan doesn't—love."

"In my dream, Grandma told Brittany that love is her strongest weapon."

"It's ours, too. Believe it."

She nodded, meeting his gaze with a strong one of her own. "I do."

Zach watched in awe as Kristen straightened her spine and blinked the tears back. In a matter of seconds, she pulled herself together. Her expression turned cool, becoming the professional face of someone who did this sort of thing for a living. She checked her watch before saying, "We should go. If we can get there before Morgan, maybe we can set a trap for her."

He nodded his approval. "Good idea."

She bent at the waist to pick up the bag, but Zach got to it first. Slinging it over his shoulder, he followed her to the door. They had to take her car because his was still in the parking lot at school.

Kristen walked out the door. He took one last look around the house, hoping all three girls would return to it in one piece. He made a silent vow. If someone had to die tonight, it would either be Morgan or him.

23

Destroyed

Zach held one of the flashlights while Kristen tried to use magic to open the school's glass doors. He had shared a spell with her that could do the trick, but since it was new to her, she was having a difficult time with it. Feeling helpless, he stood to the side and watched. Giving up his powers while Morgan was running around loose had been a stupid idea. How was he supposed to protect Kristen?

Kristen slowly enunciated each word of the spell he'd given her. She waved her hands in front of the doors, but nothing happened. The sides of her mouth turned down in frustration. Groaning, she tried again. Still nothing. She kicked the door, swore beneath her breath, and tried it for the third time.

Zach watched with pride and awe. No matter what happened to her, the girl never gave up. His father would have said she had steel in her bones. She never ceased to amaze him. His sister was trying to kill her, but instead of running away and hiding, she was headed for a confrontation with the familiar.

Kristen sighed. "I can't do it. I can't get the door open. Any other ideas?"

One of the glass doors swung open as if it had heard Kristen's complaint and decided to comply. She looked at him with wide eyes. "Wow. That's kind of creepy."

He hoped it didn't mean Morgan was inside waiting for them. There wouldn't be any chance of surprising her with a trap if she'd set one up for them. She'd continue to have the upper hand.

Kristen started to go inside, but he caught her arm just below the elbow. Dragging her close, he whispered, "I don't like this. It doesn't smell right."

"Totally. But we don't have a choice. She has my sister, and I'm not letting Cyndi die."

He released her arm and followed her through the door.

Being inside the empty school at night was eerie. The farther they went, the less he liked the whole thing. While they walked to Kristen's locker, he tried to come up with a new plan. There had to be something he could do if they got in over their heads, a last-ditch effort to stop Morgan and save the girls. He would die if he had to, as long as dying protected Kristen from his sister.

Their soft footsteps echoed in the empty hallway, sounding like thunder to his ears. He hoped Morgan wasn't close enough to hear them. He needed more time to find a plan without any flaws.

Kristen opened her locker. She stood there for a moment, staring into the metal box until he began to think something was wrong. Had someone taken the medallion?

"Is it still in there?" he asked.

She pulled the gold chain and shiny medallion out. "It's here. I was just thinking about what my grandma told me in the dream." Kristen closed the metal door before locking eyes with Zach. Her lips barely moved when she spoke. "I have to go to the gym alone."

He shook his head emphatically, mouth tight. "There is no way I'm letting you do that."

"Grandma Noah told me I have to go alone."

"It was a dream."

"It was more than that, and you know it. She didn't have time to explain why it has to be me or why I have to go alone, but I know it's the right thing to do. Cyndi is in Room 210. Go get her. Then you can both meet me in the gym."

He stubbornly folded his arms and glared down at her. "Read my lips—*no*. You are not going to the gym by yourself. Forget about it."

"Don't be difficult, and don't make me bind you. I need your help. Please go get Cyndi."

She would do it, too. She would bind him to the floor so he couldn't stop her. Then he wouldn't be able to save her when the time for saving arrived. He started walking backwards so he could hurry, grab Cyndi, and get to the gym in time to save the only girl he'd ever loved. He pointed a finger at her and said, "Do me a favor and walk slow."

She nodded.

He bolted like a horse out of the gate at the racetrack. Running up the stairs, taking them two at a time, he went after Cyndi. But as he reached the top, he found himself face-to-face with her. She wasn't tied up or locked in a room. What was going on?

The girl was wearing a dark gray T-shirt with some band on it he'd never heard of. Shining the flashlight on her, he said, "How did you get loose?"

"Get that damn light out of my face!" She lifted her hands and squinted. After he did as she demanded, she rolled her eyes and said, "If you're going to date my sister, you need to learn to tell us apart. I'm Brittany."

Although the last place he wanted Brittany to be was anywhere near his sister, he thought it was great news. Now he could go help Kristen. He said, "Cyndi is in Room 210. Get her."

"Where are you going?"

"To the gym to save Kristen. Whatever you do, do not go to the gym. Morgan might be there, and the last thing we need is for you to join the dark side against us. Take Cyndi and go home."

"Got it."

Zach turned around and darted back down the stairs, praying he wouldn't be too late. He still didn't have a feasible plan. Hopefully something would come to him when he needed it most. One thing was for sure—if a witch died tonight, it was not going to be Kristen. If it was the last thing he ever did, he was going to destroy Morgan.

Kristen entered the gymnasium with the medallion swinging from her left hand. She went over the dream again and again in her head, searching for clues. What did she need to do to defeat Morgan? She came up empty. If her grandmother had told her, it had sailed over her head.

She stepped into the gymnasium and looked around. The large room was dark with only a tiny bit of light spilling in through the skylight. As she walked to the middle of the basketball court, memories of her days as a cheerleader came flooding back. It was hard to believe now that she'd ever thought being a cheerleader was important. A lot of the things she'd held onto back then were meaningless now.

She promised herself that if she survived this night, she was going to be a different person. She was going to devote her life to something meaningful and find a job she loved instead of chasing money and prestige.

The sound of soft clapping drew her attention to the southeast corner. Morgan Bevian stepped out from behind a row of bleachers. The girl smirked. "I didn't think you would have the nerve to show."

"Where is my sister?" Kristen knew exactly where Cyndi was via the dream, but she didn't want Morgan to know that Zach was on his way to rescue the other girl. It was better for Morgan to think she had outsmarted them.

"Don't worry about her. Worry about yourself."

"That's the difference between you and me. I love my family. You kill yours."

"Speaking of my family." Morgan grinned. "Have you heard from Zach lately?"

The stupid witch thought she had Zach locked up in their home.

Kristen played along. "Take your own advice. Don't worry about Zach. Worry about what I'm going to do to you."

Morgan laughed, and a light of admiration hit her eyes. "Whoa... Look who thinks she's all that. I'm impressed. Maybe I chose the wrong sister to link myself to."

"You chose the wrong family to link yourself to."

"Brittany hates you, you know. I might have put the idea of killing you into her head, but she couldn't wait to do it. She has always hated you. Did you know that?"

"My sisters both love me, and I love them. Sometimes Brittany might think she hates me, sometimes she might think she wants to kill me, but in the end, she'll always have my back."

"That's what you think."

Morgan crossed the floor until she was only a few yards from Kristen. They circled each other, two powerful forces on the verge of fighting to the death. They took their time sizing each other up. Neither was ready to make the first move, and Morgan seemed to be in a talking mood.

"I knew you were trouble from the moment I saw you." Morgan's gaze, filled with loathing, raked down Kristen's body. "The way you looked at Zach? Sickening. The way he looked at you? Pathetic. I knew sooner or later you would convince him to kill me so the two of you could be together."

"That isn't what happened, and you know it. You forced us to make the decision to take you out when you crushed my sister and tried to kill *me*."

Morgan smirked. "I am really going to enjoy this. You have no idea." The girl lifted her hands and flung them at Kristen in a sudden attack that caught her off guard.

Before Kristen had the chance to brace herself, a huge, invisible tidal wave hit her. It knocked her backwards and sent her sliding across the floor on her bottom. She quickly rolled onto her hands and knees, looking up through a curtain of blonde hair. She had to keep her eyes on Morgan. The girl was tricky, powerful, and deadly.

Kristen didn't bother to wave her hands. She thought of a spell and jerked her head to the side as if she had a nervous tick. The power of it blasted Morgan off her feet. Thanks to the medallion, Kristen's powers were extreme. The familiar blew backwards, rolling feet-over-head in a succession of tight somersaults. She stopped when she hit the wall on the opposite side.

They both stood at the same time.

Kristen pushed her sleeves up and steeled herself against the coming attack. With the medallion clutched tight in her hand, she was stronger than a normal witch. She just wished she knew how to properly use the power. It was too bad the medallion hadn't come with an instruction manual.

The dark-haired girl waved a hand at the ceiling, and the bright lights snapped on, momentarily blinding Kristen. She tried to keep her eyes on Morgan, but she couldn't see. Using one hand, she shielded her eyes and tried to open them beyond a slit. She saw something dark rush past her. *Pow*! She was hit from behind. The hard blow to the head knocked her on her knees.

The girl had actually hit her with a fist.

Kristen's eyes adjusted to the light. She flicked her empty hand at the running Morgan. A wave of power shot from her fingers and blew Morgan clear across the gymnasium. The girl hit the wall again, falling to the floor with a loud grunt.

Kristen ran at Morgan, hoping to get to her before she recovered. If she could reach Morgan in time, she could rip the locket from her throat. Then it would be lights out for the psychotic familiar.

On hands and knees, Morgan looked up and her eyes turned solid black. She jerked her head at Kristen, a smug smile on her mouth.

An unforeseen force lifted Kristen off her feet. She flew up and slammed against an overhead beam, just missing a row of lights. The force released her, and she fell. It was a long way down.

A cry burst from her lips. She tried to brace herself, tightening her muscles for impact. *Bam*! A blast of pain shot through her. Every inch of her body screamed in agony.

Luckily, nothing seemed to be broken.

Beaten and bruised, Kristen slowly pushed to her feet. The coppery taste of blood was on her tongue. She'd bitten it on the way down. The excruciating pain added to her anger, giving her strength. With the back of her hand, she wiped a trickle of blood from the corner of her mouth. "My turn now."

She delivered the next spell with a theatrical motion as if she were sweeping dust from the air. Morgan flew backwards, but she stopped in mid-air and hovered three feet above the floor like a demented Mary Poppins. A nasty grin spread across her face.

Morgan landed softly on her feet and said, "Play time is over. Now you die."

Her face darkened and turned red. Playing maestro, she raised her hands and beat a musical score into the air. The power rushed at Kristen like a runaway freight train. It came in the form of color this time, a vibrant blue with purplish lightning shooting from the core to the outer edges. Before it even hit her, Kristen knew it was going to hurt like crazy.

Kristen lifted both hands, holding the medallion in front of her body like a shield, and tried to use it to stop the spell. She spread her legs in a fighting stance to keep her balance, and prayed. Maybe the powerful spell would only partially put her through a wall. Maybe she'd live to fight another round.

The spell hit her hard. It sent her sailing through the air. She landed on the floor with a painful cry, and the medallion flew from her hands. It slid beneath the bleachers. A noise like ripping metal met her ears. She looked around. The bleachers were breaking away from the wall. They lifted up, ready to fall on her and smash her like a bug.

Woozy from hitting her head, she couldn't think straight, couldn't concentrate, and couldn't stop the bleachers from falling.

Groaning, Kristen flipped onto her stomach and reached for the medallion. Her fingers strained. It was an inch too far. Any second, the bleachers would crush her. She didn't have time to do anything. It was over. She was going to die this time, and there wasn't anything anyone could do to save her.

During his race to get to the gym, Zach stumbled upon several traps. He ran down intersecting hallways, and things flew at him from every direction. He didn't have powers, so he couldn't use magic to flick them away. He had to dodge them instead. A few things hit him, but he kept moving. A thick history book clobbered him. Pencils flew at him, pointy-side first. He ducked, and the tips embedded themselves into the wall.

Just as he reached the doors leading into the gym, Brittany and Cyndi popped up in front of him with a disturbing flash. Now he understood why it had bothered Kristen when he used the power to pop in and out of places. "I told you to take her home," he yelled at Brittany.

Cyndi raced into the gym ahead of the rest of them. She pointed and yelled out a spell. The medallion jumped into Kristen's hand, and she flipped onto her back, using a spell of her own to stop the bleachers from falling on her. The bleachers went backwards and reconnected to the wall with ease.

Cyndi ran to Kristen with Zach on her heels. They both grabbed Kristen by the arms and helped her stand. She looked like she'd been in the middle of a violent storm without shelter. Zach wanted to kill Morgan with his bare hands. She was lucky he didn't have his powers anymore because his anger would have shaken the building down on her head.

"No, Brittany!" Cyndi yelled.

Zach looked over his shoulder in time to see Brittany crossing the gym to meet his sister with a wide smile. Morgan returned the smug grin, knowing she'd won the battle. Kristen latched on to Zach's arm. The disbelief on her face mirrored his. This was why he'd asked Brittany to stay the hell away from the school. She was going to get them all killed.

Brittany scratched her stomach through the dark gray T-shirt as she approached Morgan. The other girl welcomed her with a quick hug and said, "I'm glad you made it. Let's party."

"Party on."

Brittany reached out a hand and touched Morgan's cheek in a friendly caress. Her hand lowered. She grabbed the locket around Morgan's throat and tugged hard. The chain instantly broke. Morgan cried out in surprise, too stunned to do anything. Brittany raced across the gym floor, locket dangling from her clutched fingers, and a huge smile on her face.

Morgan hit her with a spell, and she went down hard. Her hand opened. The locket slid across the floor, stopping at the toe of Kristen's shoe. For a moment no one moved. Frozen, they all stared at the locket in stunned wonder.

Zach ran to Brittany and helped her up. She was wearing an expression that he hadn't seen before, not on her face. Then he realized why. Incredulous, he asked, "Cyndi, is that you?"

She smiled. "See? You *can* tell us apart. It was Britt's idea for me to pretend to be her. She untied me, and then we swapped shirts."

Morgan screamed. "Brittany, get my locket! *Now!*"

Brittany snatched the locket from the floor before anyone else could.

Cyndi's face crumpled. "Brittany, no!"

Brittany's eyes closed for a moment, and she scrunched her face up tight. "Love is my weapon. I love my sisters, and I won't betray them." In control now, she handed the locket to Zach. "Don't worry. I went to see Grandma Noah, and she gave me the crystal. It helps me stay strong and fight the influence of the Crushed spell."

"Awesome!" Cyndi shouted with glee. She raised her hand for a high five, and Brittany complied. The triumphant smack made Morgan scream like a wounded animal. They all turned in her direction.

Morgan lifted her hand and started to yell out another spell.

"Quick!" Kristen told them, "Link hands. We're stronger together than we are apart. Zach, stand in the middle and destroy the locket.

Hurry! Girls, we have to protect him. The medallion will help boost our power. Let's do it."

They held hands and chanted a protection spell while Zach stood in the center of the small circle. He pulled out the piece of paper Grandma Noah had given him. First, he removed Brittany's hair from the locket. Then he got out a lighter and set the end on fire. All the while, Morgan was sending deadly spells their way.

The girls spoke louder as a strong wind filled the gym. The wind swirled around the Noah sisters but couldn't get to them. Morgan screamed louder. Their hair whipped around, and the wind pulled on their clothes. They squeezed their eyes shut and continued to blast words into the air. As long as they could keep it up, Morgan couldn't stop Zach from doing his job.

Morgan's spells visibly hit the force field around them. Obliterated one by one, they made tiny, colorful explosions. It would have been pretty if it weren't for the severity of the situation. Zach forced his mind to focus on the words he needed to say.

He burned the hair from the locket while saying his own spell. Grandma Noah had told them it didn't matter that he didn't have powers anymore. It would still work because Morgan was his sister. A family member had to destroy her. Maybe that was why she wanted to get rid of Zach so desperately.

After the hair was gone, Zach dropped the locket on the floor and crushed it under his biker boot. It broke apart. He stomped it again and again until it turned to gold dust. The wind sucked it out of the circle and blew it away. Then, the wind died down until it was completely gone.

Zach turned to look for his sister, but she was gone, too. The spell had worked. Morgan wouldn't be able to hurt anyone ever again. A flood of relief filled his body to overflowing. He pulled Kristen into his arms and held her close. At least she was okay. He kissed the top of her head.

Brittany said, "Ding-dong, the witch is dead."

"Britt!" Kristen pulled out of his arms to glare at the other girl.

"That was Zach's sister. Show a little compassion."

"It's okay," he said with a smile. "I was thinking the same thing."

Brittany held a hand up for a high five from him this time, which he delivered with cool satisfaction. Cyndi looped an arm around Brittany's neck. Kristen joined in the group hug. She laughed and said, "I love my sisters."

One at a time, she kissed them both on the cheek.

With a scowl, Brittany wiped her face. "If I wanted to be slobbered all over, I'd get a dog."

The sarcastic remark was so Brittany that Kristen laughed harder. They had the old Britt back. Kristen and Cyndi let each other go so they could motion Zach to join them. He stepped into the hug, feeling a little weird about it, but in a good way. They stood there and embraced for a few minutes, glad to be alive.

"That's enough," Kristen finally said. "We have a mess to clean up."

They looked around at the gym, and the feeling of victory died. The room was going to have to be fixed before school tomorrow, or there'd be questions. Kristen took the lead, assigning everyone a duty. The girls used their powers to repair the splintered overhead beams and ripped floor, while Zach had to do his assignments manually.

Zach wasn't sure if Morgan's spells or the protective wind had made the bigger mess. Not that it mattered. Either way, it had to be repaired. He insisted Kristen sit on the bleachers that had almost crushed her earlier while the rest of them did the work. She was amazing, but she was still human. Dried blood in the corner of her mouth and a growing bruise on her forehead had him concerned. She'd done enough for one night. Occasionally, his eyes drifted over to check on her. She smiled. Sometimes she waved. Grinning, he went back to work. He began to whistle while thinking about his good fortune. The future was a blank slate. He could live without worrying about the council being after him. It didn't matter to him how he spent the next sixty years as long as Kristen was beside him.

24

Accused

"Do you understand the charges against you?"

They were on the top floor of a silver skyscraper in downtown Chicago. Nine council members sat behind a long table at the front of the room. Each had a gavel, a short glass of water, and a yellow pad of paper in front of them, along with a couple of ballpoint pens. They were dressed in black suits, probably to make them seem more formidable. No worries there—they had Kristen quaking in her shoes, afraid for Zach and for their future together.

Zach nodded in answer to the question, but he kept his mouth shut.

Kristen blindly reached for her grandmother's hand, so glad the woman had insisted on taking them to Chicago for this ridiculous trial instead of making Zach face it alone. They sat in the back row on a wooden bench while Zach stood before the council. Grandma Noah had told him what would happen along with how he should behave. If anyone could get Zach out of trouble, it was she.

The council could put him in prison for the rest of his life. They had the power. Fortunately, Grandma Noah knew how to talk to them. Years ago, she'd retired from her spot on the council. Kristen hoped at least a few of these people still respected her grandmother for the amazing work she'd done.

The head councilman stared at Zach with cold eyes. "Do you have anything to say for yourself before we pass sentence on you?"

Grandma Noah shot out of her seat, dropping Kristen's hand. She'd been waiting patiently for this moment. Every head on the council snapped up as she strode down the aisle with purpose in her steps. She didn't stop until she was standing next to Zach. "I have something to say in Mr. Bevian's defense, if I may?"

"The floor recognizes Evelyn Noah."

Grandma Noah placed a hand on Zach's shoulder while speaking, and the show of unity did not escape the shrewd eyes of the council members. Her voice rang loud and clear as she said, "There is no excuse for what Zach did."

The council members nodded in agreement and murmured amongst themselves for a second. Kristen slid to the edge of the seat and strained to hear, but she was too far away. A silent movie about a possible life without Zach began to play in her head. She clenched her hands, digging fingernails into her palms.

She was confused. Was her grandmother trying to get Zach thrown into prison? Did she still think he was dangerous? Kristen wondered if maybe they should have left her grandmother at home. If she chose to, the woman could destroy him instead of saving him.

Grandma Noah continued. "However, he is an eighteen-year-old boy, and I am asking you to take his age into consideration. All of you have children, and I happen to know that not one of them is a saint. I dare say, some of them are quite mischievous, but I don't see you trying to put them in prison. Correct me if I'm wrong. Would you allow any of your children to be locked up?"

"Mr. Bevian did not break a simple rule, Evelyn," the councilman in the middle said, shaking his head. "Because of him, a very dangerous creature was allowed to roam free for nearly two years without the council's knowledge. She could have killed people. She could have exposed our very existence."

"That *creature* was his sister."

"I am afraid that is of no consequence to us. The boy committed a cardinal sin by hiding her existence from the council even though he knew about her dangerous powers."

"Do I need to remind the council that I sat in the very seat you are currently occupying, Trevor? I know about our laws and don't need you to remind me of them. I also know you have the discretion to let this go."

"Let it go?" Trevor exchanged a disbelieving glance with the other council members. "This young man put the entire population at risk, and you want us to slap him on the wrist? I think your recent years of idleness have softened your mental faculties."

Grandma Noah raised her voice. "This boy has suffered enough! He lost his family, his sister, and his powers. There isn't anything he can do to hurt you now, even if he wanted to—which I happen to know he doesn't. It's over. Let it go."

"Isn't he currently dating one of your granddaughters? That gives him access to power. He could talk her into doing something nefarious. She would not be the first good girl led astray by a bad boy."

Kristen's mouth dropped open. They were going to use her against Zach? Fearing the worst, Kristen slowly rose up on trembling legs. She was not going to allow them to put Zach into prison, especially not their prison. She'd heard horrible rumors about the place. It made foreign prisons look like tropical vacation resorts. He wouldn't be able to survive it after losing his powers. If he were put into their enchanted prison, he would die.

"I'll give up my powers," she said in a barely audible voice.

No one heard her.

Kristen forced her legs to move. She hurried to stand between her boyfriend and her grandmother, determined to be heard by the council. Her entire body shook with fear, but she wasn't afraid for herself. Grasping Zach's wrist, she tried to mentally suck some strength from him as she said, "I'll give up my power."

A few explosive gasps punctuated her statement.

Grandma Noah leaned over and whispered in her ear. "Let me handle this, dear. I can get him off without you sacrificing yourself."

The woman's familiar perfume wafted over Kristen, calming her nerves. For the first time in weeks, she knew exactly what she was doing. The possibility of losing Zach made her face a sharp reality. Getting a college degree or running her father's offices in Hong Kong, none of it mattered. Love was the only thing worth risking her life for. As long as she had Zach by her side, she could be happy.

"I know what I'm doing," she said.

"Do you?" When she nodded, Grandma Noah added, "Nothing will ever be the same if you give up your powers. You won't be a witch anymore. You won't be able to protect yourself or influence people as you get older. You'll be an ordinary girl. Is that what you really want?"

"Will I still be the same person inside?"

Her grandmother nodded and smiled. "Of course you will, dear."

"Then nothing else matters."

"And what if things don't work out with Zach? Will you still want to be an ordinary girl? Or will you have regrets?"

Kristen repeated the questions in her head. Would she regret giving up her powers if Zach broke her heart someday? Slowly, she shook her head, and a soft smile curved her mouth. "No regrets. Promise."

It was Zach's turn to voice his opinion. He took her by the shoulders and pulled her around to face him. His fingers gently tightened in a reassuring squeeze. "You don't have to do this."

"I want to," she insisted.

"You shouldn't have to sacrifice yourself for me."

She stepped into his arms and gave him a quick hug before turning to the council. "If I let my powers be taken, will you let Zach go without any punishment? Will you end this now and forever?"

"We will," Trevor said. "Are you prepared to give up your powers?"

Both Grandma Noah and Zach protested loudly.

The head councilman banged his gavel. "Silence in the courtroom."

Ignoring them all, Kristen straightened her spine and nodded once. "I am."

The head councilman turned and spoke to the council members on his left before conferring with those on his right. Decision made, the stern-looking man said, "Very well. You have three days to forfeit your powers, Miss Noah. If you fail to do so within the required time, we will put a bounty on Zach Bevian's head, and every hunter in the region will be on his trail. There won't be a safe place for either of you to hide."

Grandma Noah gasped in outrage. "How dare you threaten my granddaughter!"

"It's okay, Grandma," Kristen said. "I'll do it before the three days are up."

Grandma Noah and Zach began to protest in earnest now, but the head councilman struck the table with his gavel twice, ending the trial.

Kristen stood silently between two of the people she cared about most in the world. Despite her bravado, she wasn't sure if she could handle life without her powers. But she knew for sure she couldn't handle life without love.

Three days later, Zach drove her to school. An awkward silence filled the car from the beginning to the end of their trip. Once he parked in the rear of the lot, he turned to Kristen with an anxious expression on his face. The grace period had ended. If he didn't accuse her today, the council would take him away in chains. She'd wanted to do it right away, get it over with, but Zach had insisted on waiting until the last possible minute in case she changed her mind.

That wasn't going to happen. She had decided she could live without powers a lot easier than she could live without him. So when he turned to her, ready to argue the point again, she was ready. Holding up a hand to stop him, she said, "We're doing this. Today. That's all there is to it. Stop trying to talk me out of it."

"I don't want you to sacrifice yourself just to keep me out of trouble."

"It isn't that big a deal. You don't have powers, and you seem to be adjusting." A thought popped into her head, and she glared at him, eyes narrowed. "Wait a second. You don't think I can handle it. You think you're stronger than me."

"No. No. No. That's not it."

"I think it is."

Unbelievable! He didn't know her at all if he thought she was going to crumble. Lifting her chin high, she said, "I can not only face this challenge head on, I can beat it. In fact, I'm willing to bet that I can do a better job living without powers than you can."

His eyes widened a fraction. "Don't get me wrong. I like your competitive side, but this is serious. After I accuse you, it will be too late. Your powers will be gone. What if you decide you can't do it then? You'll blame me because you lost them."

So, that was the problem. He was afraid she was going to grow to resent him if life wasn't an easy ride later on. She stroked his bare arm where the T-shirt ended and said, "I want this. I really do. You may not believe me now, but I was thinking about asking you to accuse me even before the witches' council intervened. If we're going to be together, we need to be equals.

"Anyway, I've spent my whole life overcoming obstacles, facing challenges, and defying the odds, but I ignored what could be the biggest challenge of my life—living without powers."

He leaned over and placed a quick kiss on her mouth. "You are incredible. Do you know that?"

She blushed. "I think you're pretty awesome, too."

"Did you tell your sisters about giving up your powers?"

"No way. Brittany would have knocked me out to keep me from doing it. She's better at dealing with things after the fact than she is before they happen." Taking a deep breath and smiling big, she added, "Let's go do it. I'm ready."

Some of the kids were eating breakfast in the cafeteria while others sat around, talking to their friends. Brittany and Cyndi approached them as soon as they entered. The two girls were arguing and wanted Kristen to play referee.

Neither of them seemed to notice Kristen's distress.

Cyndi stood directly in front of Kristen and said, "Brittany wants to curse Jack and Gina. She won't listen to me, so maybe you can talk some sense into her."

Arms folded across her chest, Brittany said, "They deserve to pay after what they—"

"The universe will—"

Brittany made a rude noise. "If you're going to wait for the universe to get even for you, you'll be—"

"I don't care." Cyndi flicked her eyes to where Jake and Gina were rising from a nearby table. "Jake's a total jerk, and I know that now, so I'm glad we aren't together anymore. I'm glad he found Gina. He can make her miserable now instead of me."

Kristen and Zach exchanged amused glances over the twins talking in code. Kristen tried to intervene in the argument, but neither of the girls would let her fit a word into the conversation. Then it became a moot point. As the happy couple passed them, Brittany waved a hand in their direction.

"Britt!" Cyndi scowled. "I asked you not to do that."

Kristen stared after Gina, sort of hoping to see a giant wart growing on the end of the girl's nose, but nothing seemed to change. "What did you do?"

"You'll see," Brittany said in a singsong voice.

Gina began to walk from table to table, insulting everyone. She was digging a deep hold with her sharp tongue, a hole she wasn't going to be able to escape. Jake followed close, trying to stop her, but she wouldn't listen to him. In fact, she insulted him, too.

"Popularity elevator," Brittany said and chuckled, "going down?"

"You didn't have to do that," Kristen said.

"I didn't do it for you. That girl took advantage of me when I was cursed by Morgan, and she used me against my own sister. She had to pay."

Cyndi pleaded, "Don't do anything to Jake, at least. Leave him alone."

"Are you kidding me? After what he did to you, he's lucky to be breathing. I'll get him tomorrow."

"No. Please don't."

Brittany asked, "Are you still—"

"No. I just think—"

"You're right. Gina will make him suffer enough with her—"

"Totally," Cyndi said.

Zach shook his head. "I'm getting dizzy."

"Welcome to my world," Kristen said with a laugh.

The twins walked off to talk to friends, and Kristen remembered her purpose for being in the lunchroom with Zach at her side. It was time for her to give up a part of herself in order to save the best parts of her life. She hoped Brittany didn't figure out what Zach was doing in time to hit him with a binding spell or something worse. Brittany wouldn't hesitate, wouldn't wait for answers before attacking.

Kristen and Zach stood in the open doorway without talking or moving. This was it. No turning back now. She squeezed his hand for reassurance they were doing the right thing. In a few minutes, it would be over. He had told her what to expect, but hearing it and experiencing it were two different things. The unknown scared her more than she wanted to admit.

One look into Zach's blue eyes, and she knew everything was going to work out. The two of them would take care of each other, love each other. They had the rest of their lives to figure out how to live as normal people. Maybe she wouldn't become a tough executive, but she'd do something. Maybe she would find something she enjoyed doing.

"Are you sure?" he asked for the millionth time.

"*Yes*."

He shook his head and rubbed the back of his neck. "I feel like I'm screwing up your life just to save my own butt. We should find another way to keep me out of prison. There has to be another way. We can ask the council or go to your grandmother."

Kristen sighed. "You are so stubborn. We've been over this and over this. I want to do it, okay? Look, if you can't bring yourself to say the words, I can ask Cyndi. It's no problem. I'm sure she'll be willing once I explain the circumstances."

"No. I'll do it. I just, I want a guarantee that you aren't going to regret it later. I don't want you to hate me in ten years."

Folding her arms over her chest, she glared up at him and asked, "Am I the same person I was when school started this year?"

"No."

"Am I a strong, independent, capable person?"

"Yes."

"Are you going to love me any less when I don't have power?"

"No."

She threw her hands into the air. "Then I don't see the problem. The council will send you to prison if we don't do this today. They'll have hunters tracking us down. I am not going to sit back and let the love of my life be taken away from me."

His lips twitched and an amused light entered his eyes. "Am I the love of your life?"

"Yes, jerk." She playfully punched him in the gut. "Now, get out there and do it, or I'll call Cyndi over here."

Zach walked to the center of the lunchroom and gracefully leaped onto one of the center tables. Every eye turned his way. An excited buzz hummed through the crowd of kids as they waited for him to make his announcement. More than one student got their cell phone ready to start texting the news, whatever it turned out to be.

He raised his hand and pointed at Kristen. Reluctant, he took his time in forming the words. Pain and sadness filled his eyes, but he tried to smile while performing the horrible task.

She swallowed before taking a deep breath and holding it.

Zach said, "Kristen Noah is a…"

Brittany and Cyndi were standing off to the side, talking to friends. When Zach had jumped up on the table, their eyes simultaneously widened. Brittany dashed forward. She was going to hit him with a spell. Kristen clenched her hands into fists and prayed Zach would hurry.

"…witch."

"*No!*" Brittany screamed.

The invisible spell hit Kristen in the chest, knocking the breath out of her body. She grabbed onto the metal doorframe to keep from falling over. The color left her face in a chilling rush, and her legs turned to gelatin and refused to hold her up anymore. Panicking, she grabbed onto the wall harder as gravity tried to take her down.

Zach leaped off the table. He was beside her in an instant. His arms wrapped around her, holding her up, while his warm mouth pressed against the side of her face. He whispered, "You're okay. You'll only feel drained for a few minutes. It's okay. Everything is fine. I've got you."

Brittany charged at them like an angry bull. One of the girls hanging out with her in the small group yelled after her, "Hey, it's not like he called her the *B* word or anything. Lighten up."

"I'll kill you," Brittany stage-whispered.

"No, you won't." Kristen put a hand on her sister's arm, hoping to make her understand. She spoke in a soft voice because yelling wasn't going to help. "I told him to do it."

"*What?* Why? Are you stupid or just drunk?"

Cyndi joined them with a puzzled look on her face. "What just happened?"

"I'll tell you what happened." Brittany jerked a thumb in Kristen's direction. "Our idiot sister has given up her powers to be with tall, dark, and scary."

"That is *so* romantic."

"Only you would think so. It's stupid is what it is."

Kristen explained as fast as possible about the hearing in front of the witches' council, the threat of prison, and her feelings about losing her powers. She ended with, "Be happy for me. Zach and I love each other, and he's super supportive. He's decided to join me at whatever college I want to go to, and we're going to have a great life together."

Cyndi asked, "Are you still planning to get a business degree and work for Dad?"

Kristen shrugged. "Actually, Zach pointed out that I don't have to decide my whole life right now. There's plenty of time to make those kinds of decisions. I'll get a degree in something, maybe even business. I don't know. I'm thinking that I want to try some different things and see where my heart tells me to go. Hopefully I'll find a dream to chase, something challenging."

After Brittany blasted Kristen with how stupid she'd become, the girl stalked off, but Cyndi shrugged and said, "I understand why you did it, and Brittany will come around. She's just had a bad day."

No longer dizzy and weak, Kristen found she could stand on her own feet again without assistance. She pulled away from Zach, but he kept a hand on her back to keep her steady just in case. A new warmth filled her from head to toe as she realized Zach Bevian loved her.

Looking smug, Cyndi wiggled back and forth in an impromptu dance as she admitted, "I told her I wasn't going to dress like her anymore and blew her mind. She doesn't get it, but I had to stop dressing like her at some point. Like I told her, if we're wearing the same clothes when we're forty, it will confuse the kids, or husbands, and that could be embarrassing."

Cyndi looked from Kristen to Zach and then back again. She asked, "Are you sure you can handle life without your powers?"

"Why does everyone keep asking me that?" Kristen laughed. "I'm fine. Besides, if I need some magical help, I can always call you. Right?"

"That's what sisters are for."

Kristen and Cyndi shared a hug before the other girl returned to her friends.

Zach wrapped his arms around Kristen, holding her tightly as they walked back to the parking lot. They had made plans earlier. First, they would go to his house. He wanted to get rid of everything that reminded him of Morgan-his-familiar while holding onto mementoes of Morgan-his-sister. Kristen was going to help him sort through the stuff while he told her about his sister, the one she hadn't had a chance to meet.

Then, they were going to go to her house. She was going to introduce Zach to her father. Kristen wasn't worried because her dad would see how much Zach cared about her. Plus, it didn't hurt that Grandma Noah had said she would vouch for him.

Finally, they were going to make a list of things they both wanted to try, new things they could explore together. Kristen knew that whether her future was in business, charity work, or a life of travel with her rich boyfriend, it was going to be an exciting rollercoaster ride, and she couldn't wait to get started.

About the Author

If you ask Kasi Blake how old she was when she started writing, she will probably say twelve. That's when she wrote her first short story. But it started long before then. Her first characters were invisible friends she played with as a child. In the third grade she wrote a one-page story about a mummy for an assignment, and the teacher read it to the class. Even though she was embarrassed, the other kids laughed in all the right places, and she realized she could affect other people through her writing. She loves to get lost in emotional stories, crying and laughing with the characters, so she thinks it's the most amazing thing in the world to be able to do this for other people.

Kasi is a hardcore Supernatural fanatic and practically has the shows memorized line for line. If you want to see her freak out, tell her you've never watched an episode. Then be prepared to listen to a long list of reasons why you should. In her spare time, when she's not reading or writing, she does nail art, engages in day-long shopping trips with friends, and takes care of her many animals.

Originally from California, she resides in the Midwest on a farm with cows, chickens, ducks, a dog, and two cats.

Acknowledgements

First of all, a shout out to the ladies at Clean Teen. Rebecca Gober, Courtney Nuckels, and Marya Heiman. They each have their own specialty and do it in such a way that it looks easy to the rest of us. Also, Cynthia Shepp, Melanie Newton, and Chelsea Brimer had a part in making this book what it is.

Secondly, my beta readers. They got to read it first, comment on what worked and what didn't, and it wouldn't be the great book it is without them. Shirley Poe, Stacie Schott, and Amber Scott.

If I forgot to name anyone, please forgive me, and let me know so I can include you in a future book.